Eternal Y

Book 1

A novel by

Alexander Williams

This is a work of fiction. Names, characters, places, and incidents either are the product of the author's imagination or are used fictitiously. Any resemblance to actual persons, living or dead, events, or locales is entirely coincidental.

address:
Alexander@alexanderwilliams.com

The Two W.H Auden

You are the town and
we are the clock.
We are the guardians of
the gate in the rock
The Two
On your left and on
your right
In the day and in the
night,
We are watching you.

Wiser not to ask just
what has occurred
To them who disobeyed
our word;
To those
We were the whirlpool,
we were the reef,
We were the formal
nightmare, grief
And the unlucky rose.

But do not imagine we
do not know
Nor that what you hide
with such care won't
show
At a glance
Nothing is done,
nothing is said,
But don't make the
mistake of believing us
dead:
I shouldn't dance.

We're afraid in that case
you'll have a fall.
We've been watching
you over the garden wall
For hours.
The sky is darkening like
a stain
Something is going to
fall like rain
And it won't be flowers.

When the green field
comes off like a lid

Revealing what was
much better hid:
Unpleasant.
And look, behind you
without a sound
The woods have come
and are standing round
In deadly crescent.

The bolt is sliding in its
groove,
Outside the window is
the black remov-
ers van.
And now with sudden
swift emergence
Comes the women in
dark glasses and the
humpbacked surgeons
And the scissor man.

This might happen any
day
So be careful what you
say
Or do.
Be clean, be tidy, oil the
lock,
Trim the garden, wind
the clock,
Remember the Two.

This book is dedicated to Maria Allen, who's gentle encouragement and kind ear helped me fight the darkness

Caroline Owen turned over on the bare mattress in the throes of a nightmare, kicking the duvet away and exposing her long pale legs. Beneath the black waters of the dream she sat before an old typewriter in the middle of a large circular room. The walls were black, the floor was black. She looked at the typewriter and saw her own name typed on the page. *Caroline.* Before her eyes the machine came to life. The keys moving of their own accord spelling more names below hers, names she didn't know: *Emily Partington, Miranda Hart, Dayna Andrews, Lucy Cunningham, Sarah Owens, Maxine Croft. Click Click.* It typed faster: *Paige Reynolds, Sally Silvers.*

Caroline stood up, wanting to leave, wanting to wake. As she tried to move, she felt her feet sink through the black floorboards, their texture like liquorice, like quicksand. She struggled to move. The typewriter clicked on and on, the noise of the machine growing louder like a swarm of flies drawing ever nearer.

She staggered, pulling out one foot free of the floor, and then another, panic growing inside her belly. The floorboards oozed black tar around her feet. She felt herself sink deeper into the darkness. She opened her mouth to scream and sat up with a shout, her hand coming up to her face to block out the sunlight coming through the window. Her palms came away wet with perspiration. She kicked the duvet out from around her legs, the images from her nightmare scattering like leaves in the wind, breaking away, receding into nothingness.

Caroline thought her nightmares were long over. The bad dreams and the daytime hallucinations had vanished when she started taking medication and stopped doing drugs. Her medication was a mixture of mood stabilizers and antidepressants. They were strong. Missing even one dose caused the nightmares to return, along with seeing things during the day. Bad things. Taking mood stabilizers left her feeling jetlagged and tired. Her sleep was a coma sleep and coming awake was always sudden. The side effects from the pills were a small price for peace of mind, she thought, getting out of bed and stumbling blindly to the bathroom.

Leaving the shower with her towel wrapped around her, she saw the pink pill she should have taken the night before bed lying smugly on the bedside table. Light pink and no bigger than a tic tac, it was all that stood between herself and madness. She took it without opening her eyes and dry-swallowed, immediately feeling the damp fog begin to cloud her thoughts.

The phone on the floor rang, making her jump. "Hello?"

"It's Michele. I'm at the café, wondering where you are."

Caroline's eyes went down to the alarm clock on the floor, the red numbers flashed at two in the afternoon. She slapped her forehead with the palm of her hand in frustration

"I'm so sorry. I totally forgot to set my alarm before bed. Is it too late to see you now?"

"I have to go now but I'll let you know when I'm next free."

"I overslept. I wanted to see you."

"Don't be sorry, Carol. How are you feeling?"

"The same, fogged out."

"Call me if you need anything, won't you?'

"I promise." *Click*: the sound of the dial tone droning in her ear.

Caroline looked around the small room of her self-contained bedsit. Had she remembered to lock the door? She gave the door a cautionary look and tried the handle. Locked. Good. Loonies stay out; Caroline stay in.

She had done her best with the room. When she had first arrived in the hostel, she had spent the first two days cleaning. Michele had visited every day bringing things her parents wouldn't miss from their large home. Her father owned a company that built house extensions for rich people and Michele had told her he was now building sheds in the garden to store all the stuff he had bought. She had promised to bring Caroline a second-hand coffee machine very soon.

The floor was a linoleum of light brown imitation wood, far lighter than nature ever intended. The mattress was laid across a box that had been slashed open and hollowed out by a previous tenant. Inside were a lot of crumbs, dust and a crowbar which Michele told her to throw out: "Previous tenants' karma is never good." But Caroline had kept it, slipping it between the cushions on the sofa.

The kitchenette ran along the back wall: two small counter tops and a stove which didn't switch on. The front door had a numbered lock on it, along with a deadbolt. There was a cupboard-sized shower room with a toilet.

Caroline sat on the edge of the mattress with her head in her hands, feeling guilty at missing a chance to see her friend and escape the gloom of the hostel for a few hours. There was only one small window in the room that never seemed to get enough daylight. Caroline couldn't remember when she had last gone out and decided to try and get some fresh air.

She bent over to paw through the laundry on the floor for something clean to wear to leave the house in. Getting out of the hostel was difficult. She had to get enough of herself together to operate her limbs to walk, then make sure the hallways of the house were empty before making a dash for the front door. She was always frightened one of the other tenants would pop out of their rooms and catch her. She had yet to see any of the other occupants of the hostel, yet she heard them throughout the day through the thin walls of her room, and at all times felt their presence.

As she hit the pavement, Caroline felt the pores of her skin opening as the sunlight washed over her. The high street was narrow, and she had to weave in and out of people to avoid making contact. She didn't want flashes on top of bad dreams. The medication blocked out the visions, but it was not perfect.

Caroline stopped to lean against a lamppost, feeling dizzy. The doctor told her there would be dizziness and weakness that would eventually pass. She looked forward to a time when she could live without the side effects of the pills. *Deep breaths. Push on.* Where was the cafe she would have met Michele? Why not go there? Michele was always raving about it. She could think of nothing better than a big slice of cake and a tall caramel latte. The only high she got to ride on since getting clean was a sugar high.

She took a deep breath and kept walking, wrapping her arms around herself to avoid the crowds and loiterers that hung around the shop doorways. After passing a repetitive strain of estate agents, the Café Lavish Habit appeared, sticking out brightly against the bleak backdrop of the city outskirts.

The cafe was full of shabby chic school desk tables and old furniture. The walls were decorated with artwork priced for sale and homemade jewellery hanging from hooks. Caroline made a quick scan of the room and saw a table in the far corner against a wall. She sat down and took deep breaths of the scented air, a comforting blend of caffeine and baked bread.

A waitress spotted her and came over wearing a denim apron. Caroline fumbled to get her purse out of her pocket. She knew she was broke but had been putting off finding how broke. The change jingled as she took the purse out of her jeans pocket, raising her hopes. A few silver coins and many coppers lined the bottom. She shook the change out onto the table. "How much is a caramel latte?" she asked.

The waitress smiled at her. "How much you got there, Hun?"

Caroline counted. "About £2.30."

The waitress winked and turned about to walk away. Caroline grabbed a handful of change and thrust it out to her, but the girl turned her back as if she hadn't seen. Caroline watched her go behind the counter and begin turning knobs on the espresso machine.

The waitress brought the coffee over and laid it down with a small silver jug. Caroline's heart lifted as she looked in and saw gold syrup inside.

"In case it's not sweet enough for you."

Caroline beamed at her in silent gratitude, feeling the weight of the night terror slip off her, feeling happier than she had in a long time. She tipped the dainty jug over the drink and watched the golden liquid pour like Midas tears into the mug before lifting it to her lips and taking a deep gulp, not caring that it was too hot. She sat back in her seat feeling her belly glow with the warmth of the coffee.

Around the café contented groups sipped their cappuccinos, some talking with friends, girls laughing. One man sat alone on his laptop with his eyes staring at the screen. To Caroline everyone seemed at ease with their lives.

The scent of the coffee reminded her of men's aftershave. Caroline felt the pull of memory creep over her. Her boyfriend Tom had worn aftershave. It was Tom who she'd lost her virginity to, Tom who had shown her the joys of shooting up. In her mind she went back to the first night he had shown her the dark pleasures of getting high. Caroline mouthed his words with her eyes closed as she sipped her drink. "Babe, let me show you how to fly..." He had taken her arm and she remembered crying out as the wasp sting of the needle slid into her. He had taken the needle out and put the rest into his thigh, keeping his eyes locked on hers the entire time, silently telling her that they were now joined in something far deeper than mere intimacy. She remembered that first rush vividly. How everything she'd worried about, her parents' approval, school, even worries that Tom would one day find her boring and leave her had, in a few seconds, become meaningless. He had grabbed her in his strong arms and thrown her up into the air. She had felt herself go through the ceiling, and out into the sky. Her eyes opened remembering the comedown afterwards. The morning after she'd felt like hell.

She was startled out of the memory. Something caught her eyes in the far corner where the man was sitting, the one with the dead-eyed stare locked on his computer screen. Her eyes narrowed, searching for what had drawn her focus. Just across from him on a small end table completely out of place was a typewriter. Caroline pinched the bridge of her nose between her eyes. A flash of something broke through the haze of medication, a sense of déjà vu. She'd never used a typewriter before in her life. In school she'd written longhand.

Had Tom owned one? He might have. She saw him clearly in her mind's eye. His strong jaw and dark eyes. Tom who had all the answers. Tom who had seemed both youthful and yet old at the same time. He read poetry by Wordsworth and Auden. She remembered him reading aloud from a notebook, a rolled-up cigarette behind one ear, his tongue piercing flashing at her as he recited the words. He wrote in books; he never used a typewriter.

So why did the typewriter remind her of something awful?

She could imagine the unpleasant sound it would make if someone's fingers typed on its keys, animating it to life. *Clackety clack.* Like a swarm of flies

She stood up, wanting to leave. Today was not the day for leaving the safety of the bedsit. She should have stayed in, taken an extra pill and fallen asleep. Better to go, run home, clothes off, back under the covers, down a pill, maybe wake the day after tomorrow ready to face the world again on its own terms.

She made to run for the door, hitting her hip on the table sending pain up her body like a red rod. The latte glass wobbled and fell, shattering on the floor. "Shit. I'm sorry," she said to the waitress moving towards her to help.

Caroline felt dizzy. She heard someone speak aloud in her head. *Clumsy girl* and looked up.

The waitress was smiling down at her. "Don't worry about it I'll get a dustpan."

Caroline reached out to touch the three largest chunks and yelped as a shard caught itself along her forefinger. She cried out and fanned her hand in the air.

The waitress passed her a napkin from the table and wrapped it around her finger. "Keep pressure on it while I sweep up the glass. There's a medical kit in the back. I'll get you a plaster."

"I don't want any fuss!" She could already feel the eyes of everyone in the room boring into her, judging her. Their voices growing louder inside her head chattering like birds.

Clumsy girl. Who is she? She looks drugged.

Poor thing looks lost.

Wonder where she comes from.

She put her hands to her ears trying to shut them out. "Shut up!" She looked up at all the shocked and judgemental faces leering down at her and then to the doorway. She ran for it and didn't look back.

She walked fast down the street weaving in and out of people on the narrow pavement. She bumped a bald man on the arm as he went past her and felt a bang as something passed through her head, an image lighting up in front of her eyes like an old photograph. The bald man reaching into a desk drawer, looking left and right to make sure he was alone, something glittered in his hand like a piece of jewellery, or a watch. *He stole the watch he's wearing from the office drawer of a client.*

Caroline felt a cold chill run down her spine as she picked up the pace. *Shit, shit, shit.* The flashes were coming back.

"Excuse me." A dark man in a hoody was in front of her standing by the bus stop.

No, I don't want to stop. I want to get home.

She went past him and his hand shot out. "Hey, I'm talking to you." His fingers brushed her shoulder and she recoiled as another flash went off behind her eyes like a firework. He was shaking a little girl and shouting at her face.

He abuses his daughter.

Run for it. She took off running with her blonde hair spilling down behind her. *Nearly home. Just get home, home where it's safe.* She ran across road and a cab blared its horn at her. She halted with her foot off the curb. Caroline made to run around the back of the car. The cab driver reversed, halting her progress across the road.

"Have you ever seen a car before?"

Caroline ignored him and walked round the front, determined that he would not prevent her reaching the safety of the bedsit.

"Have you never seen a fucking car before?" He sped up forward again, stopping her.

She changed direction and went around the back of his car again, refusing to acknowledge him. He reversed again, kicking the car door open as he flew out of the vehicle in a rage. "Have you never seen a fucking car before?"

She ran for it. Caroline could hear cars honking in the distance. She felt sick with fear as she turned right into the familiar street of her emergency accommodation. She slowed to a walking pace and risked one glance back towards the road. The street was empty, no one had followed her.

As she walked up the road, she saw many of the bikes chained to the street railing standing on empty air where the wheels had been stolen. Litter lined the pavement on either side of her; newspapers and beer cans seemed to be everywhere.

She went up the narrow walkway of cracked paving that led to the front door. She pressed her ear against the wood, listening for any sign that anyone was in the hallway. She'd been there six months and had managed not to encounter anyone in the communal areas. Going through the front door she stepped onto the filthy carpet that had been trodden over a thousand times by lost souls passing through the house.

Caroline closed her eyes in concentration, trying to listen to the house as it settled around her. She could hear the TV in the room next to her and something underneath that sound, like a low buzzing, as if a family of hornets had taken up residence in the room. *Whoever's in there is running a tattoo shop*. She didn't know how she knew for certain, but she knew.

Upstairs, she could feel people moving around on the ceiling above. A woman was talking on the phone in the room to her right and there a child running across the floor. A tricycle was overturned in the hallway. Nobody seemed to be lurking around. Caroline always had to choose between bounding up the stairs in a hurry which would make more noise and attract attention, or creep up slowly, not making any noise and risk someone coming out of their room and seeing her. She did not want to be seen by anyone. She'd lived in other hostels where she had been attacked by addicts. She did not want trouble.

She crept up the stairs and darted quickly around the corner, passing two doors. One, she noticed, had a large crack around the handle where someone had forced it open. She moved up the stairs to the third floor. Her door stood at the far end of the short corridor and she ran to it.

She fumbled her key into the lock and turned bringing the handle down and pushing hard. The door didn't move. She tried turning the key again. Nothing. *Come on, come on, please.* She felt the first tendrils of panic creep through her body. She tried the handle again. It wouldn't budge. Then she realised: the keypad. She had to enter the numbers on the coded bolt before the door would open. Her fingers moved frantically over the small numbered knobs: C1632Z. She turned the top handle and the bottom at the same time and pushed her way into the small bedsit, closing the door and double locking it behind her with a deep breath of relief, pressing her weight against the wood of the door.

Her first instinct was to reach for the cordless phone, call Michele and tell her about the café and the anxiety attack. Her hand froze as she went to hit the numbers with her finger. She could hear the dial tone of the deadline against her ear. *She's already had enough of you for one day. You didn't even turn up for your arranged meet.* Her thoughts stung but she was aware how tiring misery could be for others to listen to and she rationalised, placing the phone back in the cradle, that she didn't have that much to say to her, nothing important.

She shouldn't have left the house alone. She knew that now. She had taken her pill that morning before leaving the house and still she had flashes coming home. *Only because they touched you. You have to be more careful.*

She brought her knees up to her chin in a foetal position. *The pills aren't working as well as they used to.* The doctors had warned her that the nasty side effects of the mood stabilisers would fade as her body got used to them. She worried that the other effects would disappear as well. She resolved to double the dosage from now on, take three pills a day if she had to.

They were the only things - the only legal things - that brought any relief from the dreams, visions and flashes she'd get when she touched someone or sometimes for no reason at all. Out of nowhere, something would just come to her like knowing when it would rain when she was younger, and she'd close all the windows in the house even on a clear day and sure enough by nightfall it would rain hard. Her parents wrapped up in the drinking and passing out sides of life never noticed but it wasn't until she got older that she became afraid of it. Whatever the hell it was, she thought, looking up at the peeled plaster of the ceiling.

Sheila Cunningham's silver Mercedes pulled up on the kerb. The engine idled as her long-manicured nails turned the knob of the radio down, so she could speak to her daughter before she got out of the car. Lucy sat on the passenger side of the car with her face turned away watching the people walk up and down the high street.

"What time would you like me to pick you up, Lucy?"

Lucy kept her eyes looking out of the window. She could see the café across the street where her friend was waiting for her.

"I'm getting the bus home with Maxine."

Lucy felt her mother tense up next to her. The arguments between them had grown worse over the past week with Lucy's refusal to back down over her choice of friends and her mother's own pig-headed stubbornness. She didn't like Maxine because she smoked and lived on a council estate on the outskirts of the city. Lucy couldn't care less about her mother's opinion.

Sheila leaned over and rested her hand on her daughter's knee. "Call me if you need- "

Lucy opened the car door and slid out, cutting her off mid speech. She wove her way through the cars to meet her friend, growing more excited as she reached the café visualising Maxine's dark lank hair. In contrast to Lucy's girly attire, Maxine wore boys' T-shirts and ripped her own jeans. She always had her nose in a book and would have been a prefect at school if it were not for her frequent detentions from being caught smoking in the girls' bathroom. Maxine was a total rebel.

She looked up as Lucy walked into the café. A book was open on the table. Her voice was low and husky. "Hey, princess."

"I hate it when you call me that."

"Sorry I didn't return your message last night. I was at the library till late. I've not been going home since Mum decided to get back with her latest romance. They're fighting again."

"I wish you could stay at my house, but my mum is being a total cow about us still seeing each other."

Lucy watched her drain the last of her coffee and shove her book into her bag. She nodded to the barista behind the counter. "Did you want to grab a coffee?"

"I'm ok. How about a bit of shopping?"

Maxine looked down at her lap. "I'm broke, so it will have to be strictly window shopping only."

The pair rose from their seats and together they walked out of the café down the street, two young teenagers in the fullness of youth, walking aimlessly as if they had all the time in the world to spare.

"On the bright side, you managed to get away today."

"I told my mum that if she didn't drive me in, I would take the bus. She tried to speak to me the whole way here about how she knows best blah blah but I'm ignoring her. She thinks she knows everything there is to know."

"How does your dad feel about me?"

"He's been okay, I guess. Mum talks him down whenever he tries to jump between us. Do you mind if I grab a coke?"

They both stopped outside the newsagents. Maxine took a small tin and papers out of her pocket and began rolling a cigarette. "I'll have a smoke while I wait. Take your time."

The bell jangled above her as she strode into the shop. Lucy had been going there since she was eight years old and her father used to take her in at weekends to buy penny sweets. Now she was sixteen and, as her eyes moved over the pick-a-mix, she felt a deep pang in her chest at how far away those days of fun and laughter were. Her parents were strangers to her now, looming authority figures that were trying to control her every move.

Lucy looked back at Maxine who was leaning against the shop window breathing out large clouds of smoke into the air, paying no attention to the adults that walked past with looks of distaste on their faces. She envied Maxine for her carefree air and confidence.

What was that? Something caught her eye in the magazine racks. Her eyes moved back over the titles: Good Housekeeping, Teen Vogue. *There.* Lucy looked up to see the sales assistant busy dealing with the customer in front of her and then reached up and drew the magazine out of the rack. The cover was glossy, alight with pungent purples and reds. Across the top in gold letters were the words BAZAAR. It was an adult magazine. The woman on the cover was spread out against a silk bedspread, her eyes darkened with mascara, staring at the viewers with unwavering confidence. Her body was shrouded in a see-through silk negligee trimmed in black lace. Her lips were red as hearts' blood.

Lucy felt something turnover inside her. Her palms felt dry. She bit her bottom lip and then without thinking what she was doing she flipped open her leather satchel and stuffed the magazine in, throwing her bag over her shoulder. She held her breath, stepping away from the rack.

Time seemed to stand still. Her eyes were closed. Her whole body tensed waiting for the inevitable sound of the alarm, a siren ringing all around, the shop assistant shouting, the police, and then worse, her parents.

No sound came. Slowly she breathed out. Slowly she looked around. The shop was quiet. A mother and child were at the pick-a-mix filling a paper bag and the shop assistant was now tidying the newspaper shelves only a few feet away.

No one had seen her. Her heart rate began to slow and then she jumped as she heard a bell jingle behind her. The assistant looked up at her, through her, as the sound came again. She turned to see Maxine against the glass of the shop front, a small fag end protruding from her mouth, her hand waving.

"Hurry up!"

Lucy looked at the shop girl who was glaring at her disapprovingly.

"Sorry, it's my fault. I got side-tracked." She took a deep breath and strode up to the counter, reaching into the mini fridge and taking a can of Pepsi out and putting a pound coin on the counter. The assistant rang up the purchase and Lucy said, "Keep the change" and hurried down the steps and out of the shop, holding her breath until she was out in the free air.

"I can't believe you stole it!" Maxine was panting with excitement, trying to keep up with her as she ran down the street. "You are hard-core. Why on earth did you take it?"

As soon as they were out of sight of the newsagents' Lucy had had shown her the magazine. "I just saw it and it looked…so rich, I didn't think, I just, I just took it."

"Rich, for sure," said Maxine appraising the cover. "This mag's like ten quid."

"No, not expensive rich. I mean, look at her. She's so beautiful."

Maxine looked down at the woman on the cover. "Don't believe any of that. It's all fake. Airbrushing and makeup."

Lucy snatched it off her, stuffing it into her bag. She didn't understand. "I wish I was like that Max."

"Anorexic?"

"No!" She punched her playfully on the arm. "Exotic. I get sick of feeling so plain and dull. I want to be different. I got such a rush from taking it. It was crazy. I've never felt like that before."

"That's called adrenaline, princess. I wouldn't get hooked on it if I were you. You can get in a lot of trouble."

Lucy felt the bulge in her bag where the magazine rested and said aloud to herself, "Getting into a lot of trouble. Now wouldn't that be fun!"

A large white cat watched the two girls pass from where it crouched in the alley, its dull yellow eyes glowing against the fading light of the setting sun.

Lucy's bedroom walls were the same shade of pink they'd been when her mother and father had moved in when she was eight years old. The reading lamp by her bed was a porcelain unicorn with a pink lampshade that her dad had bought her from an old antique shop. She'd loved it at the time and she still loved it for its kitsch value.

In the past months her bedroom had undergone a change. She had banished other girlish items from the room. The pink velvet sofa from her mother was smothered by a piece of black silk she'd bought from a fabric shop in town. Her Barbie dolls and princesses were boxed up along with the My Little Ponies and teddy bears into airless cardboard tombs under the bed. Exiled, they now held court with dust bunnies and spiders for company.

Lucy had tried sincerely to rid herself of the previous decade's girly girl Cunningham. But she found getting rid of the family photos and more sentimental items like the unicorn lamp difficult: she and her dad in Disneyland, Micky and Minnie waving; she and her mother on her twelfth birthday with pink balloons everywhere; a young Lucy in a neat school uniform with her hair neatly combed and wearing a headband smiling out from a gilded frame.

She removed each photo from its frame and placed them in a black leather-covered photo album with the frames placed in a large unused shoebox to join the princesses beneath the bed. She wanted to make new friends, new memories. Time to break away from the old self and crawl out from under her mother's thumb once and for all.

Lucy waited till after dark to retrieve the magazine from her satchel bag. From her bedroom, she could hear the TV in the lounge switch off and her parents climbing the stairs. She saw the light under her door black out for a moment, before they passed on heading for bed. Finally, she heard their bedroom door close with a click.

Sliding out of bed sideways, Lucy made her way soundlessly across the plush carpet in her bare feet. She had had a bath before going to bed and her hair hung still damp around her, lightly crimped and wavy. She slid the magazine out from under the wardrobe and climbed back onto the top of the bedspread.

She heard her own mind speak silently in her ears. *Today you stole from someone.* Her mind answered: *All animals steal; morality was invented by humans.* Then a deeper, more primitive part of herself spoke up: *Animals steal to survive. They steal food to eat.*

But wasn't that what the magazine was to her? Nourishment of some kind? Didn't she feel, as she had felt since her sixteenth birthday, that some fledgling thing had begun to grow inside her? Some seed of independent nature that seemed to be flowering, in the nail polish, the new music, a new choice of friends that were totally outside of what her normal life had been before? Was she not seeking something out in the way she was dressing? This thing, whatever it was, needed nourishment and the magazine cover promised that. The woman on the cover with her crimson lipstick and dark eyes beckoned to her. Lucy looked at her thinking over and over: *I want to be you.*

She could tell Maxine didn't like fashion magazines and, in truth, Lucy had never noticed them until recently but something in the woman spoke to her. She possessed some magic. No, not magic, she had *glamour* and Lucy wanted it too. Some new voice, unheard until now, had spoken in her ear at the newsagents'.

She took off her pyjama top and looked down at herself. Her breasts were beginning to show. She looked back at the cover and took a make-up bag out of the drawer next to the bed and carried it across the room. Seating herself before her dressing table mirror she opened the make-up bag and rummaged through the used sponges, bubble gum lipstick, peach gloss nail polish, glitter nail polish, and finally, her fingers brushed against a small bottle.

Still looking ahead at the mirror, she took out a long vial of crimson nail polish and slowly twisted the lid widdershins drawing out a small brush coated in dark red paint that shined in the dark of the room. Slowly Lucy began to paint her fingernails, each stroke done with the utmost care and precision.

Charlie was looking into the mirror examining his face the same way a teenager hunts for blemishes. He appeared to be in his early forties and had a strong toned muscular body with snake and dragon tattoos running up his arms.

Peering into the mirror he could see his face was showing the first signs of age. His eyes that once were a deep ocean blue were now a pale grey. His hair was jet black with spots of grey flecked across his scalp.

He had the body of a man who worked out regularly at the gym, who probably had a well-paid job at a respected firm in the city. His teeth were white which he was glad of as he liked to smile. He looked at the old clock on his bedside table. It was time to administer his lover's treatments.

He walked to the other side of the room stopping in front of a transparent glass tank much like the sort used to keep exotic fish in. The tank had no water in and seemed empty save for a small log tunnel placed on one side. He tapped the glass and fixed his gaze on the log pile surveying the interior of the tank hopefully. There was no movement inside. He sighed to himself and pulled on a plaid shirt and left the room, closing the door to his bedroom behind him.

He walked down the dark corridor. The curtains of all the windows were drawn tightly against the intruding daylight. The walls were covered in a wallpaper that had once been a bright sunshine yellow but had now faded and peeled to the colour of a wilting daffodil. An antique writing bureau caked with dust stood in the corner. Atop was a vase of roses that looked as if they'd been dead for months; shrivelled petals were heaped around the vase.

He paused outside her bedroom with his hands on the round knob. He prided himself on his manners.

He knocked twice on the door softly and opened it a crack. "Babe? Are you awake? I'm coming in."

Her treatments were complicated and he expected her to stay in bed for whole weeks at a time which is why he went to the trouble of securing the large four-poster bed that dominated the room. It was draped in a gauzy tulle to give her privacy. "Rosie? I'm here."

A muffled sound from the bed let him know that she acknowledged his presence. He heard another moan from the darkness of its deeper recesses. The sound made him spring to action making him move swiftly into the en-suite bathroom where he kept her medicines.

The bathroom itself was spotless, having never been used. The bath was a deep rose pink which matched the sink and tiles. There was a large glass cabinet on the far side of the wall that went from one end of the large bathroom to the other filled with various bottles, jars and capsules in boxes.

He rummaged around hoping the tinkling of the glass would let her know he was there and that she wouldn't have to wait long. He took various bottles out, a cardboard box filled with tablets, a small leather case, an inhaler and a crystal glass from the cabinet. He put them on a steel tray and carried them into the room hurriedly without bothering to close the cabinet door.

The sight of her never bothered him. He did not turn on the light and found his way around the room, feeling his way by touch. He knew the light caused her pain as her eyesight had deteriorated. She could only tolerate the low burning of a candle. He struck a match lighting a small candle next to her bed.

He placed the tray on the bedside table and mixed the liquids into the crystal glass, stirring them all together carefully with the practiced hand of a trained doctor. After so many years he could have mixed her remedies blindfolded.

He opened the small leather case and took out a glass syringe and pulled the plunger back, his grey eyes watched the tube fill with the darkness of the brewed mixture. He flicked the glass with his fingers to make sure there was no blockage and laid the syringe down on the tray. He took a silver spoon out of the bedside drawer and pushed two capsules out of their casings and placed them on the spoon.

A hand reached through the veiling of the bed and clutched his wrist. The blue veins stood out prominently over the worn wrinkled flesh. The skin of the hand was smothered in liver spots. He gently wrapped his other hand around her bony fingers and took it away, placing it back on the sheet.

He parted the hanging gauze from the bed and, at first, could not make her out at all. His eyes had to adjust to the deeper darkness beyond the veil. Only her head and arm protruded from the vast linens that covered her. Her eyes were sunken in and barely open and she looked like a small doll against the vast size of the bed, a fragile thing flung carelessly onto it.

He wondered for a moment if she had gone back to sleep when a strangled cough erupted from her mouth and her body began to writhe about as she gasped for air. He reached over and put the inhaler in and pushed the button sending a jet of clean oxygen down into her ancient lungs, once, twice, three times. She took two deep breaths without the aid of the inhaler and her breathing resumed. She lay still again, her head sinking gratefully back into the pillow.

He folded the sheets down to her waist. Her body was shrunken with illness and twisted by the spinal cancer that ran rampant through her body. Her facial skin was pulled tight over her skull and crow's feet gouged crevices around the eyes.

He reached over her with his strong arms and took two large pillows from the bed and put them against the bedstead and then wrapped one arm under her back for support. He picked up the silver spoon holding the two capsules and lifted them to her dark purple mouth. She opened it instinctively when she felt the coldness of the metal, her single yellow tooth revealing itself against her rotten gums for a moment as she swallowed the pills before bringing the water to her lips.

As she drank, he stroked the grey gossamer threads away from her balding scalp. He put the glass of water back on the table and picked up the syringe. He took her hand, brought it once to his lips to kiss her wrist before turning it over to show a prominent blue vein. He slipped the needle in. She made a small groan as he compressed the plunger delivering the serum into her veins that would bring her some relief against the ravages of age. He put the syringe back on the tray and took everything back to the bathroom, placing the medicines back into the glass cabinet.

He went to the corner of the room and grunted as he lifted a carved armchair and dragged it over to her bedside. Sitting down he took one of her hands into his own. She turned her face to him and her eyes opened.

They were white eggs bulging out of her eye sockets, utterly blind. She whispered something he couldn't hear and he leaned in closer. He didn't flinch from the stench that came from her mouth as she spoke three words to him.

"How long, Charlie?"

He sat back in the chair and looked thoughtfully over at the far side of the room where a mirror hung, draped in black velvet, blind to the room, and then back to the shrunken old thing lying in the bed. "A week Rose, maybe two."

She gave no sign she'd heard him and he remained sitting in the chair for some time watching the candlelight flicker, illuminating her decrepit features. Slowly he saw a small smile begin to play over her lips. With her treatments completed he folded the bed linen back up to her chin lightly and stroked the thin gossamer strands of grey away from her face, blew out the candle and crept out of the room without a sound.

The heavy knocking coming from the bedroom door sent pounding wooden stakes into the heart of Dayna's hangover. She opened one eye from where she lay on the bed as Wanda's voice intruded into her bedroom. "Day? You alive in there? Wakey, wakey! I've got coffee here for you and porridge in the kitchen."

Dayna sat up in bed and shouted back. "Why not bring it in here for me?"

"No way. You get dressed and join me in the kitchen. I know if I bring it in there, it'll just join the ranks of all the other kitchen crockery that have wandered into your bedroom and not returned. Haul that arse of yours out of bed. This is not the Savoy."

"Love you too, Wanda!' she shouted back, letting herself drop back against the pillow.

"It's for your own good, angel pie."

Dayna could hear Wanda's high heels echoing down the long hallway back into the kitchen.

The room she lived in was Wanda's spare room that she'd used for storage before Dayna took up residence. She couldn't see the floor because various old clothes had been strewn about. Amongst them were old coffee cups and dishes that she had taken to her room and never got around to bringing back to the kitchen to wash. She felt bad enough as she was crashing rent-free in her friend's house. She wanted badly just to keep out of the way and leave no sign at all in the flat that she was there.

Dayna could tell that Wanda kept the facade up that their breakfasts were just girly breakfasts shared between friends, never bringing up the bad state that Dayna had let herself get into with her drinking, nor the state of the spare room or how long she was staying for. Dayna didn't know the answers, and Wanda never asked.

She got onto the floor on all fours and rummaged through the dirty laundry until she came upon some plain white briefs and a man's T-shirt. *Who the hell does this belong to?* She slipped it over her head and ran her fingers through her auburn hair to make herself look somewhat presentable before venturing out of her room.

The clinking of the mugs in her fingers against the dishes announced her presence as she entered the kitchen. She felt Wanda's eyes follow her from behind the magazine she was reading at the kitchen table.

"Well, well, sound the trumpets. Her ladyship has arrived."

Dayna dropped the used crusted plates and dirty mugs into the sink.

"And lark! She has returned thy dishes and mugs! Who are you, an imposter? What have you done with Dayna?"

"I thought you might want these back."

"I was going to order a new dinnerware set as I'd long since given up hope that these would ever show themselves again." Wanda moved towards the sink motioning to Dayna to move away. She rolled up the sleeves of her blouse and filled the sink with hot water.

"I can wash those up."

"It'll take you ages to clean all of this up and by that time your breakfast would've gone cold, and I wasn't up early to make that for you to throw it away. I don't know how you survive on a diet of coffee all week while I'm away and don't think I've not noticed the McDonald's wrappers in the kitchen bin. No wonder you're wasting away to nothing. There are berries on the counter. Help yourself."

Dayna walked barefoot over to the boxes of red berries and emptied the contents on top of the warm porridge. She put one arm around Wanda's waist and felt her body stiffen against her fingers. She put her head on her shoulder. 'You're so good. I don't know what I'd do without you."

"So, Day, tell me: what have you got planned for the day?"

“I was planning on going back to bed.”

Wanda scowled at her.

“Sleep’s good for me. It’s like dying without the commitment. No wonder I like it so much.”

“That’s not funny.” Even though it was a Sunday and in theory her day off from the office, Wanda still wore high heels and a pencil skirt. “You know you’re welcome to stay here but I don’t think this self-imposed isolation is doing you any good. I hardly see you. You’re never home at night when I come home from work and you may think you’re being clever by disabling the smoke alarm in your bedroom but my nose is still operational and that room reeks of cigarettes. You’re wasting your money and your health on those things.

Dayna yawned and stretched her arms out like a cat,

“I’ll try and cut down, but you know me Wanda, its either twenty a day or nothing at all”

“There’s a bath waiting for you in the bathroom. You can make a start on the day by washing all that make-up off your face and maybe cleaning out that rat’s nest you live in, if not for yourself then for me. Maybe open a window in there. You might feel better. I have to go and meet some friends for lunch. We can talk later.”

Dayna kept her eyes fixed down on the murky surface of the coffee. As it was, she’d be homeless if Wanda hadn’t let her come and stay and she’d been good to her without asking anything about what had happened with John. All she knew was that the relationship was over, and he had thrown her out on the street. She was relieved that Wanda hadn’t said, ‘I told you so’. She’d just pointed to the guest spare room and left a note on the fridge the next day telling her to help herself to anything inside and that she'd be home at six pm so they could talk. The talk had never happened.

During the first few weeks of her stay, she would lay comatose in bed, not asleep, thinking about John, wanting to call him, feeling the shame slither down her throat like a snake. It was John who had thrown her out, John who had beaten her. Some nights she could not stand to stay indoors dwelling on him. She would steal out of the apartment like a shade dressed in clothes borrowed from Wanda to meet men whose bodies gave her escape and nourishment to fill the loneliness of her night-time existence.

She opened the door to her bedroom and surveyed the mess with a look of deep resignation. She wanted to go back to bed but if Wanda came home and saw she had done nothing with her day, she'd be annoyed.

In the cupboard under the sink, she found a cylinder of white bin liners she needed to tackle the detritus that had collected in her bedroom for the past three months. She kept the bedroom door open to the hallway to let out the stale smell of fast food mixed with the fluids of various strangers she brought home from bars to placate her longing for company. They were men with square jawlines, like John, who wore leather shoes, and well-cut suits. She'd laugh a lot when they spoke and tried to tell them in the taxi on the way home that it was her flat.

Her men never stayed long in the morning due to the light of the day revealing her lies for what they were. After they had fallen asleep Dayna would rifle through their trouser pockets and lift what cash they had. In the morning they would snatch their clothes up from the floor, leaving tokens of their presence in the way of underpants, silk ties or leather belts concealed until now amongst her own various cast-offs, and disappear without a goodbye.

She heaped her old clothes on top of the made bed, shutting her eyes against the memory of the night that Wanda went to collect her boxed clothes that John had left out front of the house, flung there like rubbish for the passing fancy of tramps, scavengers, and prostitutes. All her clothes seemed to be missing buttons or had various marks of wear and tear. She had worried that John would have taken scissors to the lot to add insult to injury but - thank goodness for small favours - bruising her and throwing her out seemed to have been enough for him.

She tore off a white bin bag from the roll with a snap. The only thing left on the carpet now that the clothes were on the bed was the evidence of her night time binges: wine bottles and fast food wrappers dotted around her feet and in the corners of the room. Crisp packets were crumpled everywhere and looked as if they were multiplying. She dragged the full bin bag over to the far side of the room. The bottles clinked together as the weight in the bag shifted. Finally leaving it by the door to throw out, Dayna turned to face the bed where her old clothes were heaped. Now was as good a time as any to sift through everything and decide what to keep of her old life and what to throw out.

Lucy was late for school as she stepped out of the shower and sprinted across the landing to her room, rubbing her hair manically with her pink towel. The big walnut clock on the mantle of the living room was already saying nine thirty which meant the bus stop in the nearest town two miles away was out. She'd have to phone a taxi.

The possibility of truanting from school and staying home crossed her mind for a moment as she dried herself off, but it would never have worked. Her mother would love to come home and find her in the living room watching TV. She could just picture her screaming: "Richard! Your daughter did not go to school today. The school you work hard to pay for. You talk to her. I can't talk to her!" She wouldn't give her the satisfaction.

She looked around her bedroom, her one safe place where her parents and their views could not reach her. She had real friends for the first time in her life and her mum hated it. Maxine's mum lived on a council estate and Max hadn't seen her dad in years. At least Max's mum wasn't preoccupied with appearances or spending thousands of pounds getting the living room decorated where the curtains had to be the exact right shade of beige to be harmonious with the cream carpet and the ivory leather sofa that her dad was probably still paying off on his credit card. Phoneys, both of them.

She pulled on her school uniform, a white blouse with a grey skirt and an emerald green blazer that had the school's crest embroidered on. Her father paid a private fee to send her there and the school kept a close watch on attendance. Truancy from anyone was an automatic letter home to parents.

She grabbed her leather satchel and raced down the plush carpeted hallway passing gold-framed photos of family holidays and off down the stairs.

Her father's study was Richard Cunningham's private world of walnut wood and dark leather. A small picture of Lucy stood on the corner of the desk. If there were spare cash anywhere in the house, she'd find it here. Pulling open his desk drawers she found a silver letter opener, a fountain pen, ink cartridges and his address book. She opened it and flipped through. There was a small fold of cash inserted in the middle of the book. Jackpot! She put the bills into the breast pocket of her blazer and closed the drawer of his desk. She picked up the cordless phone off one of the black granite counter tops and rang for a cab.

Allard's Prep School for Girls was in the centre of the city. The school itself was built around a church that had been converted into a two-storey teaching space with extensions of new classrooms added.

It was twelve noon when Lucy finally stepped out of the cab and ran into the admissions office. She knocked on the door and prayed to herself that Jaye Tucker, the kinder of the women that worked there, would answer the door. Her luck was not in when Connie Francis answered instead. Her voice was clipped, while her wrinkled face wore a permanent look of annoyance.

"Yes?"

Lucy's heart sank. Connie was a short woman in her late fifties who spoke to all the students as if they were cockroaches which, along with their hopes and dreams, should be crushed as quickly as possible. Lucy imagined her dream was of an empty school building in which the loud laughter of various girls and the echoing footfalls of the two hundred plus students that attended was a distant memory and where Connie could spend the days in her office working on her paperwork without incident or interruption.

"Hello Miss Frances. Could I speak to Miss Tucker, please?"

"What do you need to speak to her about?"

"It's something private. I only want to speak to her about it, please."

"If it's something to do with attendance, then it falls into my department's remit and you can speak to me."

Lucy took a deep breath. "Look, it's urgent that I speak to her. I think I just saw someone drive off in her car."

Lucy watched with silent glee as Connie's face change from annoyed to worried. She disappeared into the office and shut the door.

Jaye Tucker's smiling face appeared in the doorframe and she stepped out of the office and closed the door, allowing them privacy. "What is it? Connie said it was urgent."

"I was late today as I missed the bus. I didn't get up on time but I'm here now and I wanted to know if you would write a letter home. My dad would freak out if he knew I missed classes."

"Oh, I see. Well, you're here now. You were marked absent this morning but I will put a note on today's attendance saying you were excused from the morning period but make sure you find your morning teacher and apologise for missing their class. Your attendance is usually good so I'm sure it would be alright."

Jaye disappeared back into the admin office. Lucy felt relief lift her as the doors closed. Crisis averted.

Lucy saw it was lunchtime and decided to go looking for Maxine. Peering around the crowded canteen, her eyes flitted across various girls with identical green blazers sitting around in groups of four and five, eventually resting on a dark-haired girl sitting alone looking down at an open book on the table.

Maxine, feeling the weight of her gaze, looked up and her serious face slowly brightened as she recognised Lucy.

Lucy made a beeline over to her, threw her satchel down on the table and plonked herself down in the empty seat next to her friend.

"Where have you been? I figured you were ill or something."

"My mum didn't drive me to the bus stop like she usually does so I had to find my way here alone."

"Shit! She left you home on purpose?"

"Yeah, I figured it's her way of getting back at me for seeing you at the weekend."

"She's a total bitch. You can't count on parents for anything. Trust me."

Lucy turned to look at her properly. Maxine had her hair side-parted over one eye that upon a closer look had a bluish bruise that was fading to an ugly grey.

Maxine looked away from her and moved the book up to cover her face.

"Jesus, Max. What happened?"

"Mum's new boyfriend. They were carrying on Sunday night and I got between them. The fist that was meant for my dear mother got me instead but I'm glad actually because it made calling the police simple. Usually when authority comes knocking, Mum gets herself out of her drunken state for long enough to tell the police that her out-of-control daughter called them as a joke and they don't come in. This time I had proper proof, and they got his sorry arse out of my house."

"Why didn't you call me? You could've stayed at mine."

"It was like one am on a Sunday morning. I didn't want to wake your folks up. They dislike me as it is."

"I didn't even know your mum had a boyfriend."

"He's new on the block. I'm hoping she gets rid of him quick. She always needs someone to go out drinking with. Otherwise she has to stay home and drink alone. I can't wait to get away. Not long now."

Maxine's face darkened and Lucy didn't know what to say to her. She looked at the book she was reading. It was 'Flowers in the Attic.'

"What's your book about?"

"This?" She looked down and then back at Lucy and smiled the smile that one conspirator gives to another. "It's great. It's about a mum who locks her children in the attic as the children's grandparents hate them and won't give her money in the will unless she keeps them locked there."

"That's horrid!"

"Yeah, it's dark stuff," Maxine said with a wicked smile. "I'm doing an essay on it for English."

"Have you told anyone in the Student Support office about your mum?"

Maxine laughed out loud. "Oh, they know all about my mum, but I don't want to report it as they'll just call social services and they're useless. They do nothing, and I don't fancy being put in some stranger's house. I'm only angry when it kicks off on a school night. Good grades are my ticket out of that hellhole. I want to finish sixth form and then go far away to university."

"Ha! Well, be sure to write occasionally as I'll miss you."

"Are you kidding? You're coming with me wherever I go. We will be like Thelma and Louise, going everywhere together."

"I'm having a hard time with English, Max. I don't even know what book to write about for Lit."

"Why don't you try reading 'Carrie'? It won't take you too long to read. Plus, there's an evil mum in it who's crazy."

Lucy laughed happily.

"Sounds like a treat! I'll check the library."

"You won't find 'Carrie' in this school's library. It's written by the King. You'll have to get your copy in the city. They're down on him here even though he's a total genius."

Both turned as the bell rang, signalling that afternoon period was about to begin. Girls jumped up all over the large lunch hall and made their way out joining the crowd of girls wearing green and grey uniforms.

"Call me tonight?"

"Will do. So glad you showed up."

"You think I could go a day without you? I'd wither and die." They both laughed and hurried together out of the hall.

Emily Partington paused at the front door before stepping over the threshold into her mother's house. As she closed the front door she flinched when she heard her mother speak from the living room.

"Go and wash your face, Emily."

Nodding obediently to the empty hallway Emily went into the bathroom and took out sponges from the medicine cabinet and began removing the make-up from her face. She had gone for a drink with a colleague after work and was afraid the smell of drink was on her. Mother Joan's sight was poor but her nose was still sharp, as was her temper.

As she came out of the bathroom and went into the kitchen to start dinner, she felt her mother's gaze on her from where she sat in the armchair.

"That skirt you're wearing is too short. Cheap."

Emily sighed under her breath. "It's a pencil skirt, mother. All the girls at work wear them."

"I never wore a skirt like that to work. Go to your room and change. Now."

Emily turned the hob down and went into her bedroom. She undressed, taking care to hang up the skirt carefully. She only had two work skirts and tried to keep them clean and neat.

Her mother's voice cut across her from the living room: "Turn the light off in the kitchen if you ain't in there!"

She hurried out, passed her mother and turned the light off. Her eyes remained fixed on the screen watching a soap opera, her can of beer resting on the arm of the chair.

Her mother spoke without taking her eyes off the screen: “Mary’s not home again.”

“No, Mam. She works nights waitressing, remember.”

“She wants to pack that in before they sack her. She’s cack-handed, that girl. Always has been. She wants to get herself a proper job.”

As she turned to leave, Joan shouted out: “Girl, get me a beer from the fridge.”

She pulled out a can from the six-pack on the shelf and opened it.

Joan Partington’s hair was dark brown and straked with grey. She was a large woman with no feminine curves. The muscular body she used to corporally punish her daughters in their youth had given way to rolls of fat as she approached her sixties.

Emily reached over to hand her mother the beer can and felt Joan catch her wrist with one strong arm.

“You ain’t been talking to that white trash next door behind my back, have you?”

“No, Mam.’ Emily’s response was automatic and without thought. She didn’t know where Joan had got this from but she’d grown used to her mother’s suspicious mind, which conjured up paranoid fantasies on a daily basis.

“If I ever catch you talking to them, I’ll take you up so hard, you’ll never forget it. Emily, you hear me?”

'Taking you up' was Mother Joan's phrase for beating you black and blue.

Emily felt the grip around her wrist slacken. Her mother's gaze was once again on the television. Emily took the empty beer can away from the armrest and went into the kitchen, throwing it in the bin and walked with her head down back to the bedroom.

She dropped onto the bed with her head in her hands feeling the hardness of the day catch up with her. She longed for escape from having to endure her mother's rants and put-downs about the way she wore her hair, her clothes, anything.

Lying awake that night she vowed to herself that she would find a way to leave home very soon.

The following week she went out for a drink with Stuart again. He arrived at her desk at five past five. She had made herself look busy filing papers away and tidying her desk as she watched the other girls leave the office out of the corner of her eye, not wanting anyone to see her and Stuart leave together.

He had come into her office with his wool coat buttoned up, looking smart. He turned her around and slid her coat onto her back. She turned to face him and she could smell his aftershave as he led her by the hand out of the office. *Just one drink*, she promised herself.

Conversation was surprisingly easy. He made her laugh with impersonations of their colleagues. She thought about her mother waiting at home for her, beer can in one hand, her blank fish eyes staring at the TV screen, her large body rooted to the sofa like a poisonous shrub.

Emily glanced at her wrist to check the time and Stuart put his hand over her watch. "I've been waiting to ask you out for ages."

He leaned in to kiss her but she pulled away. "I have to get home."

His smile faltered and then gradually re-appeared. He downed his drink and said: "I'll drive you."

"No, it's fine. I'll walk." She opened her purse but he waved it away.

"Don't worry. I'll get this."

Her watch said seven thirty. She ran out of the pub door, feeling the stone in her chest increasing with every minute that passed. She started to walk replaying every minute of her date and steeling herself for the fury that no doubt awaited her at home. When she arrived she got up the two steps to the front door and opened her purse to rummage for her keys.

The front door opened. Her sister Mary stood there, her large frame eclipsing the light behind her. Her face was grave. She spoke aloud but not to her. "Emily's home, Mum."

Emily felt sick. *Here we go*, she thought, walking down the short hall and turned to see Mary disappearing into the bedroom and closing the door. *Coward.*

Her mother's eyes were staring at the television. She was taking slow sips from her beer can. Emily stood on the spot waiting for her to speak, much in the way the accused stands in the witness box.

"Girl, where were you tonight?"

She felt the weight of Mother Joan's gaze root her to the spot. "I was working late."

Joan rose off the armchair like a viper. Her balled fist crashed into the bridge of Emily's nose. Black flowers bloomed in front of her eyes as she hit the ground crying out in pain. She felt her mother's boot connect with her stomach and she shrieked, trying to turn away from the blows. Her mother's voice came again, calm and controlled, devoid of emotion. "You tell me where you were, girl."

Emily tried to get up. Blood poured from her nose. It tasted thick and metallic. The boot connected with her again. She cried out and tried to crawl to her bedroom. "Mam, I swear I lost track of time." She choked the words out through sobs.

Joan grabbed her by her blouse and brought her face close to her. Emily saw her nostrils flaring wide as she took deep sniffs. Emily had sprayed herself with perfume before coming home to cover the smell of vodka and tonic she'd had with Stuart. She prayed that it would be enough.

"You've been out behind my back, girl. You tell me now. Don't make it worse for yourself."

Emily shook her head vehemently, "I swear I've not been anywhere. Please, Mam." She kept her hands clamped to her sides. She didn't dare touch Joan anywhere. She was like a tiger: anything might provoke her anger more. *Best not to resist. Her rage would peter out. Please let it be over soon.* She felt her mother's hands slacken and slowly come away.

"Don't you go dallying again, girl. You hear me?"

"I promise I won't."

Emily felt the volcano's wrath subside. Joan sank her weight back into the sofa. She picked up the remote and flicked it at the screen causing people to reappear and the chattering of actors filled the living room.

Emily felt the cold snail trail of blood as it ran down her face and onto her blouse.

Her mum's fisheyes remained on the television as she spoke. "Clean yourself, girl."

Emily unbuttoned her blouse feeling a cold sting of shame as she looked at herself in the reflection of the medicine cabinet, blood on her face and down her chin. Underneath the shame, she felt a small pit of anger open inside her. Her work blouse was ruined. She turned on the hot tap and ran a bath for herself.

Her mother shouted from the other room: "Don't use all the hot water!"

"I won't, Mam!" She dropped the cotton blouse to the floor and sat in the bath watching the clear water slowly change to a rose pink. She tried to think back to hours before when Stuart had slid her coat on and she had brushed up against him as they walked to the pub: the smell of his aftershave, the crackle of her skin as he placed his hand on her wrist. She tried to hang on to these thoughts but it was no use, the throbbing in her nose blotted out all feelings of joy she had making a silent vow to herself never to go out after work again.

Emily submerged herself beneath the hot water of the bath blowing out bubbles as her mind turned again to the thought of escape. She didn't earn enough to make it alone. She thought about Stuart. Perhaps she could get herself pregnant. He would have to take her in then. He seemed like he was from decent stock, perhaps a family that wouldn't ever let a pregnant woman go homeless. Mother would throw her out when she showed. It would be a gamble, but could she do it? Could she be so cruel as to bring an innocent thing into an uncaring world?

She felt the bridge of her nose. It didn't feel as if it was broken. She'd still be able to go to work and explain to Stuart why she'd rushed off. *Please, let him take me out again.*

She stood up and stepped out of the bathtub and stole a glance in the mirror. Her nose was swollen and her eyes were red and puffy. She pinched the bridge of her nose again and thought that there would be one hell of a bruise there in the morning.

Falling asleep that night she felt the first embers of rebellion alight in her stomach.

The following week she found a letter from Stuart in her desk asking her if she would like to have dinner with him at his home. She said yes.

She went with Stuart from the office to his home, a small flat he rented on the outskirts of the city. He did not ask her about her bruises, and after the meal he didn't pressure her for sex, but she knew she would have given it to him if he asked. She would have given him anything, everything that she had of herself, if only he would take her in.

That night she slept with the bonfire of rebellion roaring inside her as she accepted his advances. After their passion was spent he fell asleep peacefully beside her, while she tried to doze with her head nestled against his chest wondering if mother was awake, sitting in the armchair waiting for her to return. Eventually these thoughts drifted away from her in the dark and she fell into a peaceful sleep.

The next day after work she returned home for the last time. The front door opened, and Joan was standing there, barring her way like a stone idol, her slack eyes like small furnaces glowing with menace. "Girl, where were you last night?"

Emily took a deep breath and looked her in the eyes as she spoke. "I spent the night with a friend. I've just come home to get a few things. I won't be long."

The moment the door closed behind her Joan struck, pummelling her to the ground. Emily didn't even try to get away. She withdrew into herself, waiting for the volcano to spend its wrath and then lie dormant once more.

Joan towered over her, looking down. "Get up, girl."

Emily slowly got to her feet and faced her without fear.

"Where were you yesterday evening?"

"I told you Mother, I stayed at a friend's."

"Liar!"

There was pain as her mother's fury rained down on her, a fist catching her across the cheek. She pushed Emily with her wide body down the hall towards the bedroom she shared with her sister. Emily cowered against the wall and put her hands up to shield her face and tried to work her way out towards the front door around her mother's solid body but Joan grabbed her by the hair and pulled her backwards.

She screamed into her face: “How long has it been going on!? How long have you been whoring behind my back instead of staying here and doing your duty to me?”

Emily shouted back: “I haven’t done anything!”

Joan’s fist caught her around the face again. She screamed. Emily could make out the beer cans on the chair down the hall and understood she had stayed up all night, waiting for her to return so she could dole out punishment.

“Take off your skirt and blouse.”

“No, Mother.”

The hand whipped out again, catching her across the face. She backed up against the door of the bedroom, trying to keep as much distance between herself and her mother as possible.

“Girl, you do as I tell you. You take off that tarty outfit. I’m sure he’s left his mark on you somewhere. You’ve not been minding me. You lie down on your bed and take your blouse off or, by God, I’ll tear it off. Don’t make it worse for yourself.”

Emily tried to grab her mother’s wrists. Her mother was now pulling at her blouse, trying to tear it away from her. “You get your hands off me, Mother!” She felt the blouse rip, a button dropped to the floor. “I mean it, Mother. Now stop it!” Emily watched in disbelief as her own hand flew out and caught Joan sharply across the cheek. Silence filled the room as the two women stared at each other, Emily holding her blouse closed over her breasts, Joan, large and looming, standing motionless in shock.

Joan's hand went to her face and touched where the slap had landed and then looked down at her hand as if checking for blood. "You dare lay your hands on me in my house!"

Emily shoved Joan backwards and stumbled past her into the living room. Her eyes darted around for something, anything, that she could use to fend her off.

Her mother's voice came from down the hall. "You walk to me now. You strip off your clothes and take your punishment. I'll give you to the count of three."

Emily extended one arm out to the arm of the sofa as she heard the buckle snap open on her mother's belt.

"Two!" she said, pulling the belt through the loops in her denim jeans and coiling it around her hand.

Emily's hand tightened over the beer can.

"Three!" Joan charged down the hall, flattening the carpet with the heavy tread of her footfalls as she came, balling her hands into fists like a boxer.

Emily put her right arm up, blocking the first blow to her face and brought her left arm around in a wide arc. The metal of the beer can left a gleam of silver as it passed through the air connecting with her mother's jaw with a solid "thunk". Joan gave a cry as she was caught off balance. Emily stepped forward and swung again, hitting her hard across the face driving her back. The beer can crashed into her mother's nose making Joan shriek with pain. The belt fell from her hand, forgotten as she put her own hands up to shield her face.

Emily hit her again and again, "Don't you ever touch me again, Mother. You hear me? Don't you ever touch me again! I'm leaving you here. I'm going to my room and I'm packing my clothes and I'm going tonight and if you move from this room I swear I will wrap that belt around your neck, so you can see how it feels. You hear me?"

Emily drew her arm back to strike her again and her mother cringed back and tripped over the leg of the coffee table. She felt pain in her hand and saw the beer can crushed within it.

She bent down and picked up the belt and limped to the bedroom. She kept the door open. She dumped the bag on her bed and threw in bras and knickers, her two work skirts and blouses. She got to the bedroom door and cast one look back. She had what she needed. She was leaving tonight. Stuart would have to take her in. At least, she hoped he would.

She pulled the front door open and, without looking back, strode out taking deep breaths of free air that for the first nineteen years of her life had been denied her. The moonlight lit her way out of the estate and onto the road.

Eve Spencer did not like working on Monday mornings at the hospital. She never worked weekends and always loathed the first morning back after two days away. The skeleton staff that worked over the weekend, in her view, had the mental equivalence of the contents found in the bargain clothing bin of a charity shop.

She was annoyed when she came into the kitchen for her usual morning cigarette and coffee, only to find she was not only out of cigarettes but milk as well. She would have to have it black. Typical.

Eve worked in the mental health ward of Springfield Hospital and, after twenty years as a nurse, felt she had seen everything there was to see. Life held no surprises for her

Throwing her white uniform into a large carrier bag, she began rummaging around the coffee table for her keys. The surface was littered with full ashtrays and old magazines. She lifted one up to find a used scratch card nestled underneath a copy of that weekend's TV guide. Two of the windows had been scratched off but the third was still covered. Stealing a quick look at the clock to see if she had time to spare, she ran into the kitchen.

Thoughts of sandy beaches and long lie-ins filled her head as she hunted around for some spare change. She decided to use her house key. Perhaps she wouldn't have to go to work after all… Perhaps she would never have to work again. There were two plums already scratched out. If the third box turned out to be another plum, she was a millionaire.

She stood hunched over the ticket on the countertop and began scratching away furiously, licking her lips as the door key revealed what was in window number three. A lemon stared up at her.

"Fuck!" She banged the counter with her large ham of a fist and crumbling up the offending ticket barged out the front door.

It was only when she reached the staff entrance of the hospital she realized she'd been in such a hurry to make it on time she'd forgotten to nip into the newsagents' to buy cigarettes multiplying her sour mood threefold.

"Good morning, Eve!" some happy voice trilled at her from behind setting her teeth on edge.

She turned her head to assess whether this was a doctor (a superior to be engaged in small talk with) or a fellow nurse (inferior and should be snubbed). It was a nurse. Eve couldn't remember her name. She was young and wore one of those annoying smiles that suggested that she was happy to be at work at eight am and desperately wanted to pass on her positive attitude to everyone in the building like the carrier of a virus. Eve fetched a deep sigh while turning away from her.

The nurse shot to her side, grinning like a Jack-o'-Lantern. "How was your weekend, Nurse Spencer?"

Eve took down the nurses' chart from her pigeonhole outside the communal office and flipped through it theatrically, taking nothing in. "Fine," she said tersely and began to hurriedly walk to the mental ward, her white plimsolls squeaking on the mopped floor. She was determined to put as much distance between herself and the nurse who seemed hell-bent on engaging her in conversation and sucking the last free minute she had to herself away from her like a joyful leech.

"Oh, Nurse Spencer! Aren't you going to change into your uniform before going to the ward?"

Eve was caught so far off guard she actually turned to acknowledge the girl who was scuttling up to her like an insect. Eve could see she'd got up early enough to put make-up on. Her lips were an annoying shade of pink. "I can do the round for you while you sign in and get changed," she beamed, reaching for the clipboard that Eve was clutching.

She looked down at herself and saw that in her rush to demean her colleague and escape conversation, she hadn't changed into her uniform.

"Sharon, isn't it?"

"Fiona, Nurse Spencer. My name is Fiona."

"Yes, right, Fiona. No, I will do the rounds, as I am the senior nurse here. If you want something to do, go to the nurses' office and check that all the patients' charts for each ward are in each nurse's pigeonhole. I've got a feeling the weekend staff may have forgotten to print them all out and, if you finish doing that, you can make me a coffee: white, three sugars."

Eve took enormous satisfaction in wiping the happy look from the girl's face. She followed her up the hall in the direction of the changing rooms to put on her uniform for the day, looking scornfully at Fiona's slim figure underneath her tight uniform as she hurried towards the office.

The changing room was a small tiled room situated behind the mental health ward. There were three rows of identical lockers where employees could store their valuables and personal wear and a row of showers that were never used ran along the back wall.

Springfield Hospital was built during the 1800s and used as an asylum. The hospital grounds surrounding it were filled with looming trees and voluptuous flower beds. The bulk of the doctors' offices were on the top floor of the great five-storey house that stood at the heart of the grounds and the floors beneath served as the mental ward with various therapy rooms that bore the appearance of disused classrooms.

Eve liked the house. The period building had a feeling of grandeur about it, a touch of the traditional mixed with a foreboding; both qualities Eve felt she possessed.

Inside, the corridors were wide and long where footfalls echoed loudly, where it was all too easy to get lost. The walls were solid stone, painted magnolia and always cold. Windows were shut tight with iron handles and great pipes ran along inside the walls like metal veins. There had been an attempt to brighten the interior by hanging patients' artwork along the fading walls, but the canvasses were always so small that staff and visitors, eager to get into smaller office spaces or the fresh air of the outside grounds, never stopped to study them closely.

Eve was proud to be working in the hospital where the noble work was done for those that could not afford private care. The turnover of staff was high. Many of the younger girls could not handle the night shifts on the mental wards. The corridors late at night never failed to scare some of a weaker temperament. Rumours of patients getting out and lost on the grounds or found wandering the hall in the morning were rife.

Eve always sacked nurses on night duty who allowed such news to reach the ears of patients' relatives. She'd even sacked one girl recently for refusing to work the night shift after she'd said she'd heard whispers in the corridor late at night. Weeks later Eve had been asked to provide a reference for the girl who was going to work as a nurse in one of the private doctors surgeries in the city and had declined to reply. The girl was useless, head full of nonsense, and probably marked on. She knew young girls were always jabbing themselves for ink and needles. She had no time for her type on the ward.

Eve undressed in a hurry peeling off her tight blouse then took out her white uniform from the carrier bag on the floor. She hurried, eager to be out and begin her rounds. She adjusted her cap in the mirror. Her burnt perm had been set like a clown's wig and her nurse's lanyard hung around her thick neck. Smoothing out the creases on her uniform with the palms of her hands, she gave herself one more look in the mirror and strode out of the room into the wide fluorescent-lit magnolia hallway leading to the mental ward.

The door to the nurses' office was closed when Eve arrived. She heard voices inside and remained for a moment with her ear pressed up to the doorframe. She recognised the saccharine high voice of Fiona who'd spoken to her that morning and another woman's voice she didn't recognise.

"I said 'hello' to her this morning, but she ignored me. She's hard work, always hard work, that woman."

Eve threw open the door and marched in with her clipboard under one arm. Both of the young nurses jumped apart.

"Fiona, once you've finished with your conversation, perhaps you could do as I've asked you and check that all the patients' charts are in the correct nurse's pigeonholes."

"I have, Nurse Spencer. They're all there in the correct place."

"Good, then you can tell me what happened to the coffee I asked for before."

"Oh sorry! I forgot."

"Clearly," Eve replied scathingly, flipping through the sheets on her clipboard. "And you, Shelley." The nurse who Fiona has been gossiping with was half way out the door when Eve shouted at her. "If you've got nothing to do, perhaps you could water the plants on the ward. I doubt anyone bothered to do it over the weekend."

She watched Fiona prepare the coffee out of the corner of her eye and mentally counted how many sugars she spooned into the cup, determined to tell her off: one, two, three.

"Here you are, Nurse Spencer."

She took the mug from her hands with a curt nod and took a sip. The small clock on the wall said eight fifteen. It was time to wake the patients. She fetched a sigh. No time to finish the coffee. "Fiona, could you please unlock the medicine cabinets and take these with you?" Eve tore from a list of each patient on the ward and what medication they had each morning with breakfast. "I'll wake everyone up. After you've done that, grab whatever her name is and the pair of you can assist me in getting everyone to the patient common room for breakfast. Chop, chop!"

Eve watched her go with a grimace. Fiona was already out the door and around the corner and had to walk back quickly when Eve called her back. "One other thing. Try not to mix the patients' meds. I don't fancy having to deal with a death on the ward this early in the week."

Eve set the coffee cup down on the desk and hummed out of tune under her breath as she strode to the large double doors that would take her to the mental health ward to wake the patients. She swiped her nurses' card through the electronic reader and the door buzzed open. There was a log of every staff member coming in and out and Eve liked to review the log at the end of the month to catch out nurses on the night shift checking in late. She had caught a few in her time taking long lunches. She relished weeding out the useless ones.

The ward itself had only seven in-patients. These seven were sectioned for their own safety and, unlike outpatients who were sectioned voluntarily, these seven were not permitted to leave. Each bed had a rail encircling it with a curtain hanging around the patient for privacy. Each patient had a bedside table where they could have various houseplants that friends or relatives brought them although the turnover for plants, unlike the patients, was high.

Eve saw Shelley spraying a spider plant next to the sleeping head of Eunice Hyde, no doubt hoping to revivify its wilted look with the sheer force of good intention. "Give it up, girl. The plant's dead. So are the others. Throw them all out."

Shelley carried on spraying. "I think it's the lack of light in here, Eve. Perhaps if we opened the curtains and let some light in-"

"No amount of light will bring back these dead things. Get rid of them."

Eve moved to the far end of the ward to the largest window that looked out onto the grounds was and threw open the heavy curtains. "Right! Rise and shine! All of you." Light flooded the ward causing all the patients to come awake with groans. Eunice Hyde was trying to cover her face with her pillow to keep the light away from her. Eve began moving down the room, throwing back the curtains enclosing the patients' beds.

"Actually, Nurse Spencer-"

"What?" She turned to face Shelley cradling a dead vicus in her arms maternally as if it were a stillborn baby.

"I would speak to the doctor and ask if we could have some petty cash to buy some orchids for the ward. These spider plants aren't very cheery and I think some colour would brighten the place up."

Eve glared at her. "We don't want the patients to become over stimulated."

"I don't think there's any danger of that, Nurse Spencer." She was looking past Eve at the bed at the end of the ward nearest the window. Even though the bright light of day was flooding the room, unlike the other patients, the man sleeping there had not come awake. During Shelley's first few weeks working on the ward, she'd often come in afraid that some patients had passed away in the night, but then she'd learned that the cocktail of antipsychotics and mood stabilisers they were on caused them to sleep heavily.

Eve walked up to his bed and shook the man awake. "Time to wake up, Mr Graves!" she bellowed.

Shelley turned her face away with a frown. She didn't like how heavy-handed she was with the patients. She didn't need to shake him awake like that.

"I wouldn't bother wasting money on the plants," Eve continued. "Nothing here stays alive for long." She strode towards the double doors to fetch the medicine trolley. "These zombies would suck the life out of just about anything."

Shelley gaped at her. Eve walked through the double door which locked behind her without waiting for a reply. As far as she was concerned, the conversation was over.

Shelley walked around to Paul Graves' bedside. He had one arm across his face to shut out the light coming in from the huge window.

"Are you all right, Mr Graves?" Shelley asked, trying to take his hands in hers.

He turned away from her, mumbling.

"What, Sir?" She bent down so her face was level with his and cringed back as he shouted.

"I need to go to the toilet!"

She recoiled backwards. "Stay put for now, Mr Graves. I'll run and get the wheelchair!" Shelley flew through the double doors to fetch a wheelchair from the storage room. Swiping her card through the reader and pushing her way back in through the door her nose was hit by an overpowering smell. "Oh, Mr Graves!" The old man was half out of bed, lying on the floor. It looked like he was trying to crawl away from the soiled bed. It was all over the sheets and his hands.

Shelley ran around to him and wrapped her arms around his torso, hauling him into the wheelchair. "It's all right, Mr Graves. I'll get you cleaned up."

"What is this?" The voice cut her like a knife. Eve was looming in the doorway. "What happened?"

"Mr Graves seems to have had an accident. I'll take him to the bathroom and get him cleaned up. Why don't you get rid of his dirty bedding? I'll ask Fiona to take the other patients into the common room for breakfast."

She pushed past Eve using Mr Graves as a battering ram. She took some delight in forcing Eve's corpulent frame up against the wall to avoid being marked by Paul Graves' poo-smeared hands reaching out to clutch her.

Eve covered her face with the clipboard as he went past. Shelly had to suppress a giggle.

Fiona was coming down the corridor, running behind the medicine trolley. "What's happened?"

"Mr Graves seems to have been caught short. Could you give me a hand lifting him into the bathtub? I've told Eve to sort out his bedding."

"Does she need any-"

Shelley cut her off. "No, leave her to it. She's always so quick to remind me she's head nurse. Let her struggle by herself. If you grab his legs, I'll grab his shoulders. Here we go." They lifted him into one of the two bathtubs that occupied the patient bathroom. "Could you get him some clean scrubs please?" She turned on the hot shower and began hosing him down.

Shelley studied Paul's face as it reclined against the bathtub edge. He was smiling. "What's so funny, Mr Graves?" she asked, smiling back at him. He didn't respond but carried on watching her with interest as she hosed him down with the showerhead.

Fiona came in with some light blue patients' scrubs. "Thanks Fiona. Could you give me a hand drying him?"

"Eve wants me to bring in the medicine trolley. She says they need their meds."

"Well, she'll just have to wait, won't she? We're understaffed since she got that new girl sacked last week. If she's that desperate, she can do the medicine rounds herself."

Fiona grinned at her. "Don't let her hear you talking like that!"

Fiona and Shelley towelled down Paul Graves' damp body. "Don't you think he's a little thin, Shelley?" Shelley could make out his ribcage standing out prominently from his chest.

"Yes, he does look a little underweight. I'll put it on his file. Extra helpings for Mr Graves!"

"Right, let's get you back to the common room now you're nice and clean. Fi, give us a hand, would you?"

The two nurses heaved his deadweight back into his wheelchair and wheeled him back into the ward.

"I don't know how you deal with it."

"What, Fi?"

"The smell of shit!"

Shelley laughed. "Don't worry. You'll get used to it. There are far worse things."

"That's not the first time he's soiled himself, is it?"

"It happens sometimes, when she's on shift." She nodded to the common room door unmindful of Paul who was watching them both with interest. "I think it's his way of protesting."

"You don't think it's the medication he's prescribed, do you?"

"Not sure. Let me look." Shelley walked over to the end of the bed and looked at his chart. He's on a high dose of escitalopram and citalopram for his condition. Diarrhoea can be one of the side effects. He's on quite a high dose."

"Do you think we should mention it to Eve? I think he's on too much."

"I wouldn't say anything just now. I'll speak to the doctor when I next see him. It's just due to his condition. He needs to be heavily sedated. He's schizophrenic. We had him on a much milder dose but he often got out of the ward and went walkabout. He could be difficult to restrain when he's in the middle of an episode so we increased the dosage."

"How long has he been here?"

"I'm not sure. He's been here since before I started."

"Nobody ever visits him?"

"No, no, I don't think so. I will leave a note on his file to review his medication."

Fiona left, passing Eve in the doorway of the nurses' office. She had to breathe in to avoid brushing against her prominent stomach as she went past.

"Shelley, why is Mr Graves not with the others in the common room?"

She carried on writing the note on his file. It wasn't even noon yet and she could feel her inner fuse growing shorter. "I've left him in bed. He was sleeping when I left him. I didn't want to overdo it with him. I thought it best to let him rest."

"He needs his medication on time. If we leave it till he wakes up, it'll be off schedule."

Shelley sighed. "I'll make up his meds now and leave them next to him. He can drink it when he wakes up."

"I'll wake him up."

"I want you to let him sleep. I've also left a note on his file for the doctor. I think he's being given too much citalopram."

"He's old. The dosage is just right for someone in his condition."

"When was he last assessed?"

Eve's eyes narrowed. "I reviewed him a month ago and thought he was doing just fine. If you have any problems, I suggest you speak to the doctor."

"I will," she said tartly. "I've left a note here for him to contact me."

Eve's mouth tightened forming a crevice across her face. She walked to the sink and filled a glass with water and dropped the pills into the glass, stirring until it was filled with a ghostly white fluid. "I'll take it through to him now." Eve turned and walked through the door.

Shelley called after her. "Leave it by his bedside. Don't wake him!"

Eve heard her but gave no sign of acknowledgement. She swiped her card through the reader and strode up to Paul Graves' bed which was once again encircled by a thin polyester curtain. She could see the shadow of his body through the veil and heard him snoring. She left the glass at his bedside next to a dead brown potted spider plant and strode off into the common room to clear away the breakfast trays without looking back.

Unseen by anyone, a wrinkled hand emerged from within the curtain and picked up the glass. The milky liquid sloshed from side to side as the hand tipped the contents of the glass into the plant pot. The wrinkled hand withdrew into the folds of the curtain.

Emily had just turned out of the council estate and had passed out of sight of her house when it happened. The street lamps emitted no light for her to see by. The shattered glass of their bulbs lay littered on the pavement. Emily walked on seeing by the light of the full moon along the stretch of road that led to the nearest town.

She had some money. She thought about calling on Stuart and, if he would not have her, spend the night at a hostel if any were open. She kept having to remind herself that she had a job. She could get more hours. She would survive.

She hugged herself against the night air as she walked and imagined herself somewhere warm. She guessed by the lights in the distance she was about a mile away from the town, only an hour's walk if not shorter. She was so deep in her thoughts she hadn't noticed the car that pulled up creeping quietly along next to her, its engine quiet, its headlights cut off.

"You all right there, little lady?"

She jumped back, startled. She hadn't heard the engine. A tattooed arm came out of the window, holding something.

"You've got some blood on your face there. Here." She saw in his hand a white Kleenex tissue. She made no move to take it. She didn't take things from strangers.

"It's all right. I'm not going to bite you. Saw you back there. Girl your age shouldn't be walking this time of night."

The moon's s rays lit up the car. It was painted bright blue, a relic from the 60s. Music drifted towards her from the radio. *Pretty woman, walking down the street. Pretty woman, the kind I like to meet…* She saw his arm was covered in tattoos: snakes and dragons painted in lapis lazuli and bright oranges.

"I didn't mean to startle you, little lady." The hand withdrew back into the depths of the car.

"No, wait!" Emily touched the side of her head, her fingers came away wet. "Thank you." She took the tissue and pressed it to the side of her face. The driver made no move to show himself.

"What kind of car is that?"

"This here, girly, is a 1957 Chevrolet Convertible." Emily could see the car was an intense duck egg blue with a white roof.

"Where are you running to this time of night?"

"I'm heading into town to spend the night at my boyfriend's," she lied.

"Is he not gentleman enough to come and collect you himself?"

"He doesn't know I'm coming. I'm surprising him." She tried to place the man's accent. Irish or perhaps American.

The light went on in the car interior. The inside of the car was upholstered in light blue leather identical to the car's exterior. Everything from the leather seats to the steering wheel had been coated in the same shade of blue. Emily couldn't help but smile at the out-of-date dials and speedometer and the various levers that jutted out of the steering wheel.

She couldn't guess the driver's age as he wore sunglasses, but she could see deep lines around his mouth. She guessed he was in his late forties or early fifties. A lit cigarette protruded from his mouth. There was a wedding ring on his hand. He wore a red plaid shirt the shade of oxblood and two buttons were undone showing a generous amount of chest hair.

He took off his sunglasses as he spoke, concern showing in his grey eyes. "Girl, I've got a daughter your age and I tell you now I saw you walking back there with bruises all over you and I'm not going to pry but I wouldn't be happy if it was my little girl wandering the streets at night all marked up when she should be tucked up in bed."

The radio played on inside the car. *Don't walk away babe. OK if that's the way it must be OK. I guess I'll go on home but wait there'll be tomorrow night but wait…*

"I could drop you off somewhere. I'm headin' home to the missus now. Could take you with me if you like. She'll cook you a nice meal and get you wrapped up warm."

Emily could feel the heat from the air conditioner in the car reaching out towards her beckoning silently. She looked down the long dark road. There were lights way down in the distance where the road sloped towards the town. It looked a long way away. She looked back at the man in the car. *He's married with a daughter of his own.*

She took a voluntary step forward and her nostrils flared as she caught a faint whiff of his aftershave like a tremor of violets. "A ride would be great."

He leaned over to the passenger side and pulled the lever. The door swung open. "Hop in, little lady."

Emily slid into the passenger seat and shut the car door. The headlights came on as the car pulled off the curb and drove off into the darkness.

Emily's eyes darted around, taking in the queer interior of the car. The leather was slightly faded on the seats. All the inside doors had silver handles.

As the car picked up speed Emily tried to plan what she would do tomorrow. She could find a hostel for the night, have a hot shower and a good night's rest. Then she would focus on getting herself to work.

She looked over at the stranger. His sunglasses were back on his face and his eyes on the road. The dial on the speedometer stood at 35 mph. She watched the hedges and trees as they went around a bend and came closer to the town. The trees thinned out as more buildings sprang up.

"Could you drop me off near the bus station, please?" She wasn't sure, but she felt the car begin to speed up around her. Glancing over, she saw the speedometer creep up to 40 mph.

"Bus station? I wouldn't want no girl of mine sleeping in no bus shelter."

She felt the car pick up speed again.

"I'm not going to sleep in a bus shelter," she insisted. "I know a place round here where I can book myself in for the night. I pass it a lot on my way to work." She noticed out the window buildings had given way to trees again.

"Do you know the address of this place you wanna go?"

She looked over at him, his expression unreadable beneath his sunglasses. *Who the hell wears sunglasses at this time of night, anyway?* "No, but it's close to the bus stop we passed back there. Back there is fine."

"All righty. It's a one-way road so we'll have to wait for a turning."

Elvis was singing on the radio: *You were always on my mind, you were always on my mind.* He hummed along with the music. His hand reached over and shifted the knob into fourth gear. The car was picking up speed.

Emily kept her eyes out of the window. She had to squint to make out various trees that ran along the road going by in a blur. He crooned in the driver's seat next to her, grinning. "*I made you feel second best. I'm so sorry. I was blind. You were always on my mind. You were always on my mind.*"

"You know what, can you drop me off here? I'll walk back."

His face stayed looking forward, but she thought she saw a flicker of a smile pass across his chiselled face as he answered, “Way out here? No can do, darlin’. There’ll be a turning eventually. I’ll have you back in town in no time.”

The speedometer crept up to fifty.

“Can you slow down, please?”

He gave no sign he’d heard her. It was pitch black outside the car window. The road seemed to stretch out endlessly, a long black gravel tongue lit by the headlamps of the old car.

“I’ll need to stop off for a minute, little lady. Got to answer a call of the wild.”

She felt the car slow as he turned left off the road and into a field. He braked a little too hard, and she felt herself go forward and her head came back, hitting the headrest hard. He pulled the handbrake up, cutting off the engine as he pulled the keys out of the ignition.

Emily saw her chance and with both hands worked the silver handle on the inside of the passenger door. To her dismay she felt a dead 'thunk' as she repeatedly worked the handle up and down.

She heard him chuckle coldly behind her. “Ah yes, been meaning to fix that damn door for a while now. You just sit tight and I’ll be back in a jiffy.” He slammed the driver’s side door and the car lights went out. Looking out the passenger window Emily saw the moon bloated full in the night sky. Dense trees stood around. It began to slowly dawn on her just how alone she was and how far from home. She had an idea of driving off with the car but, looking over at the steering wheel, she saw he’d taken the keys with him. That’s when she heard his voice carrying over across the night air. “*You were always on my mind. You were always on my mind.*" She could hear the jingle of the car keys as he shook them up and down in time with his crooning.

Emily closed her eyes. *Think, think.* She did not want to spend another minute in the car with this weirdo. *Try his door.* She saw the glint of the silver handle on the driver's side door and lunged with both hands. The cold metal clunk confirmed her worst fears. He had locked her in. She heard his voice coming closer.

"I made you feel second best. I'm so sorry. I was blind."

Her eyes darted around the car. They kept straying back to the driver's side window where no doubt he would soon appear.

Her seatbelt was the only thing that stopped her falling out of the car when the passenger door flew open making Emily shriek like a trapped animal. She felt something wet clamp against her face. Instinctively she tried to turn her face away from the smell of the chemical but his hand stayed firm. Her face felt cold. She kicked against him with her feet and tried to get out but the seatbelt kept her restrained as he climbed into the passenger side to hold her down. She gradually lost feeling in her legs and her struggles became weaker before she finally gave herself over to the darkness that smothered her.

He kept the sponge on her face for a few more seconds and then took it away to put the side of his face to her mouth, like a man lifting a shell to his ear. He'd overdone it before and killed them by mistake. Rose had been furious on those nights when he'd returned home empty handed and they'd have to wait a whole month for another full moon and go to the trouble of finding another girl. He was relieved when he felt warm breath against his ear. *Good, good.* This one was pretty, and he didn't want her wasted.

He left the car door open to let out the smell of chloroform. Taking his sunglasses off he leaned back in the car and unbuckled her seatbelt. One of his large hands felt the inside of her wrist checking her pulse. It came steady. He stroked her hair softly. One of the top buttons of her blouse had come undone in the struggle and he did it back up before getting out and walking around to the back of the car.

He popped the boot and took out black tape. He left the trunk open and came back around to the front of the car, keeping his ears alert for the sound of any cars approaching. Nothing. The night was still and silent. His watch read one a.m. He needed to hurry and get home soon. Rose would be worrying. He quickly taped her wrists together, leaving some ease in the tape to keep the circulation from being cut off. He then taped her ankles together. He slipped off Emily's work shoes and threw them in the backseat, whistling out of tune as he worked.

Once she was trussed up, he stepped back to take in his handiwork. He whistled cheerfully to the night air and was faintly aware that he had an erection. The struggle always excited him, the feel of their frantic hearts beating against his. He wished he had time for a cigarette. He remembered an old saying about the best cigarette of the day is the one right after a good meal or sex. Obviously whoever said it had not snatched anyone.

Stepping away from the car in the light of the moon, he could take in her full profile. Emily's lashes rested lightly against her cheeks. Her long legs bent up to her knees; her hands were small and delicate bound together as if in prayer. He felt his groin again. Rose said she wanted a blonde one. He had said beggars couldn't be choosers but now he saw her full profile against the blue leather of the car seat he felt a sense of pride at what he'd procured, not a prostitute or a tramp this time, no sir. This girl was a true treasure.

Time for finishing touches. He took the roll of black and bit off a short length and slapped it lightly across her mouth. She probably wouldn't come to until they were at the house but Rose always said prudence was their watchword.

With a moist grunt he picked her up out of the seat and felt a sharp pain in his back as he took the full weight of her and carried her round to the open boot. He placed her slowly with reverence down in the small compartment. He regretted having to bring her legs up to her chest to fit her in, not wanting her to cramp on the long drive back but he couldn't risk having her on the backseat. He looked down at her sleeping like a lamb and spoke aloud to the darkness. "Pretty as a picture. Neat and helpless as can be. Just the way I like 'em".

He slammed the lid of the boot and walked around to the driver's side, putting one hand against his back feeling down his spine. God, he always hated it when he got old!

He got into the car and took a small packet of pills out of his jeans pocket and popped two painkillers into his mouth. It always caught up with him during a snatch, all that extra exertion on his muscles. *Oh well. Easy come, easy go.*

He popped the key into the ignition and felt his car roar to life like a rabid beast. He flipped down the mirror above and looked at himself. A few strands of grey hair were showing, but the aging was most clear around the eyes. He put his fingers to the lines there and stretched the skin back and forth. *Hey ho.* He put the gear knob into reverse. After tonight, getting old would not be a problem anymore.

No one reported Emily Partington missing. No one knew that she was. Her mother never spoke of her first-born daughter after the night she walked out on her. The office where she worked as a receptionist had only her address on file and wrote to her twice: once to inquire about her whereabouts and then to terminate her position. Both were sent back accompanied by a piece of paper her mother signed with one line written in a firm hand. 'Gone away.' It was thought amongst the few staff who wondered where she had gone that perhaps she had been unhappy in the role and had gone to work elsewhere.

Stuart was the only one who took any real notice of Emily's absence, and the following week on from her disappearance he went to her home to ask if she was there. "Never heard of her," the huge woman in the doorway told him before slamming the door in his face.

As far as the world was concerned, Emily was just another girl who'd vanished. Headstrong, perhaps irresponsible, probably pregnant. She'd skipped town one night with a man she had had her heart hooked on. She was probably just fine.

Dayna tossed and turned on the creaky bed frame. It was a Friday night and Wanda had phoned earlier to say she wouldn't be home. She was staying over at her mother's for the weekend and would not be back until Monday morning. Dayna could sense on the phone by the tone in her voice that she was suppressing the urge to ask if she was going out that night and Dayna was glad she didn't ask so she wouldn't have to lie to her.

Dayna's night-time excursions into the city were a bad habit she could not break. She resented rattling around a flat that wasn't hers all weekend, noticing that Wanda always left newspapers open to the Help Wanted section on the kitchen table, like she would start over working as a home help changing some old incontinent man's nappies or babysitting someone's smelly kid.

Lying in the dark she could see the outline of the rubbish bag full of old clothes she had packed up the days before. It was still there. She turned away from it to face the wall. It could join the long list of things she hadn't got around to doing like getting a job or registering at the local doctor's. She remembered Wanda's words to her that morning: "You need to speak to someone, Day. You were in an abusive relationship with a creep. If it was me…"

Dayna had snapped back at her. "But that's just it, Wanda. I'm not you, am?"

She hadn't meant to snap at her but she was getting a little tired of having her face up against the glass of her friend's life.

She was sure that Wanda was sensing it too, the creeping resentment. When she heard Wanda's key go into the lock she would quickly duck into her bedroom and shut the door. Wanda was too tired after work to check on her and then Dayna would hear the shower coming from the bathroom they both shared and then the bedsprings squeaking as Wanda went to sleep for the night.

But Dayna had trouble falling asleep and had not slept well for a long time. Sometimes she would pace the small room for hours muttering to herself, trying to put everything that had happened in an order that would make sense in her head. But often the pain was too fresh, and she would always end up sitting on the floor in the corner sobbing, waiting for the despair to pass.

Most nights, she would just get fed up, put some clothes on and head out into the night to pick up a stranger. If she was lucky, he'd have a place of his own he could take her back to and she wouldn't have to deal with the feelings of loneliness that seemed to cling to her like a clammy hand clutching her heart. She could lose herself for a few hours, in someone else. They would buy her drinks. Sometimes they would give her drugs. She went out for a feeling of escape and those blissful moments just before realising where she was and who she was when she'd wake up in a stranger's bedroom and she'd have no memory at all of how she had got there. On nights when she went home with strangers, she would always sleep deeply, with no bad dreams, that seemed to be in such large supply in recent days.

Enough.

She sat up in the single bed and swung her legs around and stood up. She left the lights off in her bedroom and walked out of the room wearing nothing but a pair of cotton briefs. Feeling herself being pulled down the hallway, she wondered faintly if she'd developed a problem and questioned how in charge of herself she was. Could she, if she wanted, just go back to bed? She could sleep through the night and try to start over again in the morning. She could phone the doctor's and get an early appointment, speak to someone, hopefully a woman doctor who would understand and then maybe come home and take a short nap. Then when Wanda came home, she would tell her she'd like help in finding a job. Perhaps bringing her in on it would lessen the wall of silence that had sprung up between them.

Standing in front of the door to Wanda's bedroom she knew she wouldn't do these things. Dayna looked back down the hall to the front door, willing Wanda to appear there, almost hearing the jingling of her key in the lock.

Slowly her hand closed around the brass knob on Wanda's bedroom door and turned it. She felt moths fluttering in her stomach, as she felt her feet immerse themselves happily in the deep carpet that spread from wall to wall of Wanda's bedroom. She felt giddy trespassing on her friend's private world. The small pang of guilt she had first felt when she stole in here weeks ago was a small cry in a faraway room in her mind. Coming in here was now a rooted habit she could not break and was not even sure she wanted to.

She could see the full moon out of the bedroom window, beckoning. Wanda's queen size bed was against the back wall under the window. In front of the bed was a vanity table, a genuine antique from the Art Deco era. Three huge mirrors were fixed in place by two large elephants, their heads bowed as if in reverence to the observer, their bodies made of polished wood with carved eyes filled with stones of amethyst.

She saw her face reflected three times across triptych mirror. The bruises that had marked her during John's rages had faded but there were still red lines across her cheeks from the time he'd thrown a glass at her face. She turned away from the mirror at the thought of it and looked out of the window at the pregnant moon.

Opening the top drawer of the table revealed many bottles of nail polish and lipsticks. The drawer below contained thin silver brushes and eye pencils and in the bottom drawer Dayna found sponges and small tubs of creams and foundations. Excitement twisted inside her like a dozing snake.

Using a large hairbrush on the table, she brushed her auburn hair back, she had all the time in the world tonight. She used the foundations and sponges to give her skin a pearly white sheen. She took time caressing her face with the sponges, relishing the sight of her scars fading from view. For her arms, she chose a thick body butter that smelled of almonds and she took time rubbing it in her hands until it turned warm from the friction. She rubbed it up and down her arms, watching the small scars and marks disappear, banished for the night to some lower realm where unwanted memories live.

She chose a deep nightshade purple for her nails, and painted the tips of each nail with an ink black paint, adding the finishing touch of a single black rhinestone to the centre of each nail.

Taking an aerosol can from the drawer of hair products she squirted a thick white cream into her palm and brushed it through the long auburn locks, giving it a sleek shiny effect as if starlight had been caught in her hair.

She found a small case that had some long mascara tubes in. She gave her lashes a thick coat and then used a curler to ignite them to life. Dayna batted her green eyes in the mirror, turning her face left and right to admire her own handiwork.

Walking over to Wanda's walk-in wardrobe she slid the door across revealing a small secret room and licking her lips Dayna stepped inside.

Reaching out blindly in the dark, her palm swatted the end of a string and pulled it. The closet light ignited the bright textiles of Wanda's vast clothing collection, glinting off sequins and beads leaving flashes of colour blooming in Dayna's eyes like rare orchids.

All the garments were grouped by colour. Dayna ran her hands over everything, feeling coarse wools, soft silks, leathers and plush mink furs. Her skin tingled as the glamour crept through her giving her goose bumps. She drew out a short black silk dress with a plunging neckline and thin jet crystal shoulder straps and a crystal fringe that ran along the hemline and a pair of black patent leather high heels.

She pulled on some fishnet black stockings and pulled the plush silk satin dress over her head. The woman in the vanity table mirror twirled about barefoot making the fringe tassels come to life in an eruption of crackling beads. Dayna crept along the carpet slipping out the room like a shadow.

She took some time checking herself in the hallway mirror, enjoying taking in every detail of the stranger that looked out from the glass wearing a borrowed form and feeling a confidence that was not her own.

Dayna always felt a tingle in the air when she went out as if she was leaving the worst of herself behind. The night gave her concealment. The night offered a bounty of opportunities to her and her heart beat faster she pushed her way through drunken crowds on the street. She could make out in front of her, as it loomed into view, her favourite Friday night haunt: the Bad Penny Bar.

The Bad Penny Bar stood behind a churchyard and used to be a traditional tavern until it was bought by an opportunist who saw that there was no place in the city centre for businessmen and office workers to relax after a hard day seated in front of a computer screen. The old traditional tavern with stone wheels and benches outside for people to sit were banished, replaced with black concrete slabs and a gothic iron rail surrounding it making it the ideal place for smokers to stand and talk over a glass of wine and breathe in each other's pungent fumes.

Dayna felt the eyes of various suit-clad men crawl over her as she approached the front door of the tavern. The two large men on either side of the door like stone sentinels with earpieces stepped aside as she crossed the threshold into the Bad Penny.

A tall man in a black suit pushed past Dayna as she went through the door. The smell of him made her hand to fly to her mouth to block her nostrils from being filled with the intense mix of Paco Rabanne aftershave, Merlot and sweat. "Scuse me, luv," he said, looking toward Dayna's breasts before pushing his way out.

Dayna noticed everyone was dressed like her bad-mannered friend who had just barged past. She saw a few pinstriped and navy blue suits dotted in around the crowd. It was difficult to read which were the high earners and which were the bottom feeders when the place was so crowded but, after a lifetime of bar crawling, Dayna had the antennae of a great moth which she would use to her advantage when targeting her game for the evening ahead.

She pushed through the dense crowd to the bar and slid onto a stool next to an ornate mirror mounted in a baroque style frame to observe the crowd. The barman, a man with a piercing in his eyebrow like a ball found on a birthday cake, was busy at the far end of the other side. There were three men with greasy hair and blue office shirts waving money at him while all shouting in unison their drink orders. He was peering in close to understand what they were saying over the din of the music that blared from speakers in the corners of the ceiling.

She adjusted the skirt of her dress to make sure it hadn't ridden up anywhere and waited for the barman to catch sight of her. She had less than forty pounds caught in a garter strap around her thigh. The night was young and she hoped she could get by on ice water until she caught the eye of her first mark.

She ran her painted nails through her hair and watched herself in the wall mirror thinking of Wanda. She felt more with each passing day that the thread between them, which Dayna had thought at first was a rope, was becoming more twisted and strained with the small arguments. She now felt, in the long silences, words not said, old lines drawn in the sand and ignored, that the rope was in fact a thin thread, growing fainter with each day that went by, fading away.

"Excuse me." Dayna's head shot around. The barman with the eyebrow piercing was looking at her with an expression of extreme displeasure. "You want to order something, love?"

It was the second time someone had called her that. Dayna said, "Ice water, love."

He turned away with a grunt and came back with a tall glass of water, a single ice cube floating on the surface of the glass.

She'd just caught sight of a man in a black custom-made suit seated two places away drumming a credit card on the bar awaiting service. Dayna's green eyes narrowed as she saw the pinstripe of the suit matching up on the shoulder seam. His hair was combed over and his tie was a dark burgundy silk. He wore a gold watch on his wrist.

She sipped her water, watching to see if anyone would join him. The barman put a glass of white wine in front of him, a single glass. *Good, he's alone.* She watched as his head swivelled around to observe the crowd. His eyes rested on Dayna on his second glance around. Dayna saw in the mirror's reflection the he was watching her intently. But the night was still young, and it was far too early to make a move just yet. Better to let him dangle on the end of the line longer.

She slipped off the leather stool and pushed her way into the thicket of men, letting the various males bump up against her as she made her way into the centre of the dance floor. A lot of the club's patrons had discarded their jackets and rolled up their sleeves to grind and move around to the heavy drums that pounded through the air in a monotonous rhythm.

Dayna twisted to the heavy beat, letting the music pass over her, letting her arms move freely. It was hard to switch off the worries that haunted her waking world. John's spiteful message written on her box of clothes, the white rubbish bags left in the corner of the bedroom to throw out, Wanda's face looming up in front of her unbidden. *Dayna, what are you doing here? Come home.* She closed her eyes tighter and tried to find a beat in the music. She swung her hips around and moved her wrists, turning about and ignited the beaded fringe on her dress to life. She enjoyed hearing the fringes skittle against each other as she spun faster around in a spiral. She found herself lifting above the dance floor, caught between the moments that passed, flying above the sadness that seemed to cling to her since she'd found herself homeless and sleeping in a spare room on a single bed.

The music grew louder as people joined the throng on the dance floor. Dayna could smell them, the heavy scent of aftershave and booze. She felt a stranger's arms creeping down her waist to her hips. She turned away from him with a smile, enjoying the feeling of being wanted. A man approached her wearing a powder blue shirt and curly blonde hair. She put her arms around his neck and met his smile with her own. *Let them wish; let them want.* She laughed and spun around, pushing through the crowd and came off the dance floor.

She needed something to take her away from herself. She moved with the crowd, making her way out of the other side of the dance floor to a doorway where beyond was a narrow passage in which a small group of men were standing huddled, looking down at something that was being passed around between them. One of them saw Dayna staring and nodded at his friend. All three of them looked up and separated suspiciously. She approached them smiling.

"Hi boys. I was wondering if you could help me with something."

The stoned man's face broke into a grin. Dayna could tell by his dilated pupils that his sense of where he was averaged in the region between Earth and Neptune.

Dayna tried to keep her voice high and sweet. "Do you know where a lady could score some pills?"

She could see beads of sweat on his forehead and patches under his arms. His nostrils looked red and sore. The grinning man's friend stepped forward and said, "He's in there." He put his arm around his friend and pulled him away.

Dayna strode down the hall and saw the door he had pointed to was labelled MEN'S. The strobe light was blinking in Dayna's face as she stepped onto the tiled floor. Cubicles stood out against the wall. Opposite were two sinks with a broken mirrors hanging above. She tried to ignore the smell of bleach and urine.

A cubicle door banged open and an overweight man in a suit barged past her without washing his hands. She stepped out of his way and skidded on her high heel making her put one hand out against a urinal to stop herself from falling over.

When she looked up into the cracked mirror's reflection she saw the pale man standing behind her, the fluorescent strobe lighting up his gaunt features, casting huge shadows under his eyes and making his face appear to be a floating skull immersed in the darkness of the lavatory stall.

Dayna whipped round nearly slipping on the damp floor. Unlike the patrons of the bar, this man did not wear a suit, only a tatty old vest and tracksuit bottoms. His jawbones stood out from the side of his cheeks like walnuts and his shaved head gleamed against the harsh lighting of the bathroom. She saw a tattoo of a serpent coiled around his neck. Its reptilian skin painted in shades of grey and black. The door to the gents' room banged open and Dayna looked over with a start as a man in a navy suit barged in fumbling his belt undone and unzipping his fly in a hurry to relieve himself.

The dealer held out a pale bony hand to Dayna. She grabbed it and was pulled into the cubicle. She had time to think his hand was as cold as the earth before he closed the cubicle door and the strobe light above them blinked off again plunging her into darkness.

Dayna stared straight into his cold eyes and he looked into hers. Her breath came out heavy and fast. She felt her nipples harden under her dress as his nostrils flared like an animal's. *He looks dangerous.* She was alone in a cubicle with a drug dealer. The men in suits and the night time trysts were fun but often Dayna lay passively underneath them while they fondled her in the darkness, often reaching orgasm and passing out on top of her before she'd even begun to enjoy it. There was never any excitement, only a feeling of detachment. In contrast the man before her, when he held his hand out, she felt as if she was taking the hand of the devil himself.

Her put his hand in his pocket and pulled out a small see-through bag which looked to Dayna to have talcum powder inside it.

"I'm not here for that."

"No?" His voice had a croak which sent a chill running down her spine.

"I wanted ecstasy."

His hand went into his back jeans pocket and he pulled out two small pills that had two small logos printed on them. Dayna extended her hand towards the pills. His other hand shot out and grabbed her by the wrist. She tried to pull away but his grip was like a steel vice.

"You gotta pay for these baby." He moved suddenly. Dayna felt herself pressed against the wall of the cubicle.

"I have money."

She felt his mouth breathing heavily against her neck. "How much you got?"

"I have twenty."

"Oh you've got more than that. You've got a lot more."

She felt his cold hand climbing up her leg. His fingers touched on the bills clipped to her thigh before passing upwards to her cotton briefs, the only thing she had on that belonged to her. She made to turn away from him but his other arm grabbed the back of her neck and she felt his mouth on hers and the cold sensation of his tongue crawling along the roof of her mouth. *Is this really happening?* His fingers pressed on her cotton briefs more and she moved one leg behind his. She thought of pushing against him hoping to trip him but the cubicle was small and the door was locked. She felt herself detach like she had detached so many times before when sleeping with strangers.

She felt her hips thrust in time with his hand and she let out a deep gasp and brought both arms up around his neck. His tongue slid out of her mouth giving her the air to let out a high moan as he pushed her briefs to one side with his hand. Dayna felt a deep surge rise inside her and she jammed her feet down to the floor, unmindful of the crack she heard. All she could see were the graffitied walls of the inside cubicle and the tribal snake opening its jaws on the dealer's neck. With a surge of effort she gripped his shoulders and he hoisted her upwards. She felt herself break open and Dayna cared nothing for where she was. She grabbed the dealer by the scruff of his vest and put her lips on his. Cold, cold as the earth, walking barefoot on the cold earth. She kissed him deeply and together they went down into the dark.

Caroline was in her room trying to decide to whether to phone Michele to talk about the flashes she had had when she touched the people on the street. There was a grubby sofa pushed up against the side of the bed which she rarely sat on due to its dilapidated condition but tonight, with the full moon coming in through the window, Caroline sat there now, with her knees up to her chin, eyeing the phone on the cradle, one of

Michele's parents' cast-offs. Should she call her? Should she go to sleep?

She thought about eating but had little appetite. Her eyes went to the fridge. She remembered the doctor's words about the many side effects of taking the mood stabilisers: loss of appetite, drowsiness, weakness. She had spoken with sympathy as she'd asked her a question: "When were you last happy, Caroline? Perhaps think about when you were last happy, and try and work your way back to that. What were you doing?"

Caroline had closed her eyes and thought about all the nights at clubs when she would shoot up with Tom and the wild colours that exploded in front of her eyes like butterflies. They would get high and have sex. She thought of the crushing lows that followed in the morning. She couldn't remember being happy without the aid of drugs.

She got up and went to the one window in the room and gazed out into the night. She slid the window up, letting in a fresh gust of night air into the stale room. The carvings on the window ledge drew her eyes down and she read: **Chantelle was here 24/12/92. Lucy Partington 13/05/94.** Caroline's eyes moved along the wood. There were more, so many more: Judy and Baby was here 28/02/99. There were so many, some carved and filled in pen, smudged to barely legible words by the rain. How many lives had passed through this room? Caroline felt sick looking at all the names and dates written over and over like the repetitive babbling of an insane inmate. Her fingers moved over the cracked wood feeling vaguely sick as feelings that weren't hers passed through her making her blood run cold. It was as if the sadness of countless victims had been pounded into the wood and she could hear all their voices speaking out in deafening screams of silence.

Not one, Caroline thought, not one of them had anyone to talk to. They were all shut away in here.

She went back to the bed and lay down. She tried to slow her breathing, trying to cast her mind out, burrowing under the smell of bleach, and search amongst the hidden corners and under the piles of dust and flakes of skin, and eventually she felt traces of them: those that had come before her.

Michele didn't understand. She never wanted to linger in the bedsit. She always wanted to meet Caroline at cafes.

Perhaps tonight she could speak to someone who understood. She shuddered at the thought. *No, no way.* but she could do it, couldn't she?

Caroline had known how to do things. The flashes on the street had been a nasty thing to live with, like knowing what was happening in other people's houses, knowing who shoplifted and who didn't, knowing when boyfriends cheated, and worst of all, when she saw people walking in the street whom she knew were not alive. Sometimes they would see her and wave to her.

Then Caroline had found heroin and afterwards the ghosts had gone away, as if the poison of the drug cured of her second sight.

I may not be able to still do it. I've shot up too many times, taken too many anti-depressants.

But she knew, as she looked up at the moon, that the power was still there, sleeping inside her, like a monster, stirring, waiting to open its jaws wide and howl. *Don't do this. Call Michele. Take a pill, go to sleep.*

She stood looking at her reflection in the small oval mirror in the bathroom. Looking down she saw the cardboard box on the sink's edge that contained the cellophane strips where each pink pill was sealed waiting to be broken open and swallowed. *Am I really going to do this?*

Caroline popped out two of the pink tablets, turned on the faucet of the cold tap, and let the pills drop into the sink. She watched them spiral around the white porcelain for a moment before disappearing down the plughole and out of sight. *No going back now.*

She knew what she would do even if it didn't have a name. She was so tired of being doped up, tired of feeling outcast. She glanced out towards the window where the moon was still hidden behind the clouds. She bent down and drew the crowbar out of the gap in the sofa and closed her eyes.

She felt something move through her and her lips began to frame words that were not her own and she spoke aloud to the empty room in a man's voice. *"I'd rather have it and not need it than need it and not have it. Lock on the door might not be enough. Gotta be ready, ready for anything. Gave them a fake name but they might figure it out and come knocking. Gotta be ready, ready to fight. They won't take me alive. I'll bash their hands in. Got to be ready to-"*

Caroline's hand flew to her mouth and she pressed her fingers hard to either side of her temple to block him out. The thoughts were hard and pressured. *Addict.* She knew it. *Heroin addict. Owed people money. I wonder what happened to him?* She thought she heard a whisper come to her in a reply from somewhere, everywhere. *No one gets out of here alive.*

Caroline jumped, feeling someone standing just next to her ear. She screamed with a start as she wheeled around seeing something out of the corner of her eye. It was only the refrigerator, humming softly in the quiet of the room.

She thought of going back to the bathroom and taking the pills and letting the fog cloud her out. *Take three pills. Hell, take four. Drop into a coma where there are no bad dreams.* But she thought off all the names on the windowsill again and what she had to do. She let her mind drift on the wind that blew in from the window. She could feel the vibrations from the rooms around her, the shouts of the woman from the room above as she tried to quiet her children to sleep.

She let herself fill up the empty places and, beneath the bed, Caroline felt them, in the gathering dark, the whispers of those that had lived there before. All that despair and loneliness building as silently and as deadly as interest in a bank account. Dust was skin. Skin was flesh and the flesh had memories.

Goosebumps began to break out over her pale skin as the room grew colder. The ritual began. The room fell silent. Dust motes filled the air like a fog, called up by a spirit wind that rattled the door on its hinges. The room was eerily still and Caroline felt a humming in the tips of her fingers.

She heard a quiet click as the double bolt on the door slid back and a creak as the door to her room opened slowly making her heart skip a beat. *What have I invited into this house?* She kept her eyes squinted shut as she heard noise gather around her, the sly dragging of feet across the linoleum floor, the sense of something passing by her face making her shudder. She didn't open her eyes to see them though she felt them, called up by her madness, the nameless many that found their way here, to this place of despair. She could see them in her mind's eye: their bodies empty, mere mist lit by the candle of memory burning out as they walked through the room unnoticed.

She lay still, scared to breathe as the dead procession made its way within inches of her face. She felt the faintest breeze on her cheek as they walked through the still room. She spoke aloud to herself over and over to try and quell her building terror. "Only memories, nothing to fear, only memories. I just want to talk. I just want to talk. Leave me unharmed. I just want to know how you came here. How did you go?"

Caroline turned over and opened her eyes. Slowly her sight adjusted to the gloom as she watched them come, faint outlines like spiders' web, not ghosts, but memories marching through the room like soldiers returning from war who had lost their way. She saw them all different yet all alike: grey shades outlined by the moonlight which shone through their faces like rotten apples. She saw a woman carrying a baby, a young girl who couldn't have been older than thirteen, her hair in pigtails. Caroline noticed she had her ears pierced, the hoop earrings glowing faintly, and a tall emaciated man who looked like a scarecrow that had been mistreated by small children, much taller than the rest, his arms hanging limply at his sides as he walked.

Their faces were all downcast, and their footsteps slow and dragging as they crossed through the door that stood ajar and out through the open window where they each hung for a moment like divers going off a board before dissipating into the night. *Am I really seeing this?*

She saw a man standing in front of the bathroom door. Caroline could see his eyes fixed on hers from across the room, standing apart from the rest, making no effort to join the others that walked on. *He's looking at me.* She could make out a rope of hemp hanging from his neck where Caroline could see lacerations raised like welts on his skin. His eyes glowed with a faint light. Caroline had to squint to make him out as he wavered in and out of view, like a candle flickering in the dark.

His dim form gave her the impression he had been standing there for days and only now by the light of the moon shining through the paned window could she see him as he was, so transparent that she was scared to blink in case he would vanish.

She watched him raise his arm, palm outstretched, as if he was beckoning to her. Caroline knew that he was the most recent occupier of the room where she lived, the one who owned the crowbar. The look on his face was one of deep resignation and despair. She could see his hair hanging long and lank, floating around his face as if caught by a faint breeze that did not blow through the room.

Caroline could feel the cold reaching out to her from where he was making her shiver, as if a bitter winter had followed him here. Her eyes continued to move over him, unable to help staring, taking in details. His clothes were a jumble of stained old things. His hooded fleece hung lank around and, as if by her seeing him, more of him became clear. She could make out the lines around his eyes as if deep cracks had been gouged in his skin. Various pockmarks were up his arms. They were from needles. *He's a drug dealer. Be wary. He can lie.* Frayed denim hung limp like dead weeds from his jean bottoms and he became more detailed to Caroline, like an oil painting running into life. She saw he cast no shadow on the floor. *There are limits. Be thankful for small favours. I brought him here but he can't manifest completely. I can send him away. I don't know how but I can send him away if he doesn't answer my questions.*

She raised one hand up, palm out and opened her fingers like a fan. "Hello." Caroline spoke and let the word hang in the air. He gave no sign he had heard her at all and continued to gaze at her. "Tell me your name! Tell me how you came here!" She tried to shout but the words caught in her throat and they came out as barely a whisper.

Caroline shivered in the growing cold. *It's the chill, the chill of the grave. He brought it in with him. I don't know how to stop this. How do I turn it off? It was mistake.*

"I'm coming," she said. And she took a small stride forward. *Nothing to fear from him. Perhaps what he wants is to climb inside me, have a second go round, or head out on the town and shoot up one more time, but he won't have a chance because I am in charge here and if he so much as flinches the wrong way I'll send him back to whatever hell he came from. He did a stupid thing with that rope and it doesn't matter if he knows now it was stupid and thoughtless or selfish. It's just something he will have to live with.*

She took another bold stride forward towards the intruder. The crowbar clenched in her right arm. Her eyes stayed fixed on him. His arm remained outstretched and then in her head she heard it: a small voice sounding in a whisper, as if spoken by a small child in a distant room; or perhaps the voice had spoken loudly, not from the place where she was, but somewhere further, somewhere grey and cold that never felt the warmth of sunlight. *I can't live with it. Caroline, I'm dead.*

"Get out of my head!"

I only want-

"Get out of my head!"

She saw him flinch and fade back into the wall as she threw her thoughts at him, getting her will behind them like a battering ram. All his physical form diminished. His face became a blur and his thick long hair and beard unravelled before her eyes becoming indistinct, his whole form reduced down to angry child's scribbles. His clothes were once again shapeless and foggy. His eyes though, the old coins that were his eyes still shone with malignant power.

Caroline took another step forward. The procession of phantoms was inches from her face now. "Why are you here?"

She heard his voice whisper inside her head. *I'm always here.*

"You hanged yourself here?"

She waited for him to speak again. Hairs stood out on her arms. His eyes glowed faintly across the room like two small moons.

I came to speak for them.

Caroline didn't understand. "Who?"

Them.

She looked at the parade that was still running like a film strip and felt a deep swell of terrible pity in her heart as the spectres made their way through this place of waiting. A waiting room, waiting to be housed, freed; waiting to be put back out on the street. Caroline knew a word for a place where you waited. *Limbo. Where you waited, where you are tiny, and the power is not yours but ours.*

"Let them speak for themselves," Caroline said.

They had no voices in life but you expect them to speak in death. Stupid girl.

"Make them speak to me."

They have no speech, no names. They gave them up when they came here. They live in the moment of loss, absolute, alone. They cannot help you. They couldn't even help themselves.

Caroline felt sick. The night sky outside was no longer pitch black but dark blue. The moon was waning outside the window and she could see the spectres beginning to fade. The chill remained passing by her face as if invisible hands reached out to her as they went by, but she could feel that the ritual was ending. *Now or never*, she thought, and took a step forward into the mist of phantoms. She screamed out as the shouts of a thousand voices spoke at once inside her head making the floor and the ceiling change places, the sheer mass of countless memories knocking her off her feet. Images flashed behind her eyes like bombs detonating, images of lives that weren't hers. There was flash after flash making her blind and deaf with shock.

Her hands dropped the crowbar as they came up to cover her ears. Her legs spasmed as she writhed in agony on the floor. She thought: *I will fall and lay here and they'll have me, possess me, one after the other, fill me with their thoughts, their memories, their woes. I'll go mad. I'll go mad. They'll leave me a vegetable.*

Slowly she forced them out, pushing hard against the collective silent screaming that echoed around her head. She got to her feet and stepped through the parade of phantoms to meet the pair of eyes that hovered in front of her. The light of the coming dawn had reduced his form to nothing; only his yellow eyes remained.

She spoke to him, "Tell me something useful."

As the sun rose in the east turning the sky to fire, he spoke the last words she would hear him speak, and they made no sense at all, but she knew she had heard him clearly in the rooms of her mind and in the well of her soul. His voice echoed around her head for hours long after his eyes had faded from sight.

Stay away from the woman with the beehive hairdo. She'll eat you alive and pick her teeth with your bones.

She thought he'd reappear, but an alarm was going off somewhere above. Like a church bell sounding. Dawn broke, setting the sky on fire and she continued to stare at the fridge willing him to return, to explain this last riddle, the parting message of a dead man that made no sense to her at all. It had brought her no comfort, or shelter from her loneliness. The ritual was over.

The room was freezing and empty, the door ajar. Caroline sank to the floor and cried. She had not wept since the first night she had arrived in the hostel, not since the pills had taken all her emotion away; but she cried now, for the helplessness she felt, like a rat caught in a snare, and for those poor souls she'd seen whom she could not comfort.

She rubbed her arms. Daylight was coming through the windows, moving through the room like a silent burglar stealing the shadows that were there only minutes before.

I can start warming up by closing this bloody window. She raised both her arms with the intention off slamming it down when she froze. Her eyes were drawn down by some power to the window ledge and she felt the strength leave her arms. The wood was old and the paint was peeling, but utterly bare. Not a single mark broke the surface. The names that had crowded up against each other carved into the wood by the many hands of people that had passed through the room where Caroline slept had vanished.

She stared at the bare peeling surface, wondering if she had imagined it. Back when she and Tom had shot up, she saw a lot of things, things that were not real. But she was clean now. She was not hallucinating, was she? But there was the ledge. She ran her hand over it, remembering the callus of the names carved in from before like the ones found on school desks. It was smooth against her hand. She thought of the drug dealer and then the parade of shades that came through the room. Was it a psychotic episode?

She decided against taking the pill. She was worried skipping a dose would be a mistake because it would throw all the chemicals running through her body out of whack. But she knew if she took it, then the fog would return and she'd sleep dead to the world, and nothing, not even the sound of the phone ringing would wake her.

She smiled grimly to herself as she lay down on the bed staring down at the crowbar that lay on the floor where she had dropped it. *Even if it's a salesman trying to sell me time-share, I'd talk to him. Just let it be someone living.* Her head was still throbbing and she wondered if she would have to get up and take an aspirin, but there was no need. Within moments she fell into a deep sleep where no ghosts troubled her.

Dayna sat inside the toilet cubicle in the men's bathroom pulling at her fishnet stockings. The dealer had laddered one and she was prying them both apart with her fingers. The feeling of the net cutting into her fingers was a distant feeling probably happening to some other girl. With the LSD raising her heart rate the fishnet felt tight on her skin. Finally, she was free. She balled up the old net rags and threw them into a corner.

She staggered to her feet and looked up at the towering cubicle walls that reared up on either side of her, feeling sick, closed in. She shut her eyes against the sounds of the music. *Need to leave. Can't tread on the floor. Filthy. Find shoes.*

With one hand she grabbed the empty toilet roll dispenser to keep her balance as she rocked to the side, her hands brushing against the urine-soaked floor of the tiled bathroom in search of Wanda's high heels. She had to wiggle her feet maddeningly from side to side to get her feet inside.

Looking into the cracked mirror above the row of sinks she could see a stranger looking back. Her dalliance with the drug dealer had left its mark on her face. Her lips were smeared into a mocking clown's leer, her hair was a crow's nest and there was a slight pain when she put her hand to the back of her head and felt her scalp. *Bastard pulled my hair out.*

She screwed the faucet with one hand letting cold water gush out and wiped her face removing the red lipstick and black eyeshadow that had been applied with such care only hours before but now was spread around her face. The glamour had faded.

She stumbled out of the bathroom and found herself in the long hallway that led back to the bar. *Am I having a good time?* She had to get back to the bar, sit in the chair, regain her thoughts. Perhaps she could buy another drink, re-join the party. Her hand reached down and felt up her skirt searching for the garter that had the cash strapped to her thigh, but the garter, and the money, was gone.

Live mice scurried in a small cage on the floor of Charlie's room. Rose rarely disturbed him in his private space. He suspected that she didn't like being around his pet. She didn't understand the power and beauty of the creature that dwelled within the tank. Few women did.

He got up off the narrow bed and crossed to the other side of the room, stepping over piles of dirty laundry. Jeans were flung about on the floor and plaid shirts draped over odd chairs.

He slipped on his leather cowboy boots. He didn't like walking around in bare feet. The old house got dusty and he was wary of splinters on the wooden floor. Looking after her made him paranoid about infection. Some floorboards were weak in places and often creaked under his weight. He thought in the kitchen he could smell mould in the walls. He couldn't risk getting sick, no sir. It wouldn't do if both of them were taken off their feet.

He saw himself in the mirror on the wall and saw the lines on his face. They were deeper than the previous day. His hair showed the deepest signs of age. Last week his hair was jet black with grey roots which he quite liked. He suspected he looked like everyone's daddy or uncle. Tonight his hair was iron grey and, looking closer, he thought he saw the faintest signs of his hairline receding from his square forehead. He grimaced at the idea of walking around with a widow's peak. It had happened a few times before when it was a long time between hits. In those cases, he would shave it off and don a toupee. Rose had a whole bunch of them in her closet, but they made him feel old and they were coarse against his scalp. They itched horribly, but he put up with them knowing the time between snatches hit Rosie a lot harder than it hit him.

Running his hands through his hair he thought he should count his blessings. It wasn't him lying on the four-poster bed in the next room with no bladder control, in constant pain, needing medication every few hours unable to speak. No, he was the lucky one and it was his greatest pleasure to restore her, his priestess and goddess. That made all the back pain, joint ache, hair loss and frown lines worth it.

Making love to Rose under the light of the moon while the blood of the lamb's sacrifice dried on their naked bodies was as close to heaven he would ever get. He bent down feeling his joints make a slight crack. He needed to slow down and be more careful with himself.

The mice sensed movement outside the cage and four scurried into corners to climb over each other and nip at each other's flesh. He heard a faint squeaking coming from them. It was so much like the girls' pleading and weeping when he brought them into the house. He paid them no more mind than he paid the mice. Pigs squealed when they went to the slaughter. All part of the food chain, all part of the natural order of things. Predator on top, prey on the bottom.

He pulled on a thick black latex glove he hung next to the cage from a nail in the wall: the kind used by men in factories, and with his other hand unlocked the small square door in the roof of the cage. His black hand shot in and pinned one to the floor. The mouse's whole body turned rigid, squeaking, trying to nip at his fingers, fruitlessly gnawing at the plastic coating. He felt only the vaguest pinches and squeezed tighter as he crossed the floor towards the large tank that rested in pride of place at chest height on an old dusty bureau, a thin yellowing lace crocheted cloth veiling view to the inside. The moth holes in the lace emitted a faint green light from the bulb inside as if the box contained some deadly uranium.

With his free hand he whipped off the cloth, sending a cloud of dust up into the air and exposing the full glare of the green bulb transforming the room into a lagoon of green light. He kept a tight grip on the mouse that continued to bite fruitlessly at his fingers. Its tail whipped from side to side, its claws kicking at his wrists hoping to injure, to harm, to jump to freedom.

He raised the glass lid of the tank, throwing the mouse into the green-lit nightmare world. He let the lid drop and replaced the weights, not bothering to watch the mouse's progress as it made its way through the green-lit cobwebbed hollow of his favourite pet. The green bulb within the tank brought black shadows dancing merrily along the wall in mad gangrene light.

He grinned to himself exposing his crooked yellow teeth as he heard the faintest scurrying and a cry of pain, movement, and then silence. His gloved hand played over the lace cover. He was tempted to peek in, but he suspected, eyeing the various greasy plates that he had left stacked near the bed, that his pet, like him, enjoyed her dinner in privacy.

Maxine was already at the entrance to the school waiting for Lucy when the bell rang signalling the end of the day. Lucy had missed her a lot that day. Due to studying alternative subjects their classrooms were on different sides of the school building, so they'd been unable to meet.

Lucy spent the free hour locked in one of the adult girls' bathrooms, the stolen magazine open on her lap, her eyes raking over the glossy photographs and listening out for the gossip that filled the tiled room.

Maxine had the familiar frown on her face, a cigarette defiantly poking out the side of her mouth, her green and black plaid uniform skirt riding up as she kept her legs crossed coquettishly. Lucy could see she was wearing over-the-knee knitted grey stockings which was against the school dress code. Her eyes were fixed on a book she had clasped in one hand.

Maxine looked up from her book and saw her. The shadow of a smile crossed her face, showing more in her eyes than her mouth. Lucy saw with glee that she suppressed it into a stubborn frown as she puffed away. She raised one hand to her in acknowledgement. Lucy returned the favour by waving her arm above her head in a large arc causing students and teachers to stare at her. She laughed aloud when she saw Maxine give a cry of disgust, causing the cigarette to drop from her mouth, and theatrically burying her face in her book. She descended the wall and stamped out the cigarette with emphasis as she came towards Lucy.

"Just when I think you couldn't get any weirder, Lucy, you embarrass us both with that horrid display."

Lucy envied her detachment from social normality that seemed to obsess everyone else in their school. "You know, Max, you're asking for trouble smoking inside the school like that. Would it kill you to wait until we're down the street?"

"Yes, it would." She snapped her book closed. Lucy could see she was still reading 'Flowers in the Attic' and was now nearly finished. "Besides none of them will come over here and tell me off. They're too eager to get home to their empty houses in time for 'Judge Judy'."

They passed out of the gates together along the pavement towards the city. Lucy was a little ahead of Maxine when she turned and saw her friend staring at something on the other side of the school entrance. She followed her eyes to the teachers who all wore similar grey suits moving towards the car park.

"Check it out."

Lucy looked about but couldn't see anything out of the ordinary. "What? I don't see it."

"C'mon. It's obvious."

"Notice that all the girls hang around in groups after school. No one's rushing to go home, and yet all our joyous salaried teachers are speeding to their second-hand vehicles without speaking to each other like ants fleeing a bonfire."

"Oh, c'mon. They probably all talk at school. They need to get home."

Maxine's eyes remained fixed on the cars that were pulling out one after another. There was a strange look on her face. Lucy felt the chill as evening approached.

"Nope, they don't talk to each other. At lunchtime they stay in their classes and eat the lunches they bring in. I see none of them in the canteen. They don't mix with the students. They think they're better than us."

"Don't be silly. They don't think that."

"Oh yeah?" Her friend turned to face her. "Notice how all of our so-called mentors are beelining to their vehicles paid for by our beloved parents and they all take care to keep the distance from each other. And then look how our fellow sisterhood all linger together in groups, no one wanting to go back to their parents too soon, not wanting to go home to *them*. They all hate each other. Don't you see how sad it is?"

"I don't see what you're on about" But even as Lucy spoke she did see it. All over the school, girls were laughing, sitting in circles on the ground, jumpers draped about their shoulders, others talking intimately in pairs, all with the carefree expressions of those gifted with time to spare. Then she looked again over towards to the teachers coming out of the doors, not stopping or looking around, all with the harried expressions of people who do not want to be stopped or spoken to, all wanting to leave. *Adults.*

Lucy had to hurry to keep up with her. As Maxine spoke, Lucy hung on her every word. Maxine saw things differently. "None of them speak to us outside of class. Not one of them asks me how I'm doing in class, or asks about my mum, or where my bruise came from. They don't even see us. They only care about getting us through the eight hours they have us for and then shuffling us off onto our parents. They think they're better than us because they're adults. They make huge salaries which your parents pay them to keep you busy and out of their way, and they spend their entire day here, not liking each other or enjoying themselves, and then they drive home to empty houses to probably warm up some left over takeaway and fall asleep in front of the TV."

Lucy looked at her. "Are we talking about the tutors or your mother now?"

Lucy knew Maxine's mother was too busy drinking to have ever cooked a meal for Maxine. She wondered if her friend had ever sat down to a family meal in her life.

"I'm talking about adults. They all think they're better than each other, but all the same grey clones with no lives. It will not be that way for me."

Lucy laughed. "What? You're going to be the one girl in the world who stays young forever?"

Maxine didn't smile. "I'm just going to make sure I will not end up stuck here with the rest of them believing I made something of myself when really I'm just a hamster stuck in a wheel with my head full of bogus pretension and pseudo intellect."

Lucy took hold of her hand and Maxine flinched, pulled out of her thoughts. "Just promise me wherever you go you will take me with you."

Lucy felt Maxine her squeeze her hand in return. "Totally. We're sisters... no doubt."

They held hands all the way down the road. One man on the other side of the road jabbed his friend on the elbow and nodded in their direction, a grin spread out on his partner's face. He whistled at them and shouted: "Hey, dykes! Get a room!"

Maxine kept her left hand in Lucy's right, and raised the middle finger of her right hand in return, without looking in their direction.

The pair made their way steadily from the private school building that stood outside of the city, taking a route known only to the students through the winding streets away from the main road. Maxine was quiet, and Lucy was thinking hard on her friend's earlier cynical observations. *Do I think like that? No, but I wish I did.*

They stopped in front of the bus shelter and Lucy pulled the stolen money she'd lifted from her father's study the previous morning. She doubted he'd noticed it was gone. Maxine lit another cigarette and took a drag.

"Put it out, Max. The bus will be here in a minute."

"Chill. I've got time for one more. Oh, shit!" The bus that was usually twenty minutes off schedule turned the corner. Maxine flicked the cigarette to the curb.

"Why didn't you wait for your mum to pick you up?"

"Mum stopped driving me. I think she thought I would say something about it, but I don't mind the long walk of an evening. I like having time to think."

"How far is it to your place?"

"About two miles."

Maxine's head snapped around from where she was facing the window. "You can't walk two miles in the dark."

"I haven't been, really. I've been taking cabs to the end of the street. I think she assumes a friend's mum drops me home. I think she's hoping I will crack and apologise to her. Fat chance."

"What do you need to apologise for?"

"She doesn't like us hanging out together. I think she just wants me back under her thumb." Lucy raised an imaginary glass in the air. "Good luck, Mum."

"You can't keep taking cabs. How much is that costing you?"

"I have money."

"Oh yeah I forgot which part of town you live in." Maxine laughed to herself, but underneath it Lucy heard the subtlest note of resentment, and felt a wall come up between them. "Lucy, the trust fund baby."

"Shut it. I don't have a trust fund."

"You won't have one if you keep angering mummy dearest. Hey, don't piss her off too badly. I need you for our escape fund!"

Lucy couldn't help but grin at this despite annoyance she felt at the mention of her father's money.

They drifted into silence again as the bus rolled on, both contemplating the fates that awaited them at the end of the journey. Maxine was going home to the council estate that stood on the edge of the city. She'd be letting herself in through the front door and heading straight upstairs to change without calling out to her mum who would either be watching TV in her own room with the door closed, or on the sofa with her latest romance astride her.

Lucy saw her evening mapped out. She'd get off the bus, go into the house and get up the stairs before her mum interrogated her on her day at school. She knew the end of term was approaching with the inevitable end-of-term grades being posted to the parents and Lucy's mother became increasingly unbearable during this time, poking and prodding for hints on how well she thought she'd done, always insisting on going through all the post before handing it over. She waited for that day when the grades finally arrived so she could phone up her fellow coven members and find out how their daughters had fared compared to their predicted results. Lucy hated all of them. She'd run straight to her room, slam the door, and put on some music, awaiting the inevitable bird screech of her mother announcing that dinner was ready to which attendance was compulsory and non-negotiable.

"Max, are you going straight home tonight?"

"No way. I'm heading into the city. The malls are always deserted. I was going to hang out at a cafe and do some homework till they close. Then head to the library; it doesn't close till eleven. I was going to work there and then head home."

"Can I come with you?" Lucy tried to keep her voice neutral, she didn't want to sound needy.

"I thought you did your homework at home."

"I just don't want to go home tonight, is all. Say if you don't want me there."

Maxine thought for a moment. "You can come with me, but maybe you should phone home to let the folks know where you are. Your parents hate me enough as it is."

"I will," she said, turning to look back out the window, watching the landscape change from green to grey as they worked their way into the city centre.

Lucy enjoyed the feeling of freedom within the monolith structure of glass and steel that was the city mall. The entire building was a circular dome. She could see people on the next floor through the glass flooring moving in a wide ring as they walked around. It was so trendy. The whole place to her seemed to be a world of mirrors that reflected itself repeatedly into infinity.

"Are you hungry?"

"Mmm?" Lucy was eyeing a mannequin in the shop window that was wearing a short dress of black velvet with lace sleeves. *My mother would kill me if she saw me wearing that.* "No, I'm not but I'll go with you while you get something if you like."

"Let's go in the food court and grab a burger. I'm starved."

"You wouldn't be starved if you ate at school. Where were you today?"

"When?" Maxine pushed the button to call the lift and looked through the see-through doors and upwards to see the various cogs and wheels turning as it descended towards them.

"At lunchtime. I didn't see you."

"Library. Book project. Which reminds me, what are you doing for your book report? Did you get 'Carrie'?"

"No, I didn't."

"I'm going to the bookshop after we eat. I'll try and find you a copy. Fingers crossed they have it."

"Let's take the escalator."

"Let's just hurry. I'm starving."

Charlie did not like shopping malls. He didn't like leaving the house, not looking the way he did. He felt tired. He'd given Rose something extra in her remedies that morning so she would sleep through the day.

He hated the fluorescent lighting in the malls. He felt like he was being X-rayed. They showed everything, every line and wrinkle. But it was nearly time and he wanted to be ready for when it happened. He wanted to show Rose he cared.

Christ, why on earth was is it so big? He remembered a time when there were no malls, or stores and, before that, market stalls with people selling their wares. Even before then the caravans would roll into town where you'd barter with food. Rose and he still had things from back then. Simpler times.

It was different when he came out with Rose. They could blend in well together, arm in arm, like so many of the hundreds of thousands of rubes that came to empty their wallets in this den of glass and concrete, while their fellow men slept in cardboard boxes outside in the rain.

His mouth spread into a grin. He loved the hypocrisy of it all. Only humans could've built a place like this. But he did not like the cameras. He didn't like being seen, and he felt them on him, making the hairs on his knuckles stand on end. The electric eyes. Rose assured him that they underpaid the bozos working on security: jobsworths with beer bellies and with brains like mashed potato. He still felt them crawling over his skin. They made him nervous. Still, even if they did snap him on a screen somewhere all they'd get is a fifty-something man with a slight limp in denim jeans and matching jacket. They wouldn't be able to see his hair due to the cowboy hat he wore. Let them try and look for that guy. He chuckled warmly to himself. He wouldn't have this face for much longer anyway.

"Lucy, come on!"

"Just a second." Lucy had seen it as they were about to step onto the escalator: a white mannequin wearing a red calf leather jacket with a high collar. It reminded her so much of the photos in the magazine she'd stolen only days before. "It's so gorgeous."

"Yeah and so out of our budget."

"I'm going in there."

Maxine grabbed her on the arm. "I'm about to waste away to nothing here. The mall doesn't close till ten. Can we please get some food? I swear all that junk you're reading has infected your brain."

"Excuse me?" Lucy turned from the window to look at Maxine angrily.

The shop attendant inside looked up at the raised voices coming from the doorway and saw two uniformed schoolgirls facing each other, one with an arm on the other. Both wore identical black and dark green uniforms with blazers. She hated teenagers.

"What do you mean the junk I'm reading?"

"Nothing, forget it." Maxine turned away towards the escalator.

Lucy looked after her and back at the jacket and then hurried to catch up with her friend. Max was ahead of her on the escalator floating upwards. Lucy ran up to meet her.

"What trash?"

"Oh, let it go. Just that magazine you've been glued to this past week."

"I've not been glued to it."

"Please." Maxine turned to face her. "Twice this week I've seen you sitting alone in the canteen staring at your lap gazing at that thing. It's got a hold on you, girl."

"It has not!"

"Has too."

"Has not times a million."

"Has too times a million infinity."

"You're such a loser."

"Well duh. I'd have to be to hang out with you."

"Bitch!" Lucy shoved her playfully.

They both exploded into fits of giggles, causing people on the escalator to stare disapprovingly.

He was on his way up to the pharmacy to top up on Rose's remedies when a glint of light made him stop in front of the clothing store window. The white mannequins had painted lips and glued on eyelashes with identical blonde wigs. One mannequin girl wore a dark blood red leather jacket with a high collar paired with a denim mini skirt with the word 'Juicy' made out in rhinestones across the back. "Pretty as a picture, neat as can be. Just the way I like 'em."

The Punky Fish clothing boutique catered to teenage girls and, like all stores whose market was aimed at the younger clientele, most of the customers were fathers dragged in by their spoilt daughters; so the Sales Advisor, Gina, was surprised when she turned around to see a man with leather boots and a cowboy hat moving his way through the store picking up and eyeing various dresses, seemingly unaccompanied by the usual snot-nosed brats that tormented her working day.

She felt her body straighten as her eyes moved over him. He was older, well built under his plaid shirt. He had his sleeves rolled up, showing what she thought were rather sensual tattoos. She felt a pleasant shudder run up her spine. He was not wearing a wedding ring.

She made her way around the counter, readjusting her cleavage as she came by the wall mirror. "Are you looking for something in particular, sir?"

He looked up sharply from the rail. She could only see his smile under the broad brim of his hat. The lighting of the ceiling lights cast a shadow over his eyes. His voice was much deeper than she had expected and had a slight croak to it when he spoke. *Maybe he's a smoker.* She felt another pleasant shiver.

"I'm buying presents for someone."

Gina looked over the leopard skin dress he had in one hand and the rhinestone-studded mini skirt, the tassel fringed boob tube and the pink leather jacket with the studs on the collar in the other.

"Your daughter, sir? Sweet sixteen birthday coming up?"

His grin widened. She could see dimples on either side of that grin that gave her butterflies.

"Daughter...sure, yeah," he laughed. "My brother's daughter's birthday, my favourite niece actually. Anything you can recommend?"

She gave him a 400-watt voltage smile. "So are you her favourite uncle then?"

"I try."

She laughed dryly. He smelled of aftershave which she found quite pleasant, something like Old Spice or whisky.

"I can see you've already picked out a few of our best items. There's a few more things over here which she might like. This is fabulous." Gina held up a wrap dress made entirely out of ruby sequins. The way the dress caught the light reminded Charlie of the sixties' mod dresses when he and Rose had had the best nights out of their lives.

"Retro, I like it. You've a good eye."

"Wonderful! Why don't I take these from you and put them by the till and you can have another look around. Be sure to tell me if there's anything else you need."

He gave her another grin and she thought she saw a ghost of a wink under the shadow of his large-brimmed hat.

"I sure will, darlin'. Thanks a bushel."

"You're welcome, sir." She turned and sauntered away. He watched her go, then took a single step forward into the space her body had occupied only seconds before and lifted his head up into the air and began to take deep sniffs.

Gina folded each item as it went through the till and then she noticed what he was doing. He had his head tilted up to the ceiling on the same spot she'd left minutes before next to the rail of sequined cocktail dresses. She could hear him taking deep inhaling breaths over and over, as if he could not get enough air. There was something deeply unsettling about what he was doing. She saw the faintest glimmer of saliva run down his chin making him resemble a rabid dog. His hairy hands were clenching and unclenching in the air as if searching for something.

She shuddered. She could see he was much older than she had first thought. He had grey hair across his knuckles and a shadow of grey stubble around his chin. There were deep crevices around his mouth when she came towards him. "Sir, are you all right?" She reached out to touch his arm.

He snapped upright suddenly as if startled out of a deep sleep. His smile faltered for a moment and she flinched back at how quickly he had moved. His mouth was a snarl, his composure rigid and then his mouth spread out into a smile again.

"I'm sorry, sweet thing. I guess my mind wandered for a second there."

Gina took another step backwards. "Do you want me to get you some water?"

"No, that's all right. Don't you trouble your pretty head about the antics of this guy. Say, I think you're about the same size as my niece."

"Oh is that so?" Gina took a step backwards.

"It's just I'm kind of lousy at picking things out for her. I'd hate for her to be in here next week exchanging the lot because of dumb Uncle Charlie making the wrong choices. Maybe you could try some things on for me? Let me see what looks good so I can narrow down my options."

"I'm not really supposed to leave the till unattended." Gina was looking around. The store was empty and, outside in the mall, a ghost town. She looked up at the security camera, the electric eye on a white stalk recording her every move. *I'm alone here with a total stranger. No one's around anywhere.*

She looked up into his face again and tried to read his expression, but the brim of the hat eclipsed his eyes from view. "I mean if it'll help you." *Just do it and then he'll leave.*

"You are an angel."

Gina gave him a fake smile.

"I like that dress over there and maybe this one too. How about I pay for all this first?"

"Wonderful. Would you want to pay card or-"

He cut her off. "Cash," he said seriously. His hand came out of his back pocket with a piece of dark blue folded leather he flipped open in front of her. Gina had been in the retail game since she had started as a Saturday girl at fifteen. Her wage had changed little since then and she'd got used to serving people on higher salaries. She always caught sight of the rows and rows of plastic credit cards in their leather wallets with a pang of jealousy shooting through her. She knew them all: MasterCard, American Express, Visa, Maestro. She'd even seen a private Swiss bank once or twice over the years. Peeking over as the customers paid was a bad habit of hers.

But his wallet was bare. It looked like one of those old wallets kids get given to keep their pocket money in: a little clip opened the change bit and the notes were stored in a gap inside. Usually there was a plastic window filled with the ID card or driver's licence. But the ID window was empty, along with the credit card slots next to it.

He produced a sheaf of bills and held them out to her between two fingers. Again she was struck by how grey and hairy his knuckles were. *They weren't that grey before.*

He was humming quietly to himself with his hands in his pockets, looking around vaguely. *Weird guy. Who carries that much cash and no cards?*

"Here's your change, sir," She gave back two of the twenties and one ten from her own batch in the till.

"Why don't you hang on to the change for now, little lady. I want to see how you look in that turquoise dress." He nodded to a rail in the corner that was sheathed in a huge cardboard banner reading SALE where most of last season's cast-offs were hanging like old skins.

"All right. I'll head into the dressing room and you can just pass it through to me."

"Whatever you say, princess."

She glanced up towards the security camera once more as she came around the desk and saw the green light was flashing on and off above the lens. *Good.* She saw him move over to the sale area where he picked up a bright emerald green stretch velvet dress and a sheer see-through gold lace dress lined in Lurex.

He followed her into the narrow aisle to the right of the cash register that had a mirror at the end of the hall and two curtained cubicles on either side. Another security camera was in plain sight above the mirror, its single lidless eye fixed ever open to deter people with sticky fingers. She was worried for a moment he'd lunge forward, grab her, hurt her, or maybe push her and run off with the garments in his hands; but glancing around she saw him standing passively, a good few feet away at the entrance to the fitting room, as if he had all the time in the world.

She pulled back the curtain and he held out his arm, the two hooks of the coat hangers dangling from his thick fingers. She grabbed them and went into the fitting room, throwing the curtain closed and began hurriedly to undo her blouse. She kept her eyes on the floor beneath the curtain expecting to see his shadow appear there, but she could hear him humming to himself from the other end of the corridor.

Sheila managed to get her house key into the front door on the third attempt. Sharing a bottle of wine with her neighbour had seemed like such a good idea hours before, but now with a thumping headache on the horizon and the sky and the ground threatening to change places Sheila thought it may have not been such a good idea after all.

Stumbling into the foyer of her house she shrugged off her fur coat and reached out to hang it on empty air where it fell to the floor with a dead thud. She glanced at it for a moment and dismissed it. She didn't feel like bending down. She stepped out of her shoes and went straight to the kitchen sink for a good spell of dry heaves that brought up nothing but air. She punched either side of her skull with her fingers. Her head throbbed. She shouldn't have drunk on an empty stomach.

"Richard? Lucy? Are you home?"

The clock on the mantle told her it was 6:45. Lucy was normally home by now. Richard was still at work. Her idea of leaving her smart alec daughter to find her own way to school seemed so right only a week before but now, glancing at the answering machine that flashed 00 on the message reader, she felt a cold chill down her spine.

She hadn't checked with any of the neighbours to see if Lucy was getting a lift home. She had just assumed so when she had first seen her coming through their door at six pm the first time Sheila had decided not to pick her up. She had been shocked. She had been sitting by the phone expecting it to ring, feeling herself becoming useful again, becoming needed. But the call hadn't come, and then Lucy had come through the door, and Sheila had assumed she'd caught a lift with Amanda and her daughter Holly, but she'd been with Amanda all afternoon, and Amanda had not mentioned anything. Lucy had not come home from school. *Where is she? She's out, out with Minnie.*

She lifted the phone to call Richard and ask him to ring Lucy and see where she was, but if she phoned him he would have questions, questions he had no business asking. She'd have to tell him everything. She wouldn't. He wouldn't understand. Better to wait. Better to stay home and wait for her errant daughter to return from whatever shame hole she was crouched in this evening.

She felt the worry drain away slowly as everything clicked into place. Yes, she was sure Lucy was not alone this evening. She could see them now, a whole bunch of them. Some would be holding skateboards, others clenching a two-litre Coke bottle filled with vodka no doubt. The leader Minnie would be passing around drugs, marijuana most likely. Her daughter was out drinking and possibly smoking and, before she would have time to go upstairs and shower or brush her teeth and change out of incriminating clothes that would wreak with the smell of cigarettes, Sheila would be here waiting for her, and by God she would wrest the truth from her defiant daughter. She took a seat in the dining room keeping the lights off, keeping her eyes on the front door.

Maxine finished eating and stifled a burp against the back of her hand. "Okay, I'm stuffed. Do you want my fries?"

Lucy was looking across the mall at the pharmacy on the opposite side of the food court. They had a billboard outside that said twenty-five per cent off all hair products. She was thinking about the woman on the magazine cover, how her raven black hair spilled out around her like a fan. *Black hair.*

Maxine snapped her fingers in front of her face. "Earth to Lucy. Come in, Lucy."

"Sorry, no, I'm not hungry."

"All right. It's book time!" Maxine pushed herself off the stool and threw her backpack over her shoulder.

Lucy felt uneasy surrounded by the towering bookcases. Maxine knew her way around better and was hastily weaving her way through the stacks, plucking various titles off the shelves and building a small pile in her arms. Lucy felt a small sting of jealousy towards her feeling so safe in this place of knowledge. Maxine was smart in a way she never would be.

"Max, there's no way you can afford to buy all of those."

Maxine sat cross-legged looking like a sultan amongst the piles of books. She rolled her eyes. "I can't buy them. I will make a list of titles and get them out of the library. Duh." She unpacked her exercise books and pencil case from school, looking at home surrounded by strangers and shop assistants shelving books around her.

Lucy felt a small twinge of resentment. "I might go grab a coffee. Do you want one?"

Maxine kept her eyes down on the book open in her lap. She twiddled a pencil through her fingers, grumbling something incoherent in reply.

Lucy turned around and headed out of the bookstore. She took the escalator back down to the ground floor looking around at the various window displays of identical clinical mannequins on display. She worked her way aimlessly back towards the entrance where she found herself back in front of the shop window with the beautiful calf blood leather jacket she'd seen before. The colour spoke to her of luxury and freedom. Lucy felt a prickle run along the palms of her hands. *Try it on.*

She stepped into the boutique and scanned the shop floor. The space behind the till was empty with a pile of clothes folded neatly off to one side. She moved towards the mannequin in the window licking her lips. The crackling in her fingers grew stronger. Her breathing became heavy as her heart rate increased. The shop assistant was nowhere in sight. Lucy heard humming. Her head whipped around. *Shit.* She felt her chest tighten. Her breath stopped in her throat. Her hand dropped to her side. There was a man in the dressing room. Her fingers twitched as if an electrical charge was in the air. She was close enough to smell the leather.

The man's voice echoed from the dressing room. "That dress looks damn fine, toots. I'll take that one as well."

Gina gave him a full turn, showing the plunging back "Do you want me to find you some shoes to go with this dress, sir? We have some satin heels in this exact shade of green."

He beamed at her. "That'd be swell, darlin'"

"Do you know your niece's shoe size?"

He took one step toward her, reaching out. She turned to allow him to help her undo the zip in the back when the grin on his face turned to a snarl. His head snapped around suddenly. His teeth were bared.

"Sir, are you all right?"

He ignored her. He began sniffing the air again just like before. She felt her whole body break out in goose bumps watching his body heave as if he was gasping for air. *God, what's he doing?* He was taking deep long breaths like a dog. With a bark he turned his back on her and ran out of the fitting room.

"Sir!" Gina shouted. She came running after him in her bare feet out of the boutique. She stopped abruptly to avoid crashing into his back and skidded on the foot of her nylon stockings.

The man stood stock still in the doorway of the store, running his hands up and down the archway entrance. His nose was pressed to the concrete, and he was taking deep long sniffs. *Call the police. He's dangerous.* She began to inch backwards towards the till. There was a panic button underneath there somewhere that would alert security.

Her eyes stayed on him. He was bent over, smelling the sides of the arch. Then he paced back and forth from the door to the mannequins in the window, then back to the door and then back to the window to the bare torso mannequins that stood on display. He was grunting like an animal and all the time taking deep sniffs of the air.

Gina was now level with the partition when he turned around to face her with a large smile breaking out on his face. He laughed. The sound of it made the hairs on the back of her neck stand on end.

"Well, I'll be damned," he said chuckling warmly. "Sorry about that, doll face. I just remembered I have to get somewhere. I'll take these and come back for that tasty number another time."

Before Gina could move, he strode across the shop floor closing the distance between them in four long strides and grabbed the two full brown bags off the counter and raced out of the store.

She exhaled deeply, her body sagging against the till. She looked up at the clock. It stood at 7pm. *Sod it.* She was closing up early tonight. Let them sack her. They didn't pay her enough for this shit. She switched off the boutique lights and took the day's takings into the back room and locked it.

It wasn't until the alarm went off in the doorway as she passed through it that she realised she was still wearing the emerald dress with the security tag gleaming on the bust like a brooch and her clothes and shoes were still on the floor of the fitting room where she'd left them.

When the alarm went off, she screamed loud enough to bring two security guards running to the scene and insisted that both stay in the store while she went to change back into her own clothes.

Lucy ran up the escalator steps two at a time, her brunette hair flowing out behind her. She couldn't believe she'd got away with it again. Her eyes darted around wildly.

She could hear an alarm ringing from the floor below. Was that for her? Were men coming for her now? Every fibre of her being was rigid, like a bird that's heard the sound of the gun shot. The next few minutes would decide her fate.

She thought of Maxine in the bookstore. Could she run out of the fire escape and leave her there? Make up something at school on Monday to explain her absence? Imagine Maxine's face when she saw the security guards apprehending her. *Don't let her see. Tell her you got sick and had to go home.* Perhaps Maxine would say she was with her the whole time if it came to it. Maybe she'd cover for her, her partner in crime, Bonnie and Clyde. Perhaps. *No.* Lucy knew Maxine would be disgusted with her. The trust fund baby: a common shoplifter. She wouldn't understand: the feeling of power, the rush. She felt like her whole body had become a lightning rod standing in the centre of the mall on the highest floor, feeling the high hit her again and again like thunder.

She gripped the metal rail in front of her to ground herself, enjoying the cold metal against her sweaty palms. *No one is coming. I got away with it.*

She had to move. Her bag was bulging conspicuously out of her side where the leather jacket was stuffed. She took another quick look around, checking to see who was watching her, and moved quickly toward the ladies' bathroom.

Slamming the cubicle door and sliding the bolt along, Lucy put down the toilet seat and sat down, rubbing her thighs with her hands trying to compose herself, breathing heavily. She kept waiting for the feelings of remorse to hit her like they had done after she'd lifted the magazine from the newsagent's. She remembered the feeling of having a snake coiled up inside her belly for days afterwards. She had felt pregnant with guilt. She had lain awake thinking, *I'll tell my father. I'll come clean. I'll put it back.* But she knew the next morning, putting the magazine back into the satchel to be leered over at every free moment in school, that she wouldn't, she couldn't.

And now she'd done this. But this was different. This wasn't like taking money from her father; this was stealing from a shop that probably sourced their garments in some far off country where people worked for a penny an hour, and the CEOs probably cheated on their taxes. She closed her eyes feeling relief come over her as she rationalised her actions. What she had done was totally justifiable. She hoped.

She pulled the jacket out of the bag. The leather had creases where it had been stuffed inside hurriedly. She thought of boys' eyes following her on the street when she wore it. She saw Maxine's newfound respect for her. *Girl, you look hot.* The jacket promised her things, promised change, metamorphosis. *But you can't wear it out. It still has the security tag on it.* She frowned. Sure enough it did: a smug grey coloured plastic tag, ugly and out of place against the richness of the leather. She filed it away in the back of her mind for later. *Get it home first. Get it hidden away.*

She unbuttoned her school blazer. She put the leather jacket on and zipped it up and then put on her school cardigan, buttoning it up slowly, feeling the knitted cloth stretch as it came around the thick leather and trying to ignore how uncomfortable it felt under her school blazer. She felt like an Eskimo wrapped in so many layers. Beads of sweat began to form on her forehead from piling so much on. *Not to worry. Just get home. Fade away. Be a Ghost.*

She ran water from the tap and dabbed her forehead and took deep breaths, feeling the comedown from the high she had only moments before. She felt suffocated under the layers of fabric. *Need to get out into the night air and feel the breeze.* It was time to leave.

Charlie wiped his mouth as he bounded up the escalator. Saliva was coming thick and fast. He smelled it, thick and rich, welcome as a cold beer on a hot summer day. The sweet taste of loneliness was on the air, growing stronger as he moved towards it. *Food.* He stopped dead at the top. She was close, whoever she was. *Christ, if I didn't have my back to the shop I could've seen what she looked like.* No matter, the scent was fresh. She wouldn't escape.

Now which way did she go, onto another level? Or down to the car park? He tilted his head back like a wolf and took deep slow sniffs. His lips parted in a vulpine smile of triumph. *She was still here.*

He moved away from the escalator. *I came out looking for presents to cheer Rose up. Imagine how happy she will be when I bring home this tasty treat. She doesn't smell a day over seventeen.* He let his nose lead him: perfume, sweat, but under that, loneliness, sadness and just the faintest aroma of panic.

He took a moment to gather himself. *Take her from behind. Strangle her till she passes out. Carry her down to the car. Tell security she's your daughter, and that she passed out. Let them phone an ambulance while you put her in the boot. She smells so fresh.*

He closed his eyes while he walked, letting his head turn this way and that way. *Over there.* He opened his eyes and chuckled aloud. “Well I'll be damned. Root-toot-toot.”

He saw the words written on the door: Ladies Room. He growled low to himself. He wrapped his hairy hands around the handle of the door. “Ready or not little one, here I come.” He pushed open the bathroom door and strode in.

Caroline awoke to the phone ringing. One arm came out from under the duvet and swatted at the corded phone, sending it on the third hit skittering to the floor with a crash that brought her bolt upright in bed. *Is someone breaking in?*

She saw the phone lying on the floor like a dead snake. She made a grab for it. "Hello. Hello?"

"It's Michele, Hun. Did I wake you? I'm sorry."

Caroline put her hands into her eyes, wiping sleep away. "Sorry, no. I was just in the shower, didn't hear the phone."

"No worries. I was just phoning to see how you were."

Caroline closed her eyes. The events of the previous night waded in hard, banishing the grogginess of sleep. "I'm fine. Just something happened last night. I would like to speak to you about it but I can't really talk about it on the phone."

"Someone didn't try and get into your room, did they?"

"Not exactly, no, nothing like that. I just saw something that frightened me."

"Were you awake or asleep when you saw it?"

Caroline closed her eyes. "It was not a dream. I was awake. I'd know if it was a dream. I'd say I had a nightmare and it scared me."

"It's just the doctor told us that-."

"This isn't me tripping."

"Can you tell when you are?"

She got back into bed, stretching the phone cord. "If I said yes, would you believe me?"

Silence. "Yes, I would believe you. Have you taken your pill today?"

Caroline though of the pink pill swirling around the sink, disappearing down the plughole. She thought of the ghosts. "Yes."

"Look, I'll be there at 10am tomorrow. I have to go now. Can you please be up to let me in? Otherwise I'll have to stand on the doorstep waiting for you to appear."

"I'll make sure I'm up."

"Please eat something today."

Caroline put the phone down slowly, and lay back down on the bed, turning away from the room to face the wall, feeling empty and alone.

Charlie crept into the ladies toilet slowly with his teeth bared and his hands outstretched. Coming around to the front of the stalls, he saw a tap was running. He turned it off, and took in the empty bathroom from the reflection from the mirrors above the sink. All the stalls doors were closed.

"You all right in there, little lady?" He put on his fatherly voice hoping she'd think he was someone in authority. He thought he heard shuffling inside the cubicle. Good. *Let her get dressed and come out. I'll smack her hard across the face to daze her and then push her back in to the cubicle. Nice and easy.* His nostrils flared and his fists clenched, feeling the anticipation of the hunt, the joy of the capture, the end of the chase.

He barged forward bringing his shoulder hard into the cubicle door. The force of the push onto the empty air sent him straight into the toilet. His knee connected with a crack against the porcelain rim of the bowl and he howled with pain as he felt the joint crack, sending pain shooting up his leg like a thunder bolt. The heels of his cowboy boots skidded on the damp floor and he went backwards, flailing his arms for purchase on the empty air. His shoulder hit the floor with a violent thud and he gave another low groan as he felt pain break across his shoulder blades. His cowboy hat lay on the floor next to him forgotten.

The toilet door opened. *Oh what now?* He was hit by a blast of floral perfume and thick tar cigarettes that made him feel sick. A pair of plimsolls moved into view, white and clinical, squeaking like mice as they came around the corner of the cubicle. His eyes moved up the nylon stockings, up to the denim knee length skirt, up into the frowning puddle-like eyes of Eve Spencer.

She leered over him like an idol. "Sir, this is the ladies bathroom."

He tried to stand but putting his weight on his leg sent a jagged bolt of pain up it. "You couldn't help me up, could you?" He looked up at her pleading.

She met his gaze with a dead stare. "I'm afraid not, sir. I've got a bad back."

He moved his arms underneath him, trying to ignore the pain in his shoulder. Eventually he got to his feet and limped past her. Underneath the heavy perfume was the faintest aroma of excrement and vomit. He shuddered. *Christ, she must be a nurse on one of those wards. She looked like she could live on a ward herself.*

She didn't step back to allow him much room to manoeuvre out of the cubicle. "Do try to be more careful, sir."

He grunted, picking up the brown shopping bags of his earlier purchase. He tried to pick up the scent of the girl again but breathing in Eve's perfume sent him into a flurry of coughing.

She balled up her fist and hit him on the back hard. "There you are." She smiled unpleasantly.

"You haven't seen my hat, have you?"

"Oh, is this it?" Eve squatted down and lifted from the damp floor what used to be a cowboy hat. The rim was bent and soaked in urine and bleach. The crown was squashed in the centre with the outline of a muddy footprint around it.

He snatched it off her with a grunt.

She looked him up and down and then dismissed him. Perhaps finding him too boring or needing the call of nature more. She shut the door of the cubicle. He couldn't help noticing her shoes from the crack under the door and then horribly a pair of lilac and red floral bloomers fell into view as she answered the call of the wild.

Charlie suppressed the sudden urge to vomit and staggered out of the toilet in a fury, slamming the door as he went.

Maxine looked up from the sofa as Lucy walked over. She looked as she had when she'd left, immersed in her books and content in her surroundings. "What happened to you?"

"I got lost in the mall."

Maxine took in her lumpy appearance with her eyebrows raised. "What's with the get-up? You look pregnant."

Lucy wiped the sweat away from her forehead. "I'd like to leave now. I don't feel well."

"Sure. The mall's closing soon anyway although I'm heading to the library now to carry on working. I'll walk you to the bus stop." Maxine threw her things into her bag haphazardly. "I was going to send out a search party but I didn't want to leave in case you came looking for me and wondered where I was. Are you all right? You look-"

Lucy stiffened. "What exactly?"

"I was going to say 'flustered' but don't worry about it." She threw her bag over her shoulder and stormed past her out of the bookshop.

"Max, please wait!"

Maxine carried on walking, ignoring her.

Lucy had to run to catch up with her, her triple layers rubbing with every movement, making her sweat horribly. "Max, please wait!"

Maxine turned to face her on the top of the escalator. "For your information, you wanted to come with me tonight. You didn't have to. I didn't ask you to and, frankly, I wouldn't have let you come if I knew you were going to bail on me." She turned away from her and took a step down.

"I didn't mean to-"

"Uph!" They both barged straight into the man coming up the escalator. He dropped his shopping bags as they collided with him, sending a shower of rhinestone tops and skirts over the floor.

Maxine was the first to react. "God, I'm so sorry. I wasn't looking."

"That's all right, pretty thing."

"Let me help you." She bent down and began picking up the sequined dresses that had been scattered down the metal steps of the escalator.

Lucy took a step forward to help when she noticed the man bend down behind Maxine. She saw him take long slow sniffs close to her hair. She felt a cold stone settle in her belly.

"Let's go." She grabbed her on the shoulder.

"I'm sorry, sir, my friend's in a rush. Here." She reached out to him with the clothes she'd picked up but he made no move to take them and his eyes moved from Maxine to Lucy, back to Maxine. His nostrils flared as he took long deep sniffs like a wolf. A grin spread over his face.

"Not at all, little lady. Don't you worry about it." He reached out and took the dress from her.

Lucy took Max around the waist and led her down the escalator.

"Don't push me, Lucy."

"Didn't you see what he was doing?"

"What? Slow down, would you?"

Lucy was practically running now. She looked back once, and saw him still watching them. He nodded his head to her with a wink. She shivered. "He was smelling your hair."

"As if. You're crazy"

Lucy cast another look back up the escalator. She couldn't see him. They walked on out of the entrance of the mall into the dark street. The moon was a half crescent above them.

"Do you want me to come with you to the library? So you're not on your own."

Maxine laughed aloud. "I've done this many times before. I don't need a babysitter. I'll be fine."

"Don't be stupid." Lucy cast a worried eye behind her. A few men were standing outside a bar talking amongst themselves. She couldn't shrug off the feeling of being followed.

"You're being silly. I swear those magazines of yours have rotted your brain."

"Would you leave it alone?"

"Fine. The bus stop's just around here."

The pair followed the city street as it curved around into a deserted bus shelter.

"Do you want me to wait with you till the bus comes?"

"No, I'll be fine. I'll call you tomorrow."

Maxine pulled out a small plastic carrier bag with the mall bookstore's logo printed across it and thrust it at Lucy. A small rectangular shape was inside. "Don't open it till I'm gone. You hear?"

"Max you didn't have to-." Lucy reached out, hoping Max would come in for a hug, but she just thrust the bag into her hand, turned and disappeared up the street and around the corner, out of sight.

Lucy sat alone. *I will not open this.* She could make out some illustration on the cover but couldn't quite see the title. *I will put it in my satchel and get it out tomorrow when I feel better. Where did she get the money to buy me a book anyway? She spent her own money on me. I can't believe it.*

She felt tears threatening and took a deep breath and brought the book out of the plastic carrier. Emblazoned across the front in bold letters was '*Stephen King*' and underneath that: *'Words are his power'*. A girl in a nightdress shot in black and white was printed across the cover and in dark burgundy letters: *'Carrie.'*

Lucy held the book over her heart, feeling a great stone turn over inside her belly. *I can't believe I left her to go shoplifting.* She couldn't wait to get home and tear the jacket off herself and fling it in a corner somewhere. Maybe she would throw it in the bin and then have a hot bath, call Maxine and tell her everything.

She was so deep inside herself that she didn't notice the blue car parked across the street. Elvis Presley's 'Suspicious Lives' was the only sound in the dark bus station.
But Lucy, with her thoughts turned to her warm bed that awaited her at home, took no notice of the melody that came across the night air like an eerie whisper.

Charlie watched the girl from across the street, his yellow eyes narrowing, trying to make out her shape in the dark. He couldn't see her very well. He cursed himself for not having his glasses in the car. He'd got so used to not needing them. He wasn't sure it was even the same girl he'd smelled in the clothing store. She looked a little big to him, chunky round the sides. Some loving parent was making sure she got second helpings at home. Not really the type he went for. But the window was down and he could smell the faintest trace of loneliness on the air. No point trying to make a grab tonight. The full moon was still a few days away.

He needed to get home to Rose. He ran his hands through his hair and felt clumps of it come off his scalp in his hand. He swore aloud and threw the hair out of the window and flipped the mirror down to assess the damage. Maybe it wouldn't be as bad as he thought.

It was worse, much worse. The eyes that started back at him from the mirror were cold and grey. He turned his face from side and ran his hands over his scalp, careful not to do any more damage. A large patch had come off his head right in the middle. Crow's feet were gouged into the flesh around his eyes and the skin around his once-square chin was loose and flabby. The man in the mirror looked to be in his late fifties.

He looked down at his arms. His tattoos were faded and old against the flesh that hung loose and flabby over his bones.

He turned the key in the ignition. The exhaust belched black smoke as the car pulled off the curb hard, leaving twin skid marks as it went off down the street.

Wanda came to the door when the buzzer sounded. "Yes?" She spoke into the intercom.

Dayna's voice came out of the speaker, broken and desperate. "It's me. I need money for a cab."

Wanda fetched a deep sigh. "One second. I'll grab my purse and come down." Wanda grabbed her keys out of the china bowl on the end table next to the front door and went out down the spiral staircase that led into the communal foyer.

She pushed out of the front door where there was a silver Ford parked up on the curb. She gasped when she saw Dayna through the backseat window. Her head was bowed, her expression blank, looking at the floor as if in prayer.

She knocked on the cabbie's window. He was talking in a language she didn't recognise into a headset. The window rolled down a crack. "How much?"

"Forty quid, luv."

She handed him two twenties from her purse with a grimace.

He turned away without a thank you, resuming his conversation on the headset.

Wanda opened the car door for Dayna to step out. She looked as if she had spent the night on a park bench. Looking down, Wanda saw her bare feet were muddy and cut in places. "Oh, Dayna." Her anger gave way to sadness as she put her arm round her waist and slammed the car door. The cabbie drove away in a hurry. "Let's just get you inside."

Dayna nodded her head with a grumble that sounded like the word 'water'.

"Yes, I'll get you water when we get in, dear. Just come up the steps now. Use your good foot. What happened?" Somehow Wanda managed to get her up the stone steps into the foyer where she sat her on one of the decorative chairs that was placed there for residents who wanted to read their mail before going up to their homes. "Stay there. I'll bring you down some shoes."

"I'm all right." Dayna made to stand up.

"No, Day, you'll get mud everywhere."

She remained sitting, her head buried in her hands, her auburn hair like an overgrown bush.

Wanda raced up the stairs and back into the flat where some of her running trainers were by the door. She grabbed them and ran back down, saying a silent prayer that the foyer was empty of her neighbours and there was no one around to see the display.

"Here put these on." Wanda untied the laces on both and knelt down, moving Dayna's foot into the shoe and tied her laces as if she was a child. "Right, upstairs. Now."

Dayna stood up without help this time and went in front of her up the stairs and into the apartment without taking her shoes off. She followed her into the kitchen. Dayna had her head under the tap guzzling water and then coughing as she drank too much. Wanda went to a cupboard above the sink and took out a box of aspirin and popped two out of the blister pack into her hands, thought about it, and popped out one more.

"Here." She held them out to Dayna and she took all three in a single gulp. "I didn't even know you were gone. I thought you were sleeping in."

The two women stood looking at each other for a moment. Dayna's panda eyes crawling over Wanda clad in an angora jumper and jeans, dressed relaxed but trendy for a day off from work. Wanda was taking in Dayna's torn dress and wild hair. She thought about slapping her, but couldn't. All she felt was pity for her friend who was so far from herself. "Go and lie down."

Dayna plodded out of the kitchen without a word.

Wanda retrieved a mop bucket from under the sink and walked down the hallway lined with flowers in vases on tasteful end tables to the spare room and pushed the door open. A moment of confusion went through her when she saw the bed was empty. She turned around and went back down the hall to the last door after the kitchen and pushed open the door of her bedroom.

Dayna was spread out like a starfish on her bed face down, one leg hanging off. Wanda heard soft snores coming from her and walked over to the curtains and drew them, shutting out the strong afternoon light. "Of course. Why not?" She spoke to herself and put the bucket next to Dayna's face on the floor. "Just do me a favour and don't get any sick on the carpet."

She untied the trainers on Dayna's feet and pulled them off noticing the deep cuts and gravel that lined them. *Where do you go at night? What happened to you?* She closed the bedroom door as she went out.

Sheila's head snapped up when she heard the key in the door. The grogginess from the wine slipped off her as her thoughts sharpened.

Lucy crept in through the doorway, ascending the stairs without turning on the light. Sheila reached out and clicked on a lamp on the table bathing the room in the light of judgement. Lucy froze on the stairs.

"Lucy, where have you been?"

"Out."

"Come down here. I'd like to speak to you." Sheila saw her daughter take a single step up the stairs. Her temper flared.

"Is Dad home?"

Sheila rose out of the chair. She would fetch her if she had to but she'd rather it not come to that. She kept her voice level. "Come down," she repeated.

Lucy exhaled theatrically and clomped down the stairs. She stopped in the archway leading to the living room. Sheila felt anger rise up inside her at her flippancy but she wouldn't give in to the need to shout. She wouldn't give her daughter an excuse to turn tail and flee to the safety of her room. She wouldn't lower herself to talking to her daughter through a locked door.

"Where were you tonight?

"I went into the city."

"All by yourself?"

Lucy rolled her eyes.

"Look at me and tell me where you've been this evening. You should've been home from school hours ago." She stood up off the chair and moved forward, closing the distance between them.

Lucy looked out of the window, shaking her head.

"Don't shake your head at me. I was worried about you."

"You weren't worried yesterday when I came home late. I had to walk from the bus stop when you didn't show."

Sheila flinched, then tried to change the subject. "Why didn't you call home tonight to say you would be late? You know your father and I worry."

"Dad's not home."

Sheila came forward another step. She took no notice of her daughter's blazer that was pulled tight across the chest, the buttons threatening to pop. She was too busy trying to smell out the tell-tale stink of weed smoke on her clothes. She was caught completely off guard when Lucy spoke.

"Mum, are you drunk?"

Sheila's eyes widened, her fists clenched at her sides.

"God, you stink of booze. Ugh." Lucy's hand flew up to her mouth covering her nose and turning away from her.

"Lucy, have you been smoking?"

Lucy staggered on the stairs and gave a forced laugh. "Ha! Are you serious? My God! You drink like a fish and smoke like a chimney with all your bitch friends and you think I'm the one who's smoking? My God, you *are drunk*!"

Sheila's hand whipped out, catching her daughter sharply across the face. Lucy's hands flew to her mouth in shock.

"Lucy, I-"

Lucy's hand rose to her cheek to feel the livid mark that was beginning to show there. "You hit me, you fuckin' bitch!"

Sheila cringed back as Lucy shouted the B word again, foul words she'd never heard her use, words she'd never dreamed she would hear coming from her daughter's mouth. *I know where she learned those words. I know where she's just come from. I hit her. I've never hit her.*

Lucy barged past her and grabbed the lamp that stood next to the armchair and held it above her head. "I hate you!" She threw it hard across the room where it shattered against the wall, plunging the room into darkness.

Sheila moved towards her. *For what?* She didn't know. *Grab her. Stop her. Hold her. Hug her.*

Lucy shoved her away. "Get off me!" She ran through the foyer and up the stairs.

Sheila clenched her eyes against the *slam* that came from the floor above as her daughter locked herself in the room. She slowly sat down back in the chair with her eyes closed, trying to clamp down hard on the rush of emotion that was coming up from the cavern inside her. *Stay angry. Don't get upset. Follow through. Ground her. Take her phone away. Barge in there and tell her she's grounded.* Silent hot tears rolled down her face. Her fingers came up to pinch the bridge of her nose as she felt the migraine surface from where it was hidden in the back of her mind.

Heavy metal music came on from above and pounded through the ceiling making her jump. Sheila's eyes opened and she looked up, hearing her daughter's heavy tread echo across the ceiling and various bangs and crashes that came again and again.

Lucy slammed the door and stormed around the room, hurling framed pictures against the walls. She punched cushions and shattered small ornaments, finally throwing herself down on the sofa and rubbing her face.

That bitch.

She was sweating profusely now. Her hand came away from her face wet. Music blared from the stereo, drowning out her thoughts of the slap. She tore her school blazer off, popping buttons and threw it against the wall, followed by the dull knitted school cardigan and, finally, she unzipped the scarlet leather jacket and threw it across the room where it landed in a heap on the floor amongst her cast-off school uniform.

She stood in her knickers and bra before the mirror, her chestnut brown hair hanging around her, lacklustre and plain. Her freckled face was staring back at her with faint disgust. *Plain Jane, plain Jane, plain Jane* went around her head. Her eyes went down to her chest where her breasts swelled with newfound fullness and down to her broad hips and further down to her stocky thighs. The mark on her cheek was glowing red against her pale skin.

She got up and went to the door where her leather satchel was flung casually in a corner. She fell to her knees and began rummaging around until her hand closed over the familiar shape of her school pencil case. She rummaged inside, moving aside fountain pens, biros and broken pencils and there, buried in the bottom, she found what she was searching for: a glint of silver flashed in the dark.

She looked over herself one more time in front of the mirror and raised the scissors to her brown locks. *Snick.* The curls began to fall to the pink carpet around her feet and her hand began to pick up speed, going left to right. Her eyes followed the scissors' movement mesmerised, unable to slow down. *Snick. Snick. Snick*

She relished the sound of the metal coming together, cutting away her old self, trimming away the cancerous leaves to make way for the coming of spring.

Caroline jumped when she heard the banging on the door. *Panic!* Knocking, knocking coming from everywhere: the ceiling, the walls, the door. *The ghosts! The ghosts are back!*

Her hands went for the door handle and the bolt and then retreated away from them as if they were hot. The banging ceased for a moment as if, whoever it was, sensed her movement behind the door. She held her breath.

"Carol, it's Michele."

"Oh shit, Shell. I'm so sorry." She grabbed the security bolt and pulled it back turning the knob at the same time. Michele stood in the doorway looking dishevelled with her clothes dripping wet. She wore sensible flat shoes and had a large carrier bag over one shoulder. Caroline's eyes moved to the two tall logo-emblazoned coffee cups held in a cardboard carrier in her right hand, so out of place and strange in the surrounding environment. They looked to her like artefacts from another planet.

"Coffee for my lady." She held them out and Caroline took them, placing them on the counter. She ran over to the door and slammed it, bolted it and then turned the knob, pulling the door against her to check it was secure.

"Still anxious about this place?"

"Wouldn't you be?"

Michele nodded. "Still, I'm here. You can leave it open if you like, maybe get some fresh air in."

"I won't, thanks." She checked the door was locked once more before stepping away.

Michele pointed to the coffee. "Two extra sweet, double shot, tall caramel lattes; an excuse for *still* not having brought you a coffeemaker. I'm sorry I've just been too busy to do it."

"That's sweet but I don't even drink the stuff that much." She took a sip. She wasn't used to the strong taste.

"But you'd drink more if you had one! And then you can join us addicts in the happy land of *legal* highs."

"I've had enough addiction in my life."

Caroline felt bad. She appreciated Michele trying to lighten the mood with her frankly poor sense of humour but she didn't really feel up to playing along today. "How did you get in anyway? I'm so sorry I thought I set the alarm before going to sleep."

"I was on the step for about fifteen minutes and some guy was coming out so I said I was here to visit someone and sort of walked in. I was knocking for a while. You must've been out cold."

"Yeah, I'm sleeping a lot at the moment." She put her hand to her forehead.

"Why don't you put on some clothes?"

"Oh shit!" Caroline looked down at herself clad in an old pair of shorts and a bra that she had slept in. "Sorry, Shell. God, I'm a mess."

"No you're not. I'll just put these in your fridge." She began to unpack identical Tupperware boxes filled with sandwiches from her shoulder bag and put them on the floor beside her. "Have you eaten much since I last saw you? You look very thin."

"No, I don't have much appetite at the moment."

"Oh, for Christ's sake! If you're not going to eat them, at least throw them out when they're past their peak! Jesus."

Caroline's eyes darted to Michele who had her hand over her mouth with her face turned away from the fridge door. She slammed it and began fanning the air frantically trying to disperse the smell of food that had obviously gone off. "No worries, no worries. I'll throw it all out into a bin bag and take it out with me when I go. Don't worry about the Tupperware. I've got loads."

Caroline pulled on her pair of ripped jeans and a T-shirt. The rest of her wardrobe strewn around the floor didn't show much better promise than what she already had on.

Michele slammed the fridge door and stood up. "I always wash out and use old ice cream boxes when they're finished. We get through a lot with my step mum and dad eating it all the time. Oh my God, did I tell you *they're trying for a baby*?"

Caroline laughed in spite of herself. "How's that going to work? They're both in their fifties."

"Don't get me started. She's reading all these books on finding fertility through acupuncture."

Caroline spat coffee out onto the floor, laughing.

Michele laughed too. "I'm so glad to be able to tell someone! I've been home with her all weekend measuring the spare room that's going to be her room!"

"You mean the baby's room?"

"She's already decided she's having a girl. I swear she's out of her mind. I think it's all just an elaborate plot to get my dad to redecorate the spare room in the shades of pink she wants."

Caroline lay on the sofa clutching her stomach laughing hard. She felt as if a great hole had opened in the cavern inside her. Bats of woe were now startled out of their rest and flapping violently up to the light. Tears rolled down her face.

"Speaking of redecorating, have you done something in here?"

'Hmm? No, nothing different." Caroline cast a reluctant eye around the hostel room: cooker still broken, clothes on the floor, crowbar back in its place between the sofa and the wall. *Better to have it and not need it.*

"It feels different in here. When I last came..."

Caroline's eyes moved over to the window. "Can I talk to you about something?"

"Sure. I've got the whole afternoon. We can even go out somewhere if you like, get some fresh air in those dried up lungs of yours."

"Ha! Thanks very much."

"Scoot over." Michele plonked herself down on the old sofa.

"I've been having trouble with the pills they're giving me."

Michele's look of joy vanished in an instant. "We've talked about this. The side effects will pass in time."

"These aren't side effects."

Michele opened her mouth to speak.

"No, wait a minute. Listen, they're not side effects. I don't know what day it is. I sleep ten hours at a time. I can't think when I am awake and it feels like the only time I get up is to take a wee."

"You've only been on them since you moved in here. Give them time."

"It's been six months. I don't feel any better. I know my own mind."

"Six months ago you were putting all kinds of shit in your system and you didn't know what was real and what wasn't."

"Don't throw that in my face. Besides I think I know what that was now."

"All that shit you and Tom were dumping into your system?"

"Yes, and I think there's something else as well. I saw someone here the other night."

"You mean someone who lives here came in?"

"No, he was standing there over by the fridge. A man."

Michele looked over to the fridge where Caroline was pointing. Her brow furrowed, looking at the empty space. "I don't understand."

"He was here before me, I think, or maybe further back than that, but I think he committed suicide here and that's why he couldn't leave. I'm not sure if he's gone now. I hope he is. I think I made him go."

Michele stood up and began rubbing her forehead. "Stop it, Carol. You've been doing so well."

"I know what I saw and you know I've been drug free for six months. You can take me to the clinic now and test me if you like." Caroline made an effort to keep her tone level.

Michele turned around to face her. "We've been through this before. The amount of drugs and mushrooms you were doing can leave images in your head even when you're not tripping. You can day-trip without knowing it. The doctor went through this when she spoke to us. You're supposed to call me if you feel a hallucination coming on."

"I wasn't hallucinating. I went out to the cafe where I was supposed to meet you. I had a bad day and I came home."

"Did you fall asleep?"

"I tried to. I was on the bed."

"Are you sure you weren't dreaming?"

"Yes I'm sure. I got up to take my pill when I saw him."

"Did you?"

"Did I, what?"

"Did you take your medication when you came home?"

"No." She saw no point in lying.

"Oh, Caroline." Michele buried her face in her hands as she sank back into the sofa.

Caroline's anger flared. She barged across the room and threw open the room to the cupboard that housed the sink and the shower and grabbed the carton of mood stabilisers off the sink. "You see these?" She rattled the box for emphasis. "These are wrecking me. They're not good for me. You take one and call me tomorrow, telling me how you're pissing nine times a day and feel like your head's filled with black tar. Hell, the first few weeks I was so dizzy I could barely stand up."

"But it passed, didn't it?"

"You are not listening to me. These *things* have nothing to do with the people I saw the other night!"

"You said you saw a man by the refrigerator. Did he have friends with him now?"

"No, they were... they were different." She closed her eyes trying to think. "I'm not sure what they were, but I think they lived here, before me. I mean, think about it. How many girls go homeless every year? A thousand? Ten thousand? Where do they go after living here? Are you telling me their parents just reappear and pick them up and take them back home and they get to pick up from where they left off?"

"No, of course not."

"Well then, where do they go, all the people that live here?"

"Social services told you. You get assessed and put on a waiting list for housing, or supported living depending on what your needs are."

"You're telling me everyone gets to just go on happily. You don't think anyone just gave up and overdosed here? Or hanged themselves? Michele, it was like they were all still here, I saw them."

"Stop it." She walked over to the window and looked out. "If you're having suicidal thoughts I can make an appointment at the GP and take you."

"Oh, forget the GP!"

"Well, what then?" She turned on her, her voice raised in anger. "What do you want me to do more than I've already done for you?"

"I want you to believe me. He was real. I saw him, as real as I see now. I didn't make it up and it's not some worthless bid for attention."

"You know I'm not supposed to go along with these fantasies. It only makes it more real for you."

"I know he was real. I think it would help if you believed me."

"Fine. Let's say I believe you saw a spook-"

"I did."

"How does that help you?"

"It would make me feel a lot less crazy, and a lot less alone, and maybe if I had support from someone I wouldn't feel the need to talk to these things in the first place."

Michele took a deep breath. "So you don't think I'm supporting you."

"I think you want me dosed up to the eyeballs so you feel like I'm getting better. They're not making me feel better. They're making me feel worse."

"All right, I accept you don't like being on them, but this ghost stuff... Do you want me to see about getting your room swapped? I'll call your social worker."

"Even if you managed to get that social worker on the phone, what would you tell them? My addict friend is seeing ghosts by the fridge. Can you get her a bigger room please? The ghosts are not the problem right now. I think he's gone anyway."

"What do you mean gone? Gone where?"

"If you don't want to do this, you can go home. I don't need to justify it. I know it was real. Of all people I thought you'd believe me."

"I'm trying to understand." Michele sat back gently on the sofa.

Caroline slowly paced the edges of the room. "All right. Imagine all the emotional pile-up in a room like this from everyone who's come through here."

Michele cast a worried look around. "Like your dirty laundry on the floor."

"Well, exactly, and I think when this guy died he got stuck here like a cork in a bottle and I don't think I could see him due to all the drugs I'd been on distracting me."

"So how come you know he's gone?"

"I can feel it. I think bringing them all out in the open popped the cork. There are signs they're all gone."

"Signs?"

"On the window sill. There were names, carved by the previous residents. They've gone now."

"Oh, Jesus."

"You don't have to believe me. I still love you for all you've done for me. It would just help if you did."

"I still think you should speak to someone before coming off the meds cold turkey."

"I feel clearer today."

"When did you last take them?"

"The day before yesterday."

"I'll phone the hospital and see if there's anything you should watch out for."

Caroline went over to the sofa and sat on the floor, her head resting against her friend's knee. "I want to get out of here."

"Oh honey, I know. Don't worry. With me badgering social services, you'll be far away from here soon. I promise." Michele reached over and gave her shoulder a gentle squeeze, taking care not to squeeze too hard, feeling her friend's delicate frame beneath her skin. "Let me call social today and see if there's something they do, something that will get you out of the house."

"I don't want to go outside, Shell. There are too many people." She pulled away from her.

"Maybe not yet but you can't stay here indoors all day with a load of spooks for company."

"You know he spoke to me."

"Who?"

"The dead man."

Caroline could feel Michele tense up beside her. "And what did he say?"

"He said to stay away from the woman with the beehive hairdo. Those were his exact words."

Michele was silent for a moment. "Bit cryptic if you ask me."

"I think it means something."

"I wouldn't waste too much energy on trying to understand something a dead man tries to tell you." She laughed aloud to herself. "Now there's a sentence I never thought I'd say."

"I'll try to put it out of my mind."

"Good. Now get your coat on. I'm taking you outside. Your skin's in bad need of some tanning."

"God, not that awful arty cafe again."

"Yes, that very one! I love it in there. Don't you love all the homemade jewellery for sale? I think it's all adorable."

Caroline picked an old cardigan up off the floor. "I think I'd take anywhere over being here right now."

Michele clapped her hands together. "Now that's the spirit! Now how do you open this fucking thing?" She was pulling at the door handle without pulling back the bolt. The edge of the jam kept hitting the thick bar of metal that protruded out of the door like a grey tongue.

"Here." Caroline pulled back the bolt and the handle at the same time allowing the door to swing inward and they both went through at once. They laughed when they collided together in the doorway, both so eager to leave the room.

Eve was patrolling the corridors of the mental ward like a Dalek. The morning was suspiciously quiet on the ward which, to her, was a bad omen that promised trouble for the evening shift. She was in a foul mood; her numbers had not come up on the lottery the night before. She'd been so close. She needed number thirteen and fourteen had popped out. That close. That close to winning twenty quid. There was no justice in the world. A high voice spoke behind her.

"Morning, Eve."

She grunted in reply.

Fiona walked past with a bright pink smile plastered across her face looking as jolly as a corpse dressed up for a wake. Eve didn't understand what she had to be so happy about.

"You know Mr Graves' toilet issue these past few weeks? Well, I had a little brainwave over the weekend. I found an old bedpan in the storage cupboard and put it under his bed, so if it looks like he's about to, you know-"

"Follow through," said Eve bluntly.

"Well, yes, exactly. We just hoist him up onto the potty and then there's none of the yucky mess to clean up." The smile crept back onto her face. Eve didn't like it.

"That's wonderful. However the man is a vegetable. How on earth are we supposed to know when he needs to use the lavatory?"

"He's been lucid since we reduced the medication he was on. Didn't Shelley tell you? She had a conversation with him this morning."

Eve was momentarily stupefied. "Where is Paul Graves now?"

"In the common room." Fiona caught sight of the look on her face and said, "Don't disturb him, please, Eve. He's made friends with a stray cat that hangs around the hospital. He seems happy."

"Paul Graves has been sectioned with us for well over a decade and besides inane drivel and babble I've never heard him speak a single word of sense, I assure you. Whatever miracle you think Shelley has performed with her so-called 'reduced treatment' I doubt it will last. They're all the same when they arrive. Dementia is the first sign of them fading. He's also recently shown signs of schizophrenia-."

"Yes, Shelley told me this morning. He thinks you're trying to poison him."

She continued as if Fiona had not interrupted her "Bits and pieces come back but they never recover fully. It's better not to attach yourself. He probably won't be here for much longer. I've never known a patient with his diagnosis to last longer than a few years."

"But you just said yourself, he's been here for a decade."

"Yes, well." She moved around on the spot uncomfortably. "He's obviously showing resistance to the inevitable but hanging by a thread is still just hanging. I doubt he has very long to live now."

"In that case, I'm sure we can all do our best to make his stay with us as comfortable as possible." Fiona beamed at her and turned tail running for the ward before Eve on her cloven footed feet could catch up.

Charlie felt his spirits lift as the car roared through the looming iron gates on the property. The car headlights reflected against the thick iron chains that were coiled around the bars like rusted snakes.

He got out of the car limping. His back had got steadily worse on the drive over. He felt around in his jeans pocket and produced a small bent key that fitted easily into the keyhole of the padlock. *Click.* He pulled the chains apart off the gate and pushed forward, grunting with the effort as he put his weight against one, then the other. They gave a great long sigh as they came open.

Birds took off from the branches of the yew trees that stood along the edge of the property. As he drove slowly up the winding road that led to the house, he thought the hedges could do with a trim. It was hard for him to stay on top of everything alone. He whistled out of tune with himself, as he drove along, so glad was he to be home.

He followed the road and then finally he saw the house loom up in front of him. It was a great manor that stood on the rise of the hill, the windows shuttered against the intrusion of daylight. Ivy had claimed the first and second storeys which, in the dark, made the house look to be suffocated from the coil of a great black cocoon. He could see a window on the ground floor that needed replacing where vandals had knocked it out, probably kids. He just hoped he was back to his old self the next time they tried it. He had a few toys in the cellar that he'd love to introduce them to. He pulled into the old disused barn that stood to the right of the property and cut off the engine.

He made his way around to the back of the house where the garden yawned out in waist-high grass to the edge of the trees where the wood began. He didn't bother to lock the cellar doors of the house. Visitors were always welcome. A few years ago a couple had slipped in through the gates one night looking to burgle or perhaps just on a drunken dare while he and Rosie were out at a club. When they arrived home they saw the cellar doors had been left carelessly open betraying an intruder. Rose went in through the front door while he made his way through the cellar. His yellow teeth flashed out as he reminisced on what a good night that had been.

He went down the stone steps into the dark of the cellar, feeling his way around by touch, he'd taken out the light bulbs from down there decades ago not needing them. He could see just fine in the dark. He felt around blindly in the dark before his hands brushed across a familiar shape. *Good.* He was worried that he'd left it in the house somewhere, but it was still here, right where it was supposed to be. He whistled happily as he carried it out of the cellar, taking care not to disturb the cobwebs that loomed over the cellar entrance, and up the wooden steps that led to the back door.

The wheels of the chair squeaked from lack of use as he came into the bedroom. She probably wouldn't need to use it for that long before it could go away again. He was proud of it: his creation. He'd built it himself from a rocking chair and four pram wheels. He liked to build things. There was a cross-stitched cushion on the seat depicting a bouquet of roses.

"Rose, I'm home."

A stirring in the dark. Muffled sounds.

"I've got a surprise for you."

Movement in the recesses of the bed.

He came around the huge bed and sat on the chair. Her eyes were open, white eggs that saw nothing through the cataracts that smothered them. He stroked the gossamer thread away from her bald skull, took a handkerchief from the dressing table and wiped some dried drool from around her mouth.

"I've got more than one surprise for you actually, but I will tell you once we get you into the living room. I need to pick you up now. A moment's pain and then it will be over."

She groaned and coughed.

He pulled back the duvet of the bed exposing her shrunken form, her tiny stick legs barely causing a lump in the silk pyjamas that encased them. The shrinking was something that hadn't happened before. He had to buy her pyjamas from an upscale children's boutique he'd found on the other side of town.

"Up we come." He placed her crooked wrinkled hands around his neck. He noticed all the fingers were bunched up together making her hands appear as fists, a sign of arthritis. He marvelled at how light she was as he lifted her into the air and placed her gently into the seat of the wheelchair as easily as shoving a book into an empty slot on the shelf. "There. Are you warm enough? I can fetch you a blanket if you like."

She opened her mouth in a croak. He noticed not a single tooth was left in her blackened gums. "Imp fineth, Warlie."

"All right. Get ready for your surprise. Woo!" He went behind the chair and wheeled her into the peeling yellow wallpapered hallway. The oak boards creaked below them as they progressed along the passage, passing doors of unused rooms without a glance to a door that was propped open at the end.

The old wooden record player stood in the centre of the room. Various old chairs were stacked precariously in the corner. Brown shopping bags had been put in a druids' circle around the record player.

He wheeled her in to face the record player and ran over to the corner of the room where a single dark candle was fixed in an old wooden candlestick. He struck the match lighting the wick. He saw her wrinkled face cringe back from the light across the room. The chair creaked under her weight as she shifted uncomfortably away from the flame.

"It's all right, Rose. I'm here. And look! All this is for you."

Her face was unreadable, a floating skull above the chair masked in the shadows that moved along the walls.

He reached into one of the brown shopping bags and produced a square envelope. With a flick of his hand he whipped out the black vinyl disc and twirled it twice in the air in front of her face. He thought he saw her mouth twitch in the corners, an old crone's leer. He placed the disc smoothly into the player and moved the needle with his fingers over the disc and hit the switch. The words of Dusty Springfield filled the room like a chant:

I don't know what it is that makes me love you so
and now I never want to let you go!
But you start something with just one kiss!
I never knew that I could fall in love like this!
It's crazy but it's true!

I only wanna be with you!

The music filled the room, making him tap his feet in time with it. He did a bop on the spot that made her face break apart in a dry cackle that became a whooping cough. He turned the volume down as she gasped for air.

"You all right Rosy? I'm sorry, just...do you remember this? Do you remember when we last heard it? God, that was an amazing night." He bent down in front of her and put one of his hands in hers and slowly moved it up and down as if in a waltz. "We danced all night to this one. And look I've got more!"

He turned around and began pulling out the clothes he'd bought from the brown shopping bags, laying each item carefully around the wheelchair that Rose sat on like a throne, her back straight as a queen. The rhinestone encrusted fabrics of the clothes glittered in the light of the candle like a pirate's plunder.

He saw her tongue come out and moisten her lips.

"That's right Rosy, nearly time, and better still I caught the scent of one in the mall."

He saw her eyes widen in the dark. He heard the creak of the wood as her body tensed in the chair.

"Yeah, it was definitely a strong one." He spoke to himself, knowing she couldn't reply. "I got her scent but then lost it again. I'm sure I'll pick it up again if I roam around. Don't worry, Rosy. She was a good one this time. Much better than the last one. She'll last much longer, I promise. I could practically taste the youth on her, like black cherries."

She croaked something he couldn't make out.

"I know I'm not looking my best but I think with an old rug to cover my hair and some make-up I should be fine to make the grab. Don't you worry. I'm on it. Tomorrow night. I'm positive."

He came in front of the chair kneeling before her. He pulled it towards him with a squeak. He lent in close to her so his ear was close to her lips. She smelled of mothballs and medicine. "Now you tell your Charlie which one you want to wear on the night."

Dayna slept through Sunday evening and woke up on Monday morning feeling low from the comedown of the weekend. She knew from the moment she surveyed the lavender interior of Wanda's room and the bucket next to her on the floor, that there would be trouble this time.

She got out of the huge bed, sad to leave it. It'd been the first time she'd slept in a double since John had thrown her out. She probably wouldn't get the chance again.

Wanda was sitting at the table looking down at her hands. Dayna moved to the espresso machine, took a china mug off the hook from above the sink and pushed a button. She listened to the faint hum as the machine poured the brown liquid from within its bowels.

Wanda spoke from behind her. "We need to talk. Could you sit down?"

She plonked down in the seat opposite Wanda, readying herself for the verbal barrage that was about to come out.

"We've been overdue for a chat. I'm sorry I've been so busy, too busy to spend time with you. I know when you came I said I'd help you back onto your feet and I supposed I've not done all I could for you."

Dayna sipped her hot coffee, letting her speak.

"I didn't realize how bad things were with you until you came home Sunday morning. Do you remember where you went?"

"A bar."

How many times have you gone there?"

"Does it matter?"

Wanda's tone dropped, betraying anger. "It matters to me. This matters." She dropped the black silk dress stolen from her wardrobe on top of the table. The loose beads skittered across the table and rolled across the floor. Wanda's hands moved inside the dress poking her fingers through the holes. "I just don't understand why you would do this. I thought I could trust you in my home. I mean, for Christ's sake, what happened to you? It looks like you've been through a war in this."

Dayna stood up to leave. She didn't need the guilt trip on top of everything else. Her head was pounding as it was.

Wanda's voice made her freeze in the doorway. "Don't you dare walk away from me! I haven't finished."

"I'm going to my room."

"You walk out of this kitchen and you can leave today. I'm not joking."

Dayna turned her head slowly to look at her. She hadn't seen Wanda's face like it before. "Fine. Whatever you say. You're the landlord."

"Do you even remember where you went Saturday night? I mean, what happened to your shoes?"

May as well tell the truth. Get her riled up.

"I didn't wear my shoes. I took yours."

"What?"

"I took yours. We're both fives."

"You're a six."

"OK so they were a snug fit but they were still yours."

Wanda's brow furrowed at her, searching Dayna's face. Dayna stared back at her.

Wanda put her hand to her forehead as if to shut out a headache that was coming. "Which ones?"

"They were black, shiny leather with red soles."

"I hadn't even got around to wearing them yet! What were you thinking?"

"I was thinking that it'd be fun to spend a night in your skin for a change! I was thinking I could wear the kind of clothes someone who is not sleeping on a friend's sofa with no job would wear. I wanted to be someone else for a night! I thought I'd take a break from myself!"

Wanda came around the table and took Dayna by the shoulders. "So you robbed me?"

"I borrowed them. I honestly thought I would have them back before you noticed them gone."

"Where are my shoes?"

Dayna closed her eyes trying to think. She remembered walking into the men's toilet, the skeletal form of the dealer. "I don't know. I don't remember what happened."

"How drunk did you get? I thought you were broke. You certainly haven't been paying me anything."

Dayna laughed aloud. "Like you need it."

"That's it!" Wanda snatched the cup away from her and threw the coffee down the sink. She grabbed her by the arms and pushed her into the hallway. Dayna struggled in protest as she marched her into the bedroom.

"Get off me!" Dayna's knees went from under her as she tripped over the mop bucket. Wanda reached down with her other arm and grabbed her shoulder, dragging her along, kicking and screaming along the carpet. She let her drop briefly to throw open the doors of her walk-in wardrobe. Dayna struggled under her like a cat. The mirror on the far wall showed one woman on the ground, her nightgown flapping open exposing her breasts. Her face was a painted harlequin tragedy. The other woman was as emotionless as a cyborg reaching down and grabbing her again, pulling her into the confined space of the closet.

Wanda slammed the door, shutting them both in. "Look at yourself."

"Fuck you!"

"Do you think you look like a happy woman?"

Dayna lunged for the double doors. Wanda grabbed her wrists and pried them off the handles of the door. She turned her around to face the mirror.

"Look at what you've done to yourself."

Dayna looked. Her auburn hair corkscrewed out from her scalp like a maenad. Her sunken eyes were smeared black with soot. Most of the lipstick had come off during her long sleep, making her mouth look as if she had a rash. There were small cuts and scrapes along her arms and up her legs from where she'd fallen on the road walking home.

"Whatever you're doing to yourself to come home looking like this, you need to stop. Do you hear me?" Wanda shook her. "I mean it. I'm locking this room from now on. You come home high and I'll call the police. You can spend the night sleeping off your bender in a cell. You take responsibility for yourself and your body. I'm not doing this with you anymore. The first thing you can do is wash that shit off your face, and then I'm taking you out to find a job. The party is over. You hear?"

Dayna didn't speak. She wouldn't give her the satisfaction of crying.

Wanda opened the double doors of the walk-in, allowing Dayna safe passage from the bedroom. Wanda stayed in the small space for a while longer, panting in deep breaths and rubbing her sore hands together.

The two women stood in front of the entrance to Springfield Hospital. The old building reared up making Caroline crane her neck to see the crows that lined the rooftops like bad omens.

"Why are we here, Michele?"

She felt small and tiny beneath its grand stone structure. "You're sectioning me, aren't you?"

Michele took her gently by the arm as they walked up the steps to the entrance. "No, of course not. Besides I can't. Only relatives can do that."

"Let me know if you do ever track down any of mine."

"After I saw you I had a long think. It was naive of me to think that getting you off the street would be the be-all and end-all, but I think it's doing you a lot of harm being shut in there all day like a battery chicken. I thought voluntary work would get you out for a few hours."

"Volunteer here?"

Their footsteps echoed loudly down the wide hallway.

"I spoke to a kind nurse on the phone this morning named Fiona. She said they always need help with the patients. You don't have to do anything too hard, just talk to them, play board games. It'd be good for you to help people."

"So, I'll be helping people to help myself," Caroline said sarcastically.

"Precisely. Now where on earth are we?" The corridor ended in a small square passage that had three corridors branching out in many directions.

"Let's go this way. I'm sure there are waiting rooms around here somewhere."

"I'm not sure about this. I don't like it here." Caroline looked behind her, hearing footsteps. Behind them the hallway was empty.

Michele continued to walk fast down the hall. "You haven't given it a chance yet. You may meet some interesting people, people needing more help than you."

"This place doesn't feel right to me." The feeling of being watched hadn't left Caroline since she had crossed the threshold into the hospital. 'It seems too cold in here. I don't like it.'

"You'll feel better once we find the ward. I imagine it's a very busy place. She said they can have up to twenty short-term patients and a small group of long-term ones who are permanent residents. Ah, finally."

They came to a small foyer with a high desk dominating the room. A dead fern stood in the corner.

Caroline heard a squeaking noise coming through the hallway. Eventually a blonde woman came around the corner wearing mint green nurses' overalls. She had a welcoming smile on her face.

"You must be Michele. I'm Fiona. Come through to the ward."

Michele turned to Caroline and hugged her. "I will have to head off now."

"What? You're leaving me here?" She spoke a little too forcibly and noticed Fiona raising her eyebrows.

"You will be fine. Call me tonight and tell me how it went." She pecked her on the cheek and, before Caroline could stop her, hurried out of the foyer.

Fiona wasted no time taking Caroline's arm and swiping her card into the reader on the door. "It's so good you're here. Michele told me all about you. We are so thin on the ground due to staff turnaround so we're really grateful for you wanting to come in and help. You'll find there's a lot of pleasure to be got from helping people with mental health problems. But don't worry, you don't have to clean any bed pans." She laughed. "That's our job. Just try and engage with the patients. Have a game of cards or Scrabble. There's one patient I think you will get on well with. He's been here for a few years and recently has started speaking again."

"What do you mean 'again'? He lost his speech?"

"He's diagnosed with schizophrenia, so he was on quite a lot of medication which we've reduced due to the side effects."

Caroline nodded. "I know all about those."

"And it'd be good for him to have come company. He's never had a visitor in the entire time I've been here. I don't think he has any family. I've given you both a private room here. He may say things to you that make little sense. He means nothing by them. It's just his illness."

She laughed again. Caroline smiled despite herself. She liked how cheerful Fiona was, in sharp contrast to the grey decor of the ward. Together they walked down the middle of the room. Caroline could see the old fashioned beds lining the ward. The faces of the patients seemed sleepy and resigned.

Fiona paused outside a small door. She spoke to someone Caroline couldn't see. "Mr Graves? Come in, Caroline, dear. There's someone here to see you."

The man in the wheelchair had light blue eyes and a tiny mouth. He was hunched over in the chair with his head bowed. He looked up briefly when Fiona spoke and then returned his gaze to the floor.

"I just need to fetch his medicine. He has it in water so it's easy to swallow. Can I get you anything, Caroline? Tea or coffee?"

"A tea would be wonderful. Thank you."

The walls were painted a cheerful rose pink, different from the rest of the ward. She sat down on the fold-up chair that had been set up for her.

The old man looked up slowly and moved his glassy eyes down her, taking her in. "You don't look like a nurse." His voice sounded raspy and cracked from lack of use.

Caroline hadn't expected him to speak. "No, I'm not a nurse."

"What are you then?" Paul's head dropped back down when he heard the squeaking from the hall.

Fiona breezed back into the room. She had a tray with a mug of hot tea and Caroline saw a tall glass with milky coloured water in it. She set it down on the table. "Make sure you're nice to Caroline, Mr Graves, and Caroline make sure he drinks that. I'll leave you to it." She winked at Caroline, shutting the door quietly.

His eyes came back up again. "Are you a patient?"

"I'm a volunteer."

He spoke clearly. "They say that I'm mad."

Caroline smiled. "They say I'm mad too."

He grinned showing a mouth full of crooked teeth. "They're the mental ones, them out there. She's not too bad, but you watch out for the other two. I call her Clotho. The other two are Lachesis and Atropos."

Caroline nodded, not understanding.

"Watch out for Atropos. She's the worst. She keeps trying to poison me."

He reached over and picked up the glass. Before Caroline could stop him, he'd tipped the entire contents into the dead plant in the corner.

"Mr Graves, I don't think-"

"Shh," he said, holding a hand up to silence her. "It's this stuff they've got me on. It clouds me over."

"I feel the same when I take my medication."

He sat up slowly. "What have they got you on?"

"Quetiapine."

"Nasty stuff, Quetiapine. Young girl like you shouldn't be on that."

A huge tom cat jumped up onto the window and dropped into the room. He brushed up against Caroline's legs and then jumped up onto Mr Graves' lap, purring.

"This is Snoops."

Caroline laughed. "Snoops and Mr Graves."

My first name is Paul." He reached out a wrinkled hand. The cat watched her with its big yellow eyes.

"Thank you Paul, but I don't shake hands."

"Why's that?"

"I just don't."

He nodded again. Caroline took a sip of tea.

"Snoops wants to know why you're here."

She opened her mouth to answer and closed it again when she saw his eyes. "For a man with schizophrenia, you speak very well."

He chuckled off key, like the sound of china breaking. The cat looked up at him. "I don't like to be bothered here. Please don't do me a disservice by telling them we've had a conversation. Tell them I drooled a lot and gave you a lot of nonsense."

Caroline took a sip of tea. *A sane man in a mental home?*

"How long have you been here?"

His smiled faltered. "A long time. I had a breakdown after my wife passed away. I came into contact with a lot of dark things. Then the bottle got me. Almost all of me." He stroked the cat behind its ears.

"So you sectioned yourself?"

"No, my doctor did. The ones that come in voluntarily they don't think need the help. They dope them up and then let them go."

Caroline nodded. "I know exactly what you mean, but are you happy here?"

"It's better in here. Too much bad out there. You didn't tell me why you came here."

She looked to the door to make sure no-one was eavesdropping. "I came off the streets a few months ago and I'm not doing well in a hostel, on the medication. I'm seeing things." He seemed to come more awake in the chair at what she'd said.

"What things?"

"Just unpleasant things. My friend was worried I was spending too long indoors so she said I should volunteer here."

"And what do you think about the things you see?"

"I don't like where I'm living. It's crowded and noisy, horrible place, but there's nothing I can do about it. I don't want to be on the medication anymore. It makes me feel ill."

"They're poison for people like us."

"People like us?"

"People that see things." He looked out the window. The cat closed its eyes, purring softly.

"What do you see, Paul?"

He smiled at her showing his crooked teeth. "Unpleasant things. Snoops sees things too."

"How do you know he sees things?"

"He tells me."

She laughed. "Cats cannot talk!"

The cat's yellow eyes were on her again. Gazing into her eyes inscrutably, Paul leaned forward in the chair. His voice was firm. "He can talk, but only certain kinds of people can hear him. I can hear him."

Caroline opened her mouth to reply but stopped, turning her head. Someone was coming down the hall. Paul jumped in his seat. The cat, startled, fled from his lap and jumped up to the windowsill. Paul slouched back into the chair like a puppet with its strings cut.

"So how are we doing?" Fiona came back into the room with a short stocky woman Caroline had not seen before.

"He's been fine, Fiona."

The short woman's eyes moved from the empty glass on the table back to Paul who was sitting still in the chair gazing at the floor again. She spoke in a tight clipped voice "Has he taken his medication?"

"Yes, yes he has."

"All of it?"

"Yes, I helped him drink it down."

The woman's eyes bore into her. Caroline stared back without flinching.

Fiona turned to the short woman. "Eve, why don't you fetch the wheelchair for Mr Graves while I finish up here with Caroline, please?"

The woman seemed to deflate before Caroline's eyes, and plodded out of the room.

"I'm sorry about her. She can be unpleasant. Don't let her put you off. We are thrilled to have you here."

Caroline stood up to leave. "No, it's been fine really. Would you like me to come in tomorrow for a few hours?"

"Would you like to? Mr Graves, would you like to see Caroline again?"

Paul slowly nodded his head up and down, his eyes stayed on the floor.

"Wonderful. I'll need to get some paperwork for you to fill out. It's tiresome but we need it filled in. Michele can be your referee. I'll be right back." She dashed out of the room leaving Caroline alone with Paul again.

"How are you getting home?"

"I'm walking."

Paul looked up and out the window to where the sun was setting. "Go straight home tonight. Don't stop or speak to anyone, even if they speak to you first, not even if you think it's someone you know."

Caroline opened her mouth to reply, but the overweight nurse squeaked back into the room. Fiona came running in after her carrying papers.

"Here's the paperwork. Get it all filled out tonight if you can and I will see you tomorrow. Is one pm okay for you? Michele said you have trouble getting out in the mornings."

Caroline winced. "Yes, 1pm is fine."

She glanced back at Paul as she left. She saw the short woman with both arms around him hoisting him into the chair. His eyes stared back at her, seemingly empty.

It was dark by the time she found her way back to the steps leading out of the hospital and pitch black by the time she got back to the hostel.

She sat on the end of the bed with a glass of water in one hand, taking slow sips. She felt exhausted, but too wired to sleep.

She kept seeing Paul's face when she closed her eyes, his seemingly vegetative state masking such awareness and sadness. He could've been lying but what would he gain from lying to her about seeing things? Crazy people often see things. Perhaps she was crazy. '*Don't stop, even if it's for someone you know.*' What could he have meant by that? Perhaps it was just the ramblings of a mentally ill man, but Caroline didn't believe it. He didn't seem to ramble to her; he spoke very well. *I could see he was telling the truth. I could touch him.*

She shuddered at the thought of the random images filling her brain, the feeling of vertigo as she was plunged face first into the void of someone else's mind. No, no she couldn't do that. He said he saw things too, unpleasant things. She had to see him again. Perhaps there were others like her in the world. *Freaks.*

Before going to bed she went into the bathroom, broke open each of the cellophane-enclosed capsules and one by one washed every single pill down the sink.

Lucy had her short hair concealed under a knitted hat before taking a taxi into school. It looked a little uneven when she saw it in the mirror, as if someone had hacked away at it. She put two boxes of hair dye she had stolen from the mall pharmacy into her school satchel. The leather jacket was hanging at the back of the wardrobe awaiting its first outing.

She did not bother to get a late slip from the admin office when she arrived. Attendance was no longer important. She skipped her first period completely and stood outside Maxine's class waiting for the bell to ring, hoping to catch her before she went into second period.

Finally, Maxine came out looking distant and pressed for time. Lucy touched her arm as she was about to fly past her. "Maxine!"

She turned startled. "Oh Lucy, it's you. Why aren't you heading to class?"

"I'm playing hooky today."

Maxine grinned at her. "No way, you can't!" She stopped in the hallway. Groups of girls broke apart like water against rocks to reform ahead, each casting disdainful looks back at them. The outsiders.

"Come with me, Max."

"You're crazy. I'm behind as it is. What's got into you?"

"I need to show you something."

Maxine looked down the long school hall where the thunderous sound of hurried feet were an echo in the distance and back to Lucy's face.

Her eyes had dark circles underneath them showing a lack of sleep.

"What's wrong?"

"Not here. The bathroom." Lucy grabbed her arm and took her off in the opposite direction towards the bathroom.

"What's going on? Urgh. It's awful in here." Maxine wrinkled her nose as they came in.

The walls had once been a cheerful shade of mint green, but years of graffiti and vandalism had transformed the bathroom into a den of dark repute. One girl in Lucy's year was rumoured to have lost her virginity in one of the stalls. Most students gave this bathroom a wide berth unless desperate.

Lucy pushed open each of the cubicle doors to check that they were both alone. "I need you to take me back to your house, today."

"What? Why?"

"Because of this." Lucy whipped off the woollen cap exposing her shorn locks.

Maxine gaped at her. "Oh my God. Did your mum do that to you?"

"I did it." She saw herself in the mirrors and saw how uneven it was. "Look, can you fix it or not? I can't see the back and I don't want to make it worse. I can't have anyone seeing me. I'd never be able to show my face here again."

Maxine reached out and touched the hacked ends of her hair with the tips of her fingers.

"Why did you do this? There was nothing wrong with the way you looked before."

Lucy thought back to the weekend: the shoplifted jacket turning to ash on her back in the light of Maxine's disappointment at being abandoned at the mall; her mother's crazy assumptions that she must have been out doing drugs with Maxine when in fact Max was by herself in a book store; the stench of wine on her mother's breath; the sting of the slap. Anger welled up inside her again. Hot tears came, unwelcome.

"Oh Lucy, don't cry. I didn't meant to- it looks fine really. I'm sure I'll be able to sort it." Maxine brought her arms slowly around her and let her sob quietly into her shoulder.

"Mum accused me of being on drugs."

Maxine pulled away from her. "She did what?"

"When I came home late, she was drunk. She asked me if we'd been out doing drugs, and she slapped me."

Maxine embraced her again, pulling her uniform shirt out from her skirt and dabbed her eyes. "Put that hat back on. We have to be careful how we leave. I could get a sick slip from the nurse. Let's go now and I'll meet you at the bus stop."

"You're a good friend."

"Hell, Lucy, given how your hair looks, you need a good friend."

"You're a such a bitch."

"Better a bitch than a Princess." Maxine smiled.

"Tramp." Lucy elbowed her.

"Bad seed!' Maxine shouted.

"You freak!"

Their voices continued unheard in the corridor of the school and when the bell rang, signalling end of class, they made a run for it and disappeared out through the school gates, and out down the street.

The estate where Maxine lived was comprised of rows and rows of identical grey concrete houses joined together like building blocks. Each house had an identical front door with a number. All the windows were the same. Some she noticed were broken; others had sheets of cardboard in them. Lucy kept her eyes down as they walked, taking care not to meet the gaze of the strangers that stood on the corners. Maxine whispered close to her ear

"Don't worry. The dealers are harmless. Now and then someone will come out of the houses to buy."

"Do they live here on the estate?"

"I don't think so. When I was younger and I saw them outside of our windows, I got scared and asked Mum if they lived around here. She said that they don't shit where they eat." Maxine laughed to herself. Lucy looked at her horrified. "I didn't get it then but I get it now. They live on one of the other estates and come here to sell. With the way the buildings are placed, it's easy to run if the police show up."

Lucy nodded as if she understood everything she was saying. Inside she felt sick. Maxine spoke as if all that was normal, ordinary.

"Ah, here we are. Mum's probably out so don't worry about having to explain why you're here."

"How do you know she's not home?"

"The TV would be on in the living room. Duh."

Lucy looked up at the front door, which was painted a dark green identical to all the others. A bronze number forty-six was fixed to the door. She hurried in after Maxine, eager to be off the street.

The front door opened directly into a living room. Lucy saw a staircase along the far wall and a small kitchenette through an archway in the back. The living room was a mess. An overflowing ashtray was balanced precariously on a crowded coffee table littered with magazines. A small television and a DVD player were positioned opposite the black leather sofas. Another ashtray was on the arm and various crisp packets were littered around on the floor.

"Let's go up to my room."

It was much smaller than Lucy's bedroom. Maxine sat on the bare floor with her legs crossed. Despite the size, Lucy felt comfortable. Charcoal sketches that Maxine had drawn had been fixed on the wall with blue tack and were intermingled with posters of various rock bands. All around the room books were stacked in heaps.

"Take it all in. The dark side of the moon, this place."

"I like it."

Maxine coughed deliberately.

"I do really. It's a little small but-"

"A lot small. A lot..."

"Yes but, you have privacy here. My mum and dad are always flitting in and out of mine like I'm up to something."

Lucy lay out on the bed with her legs in the air. Maxine was rummaging around in her bag. "Yeah, no danger of that here. I don't think Mum could find her way up here with a map. She usually just falls asleep in front of the TV."

"How did she end up living here?"

"I don't know. We've always lived here. I remember my dad vaguely but only bits and pieces. They put her here because she was pregnant with me. I was her housing ticket, I guess."

"Did your grandparents help at all?"

"No, they kicked Mum out when Dad got her pregnant. She doesn't speak to them. I wrote to them a few years ago but never heard back. I guess they didn't want to know me. Their loss. Aha!" Maxine produced a pair of long scissors from her bag. "I knew they were in here somewhere. Right. Let's go into the bathroom. Grab that mirror off the wall. We've only got a small shaving one in the loo."

"I think if I just even it out it, it will look better."

Maxine had balanced the oval mirror from her bedroom on the sink and was walking around Lucy looking thoughtful. She reached out and slowly snipped away. Tiny curls fell around her.

"The good news is I don't think I can make it worse than it is."

Lucy snorted. "Thank you very much for that."

Snk, snk.

"I'm trying not to take any more off. Just evening out what's there. For what it's worth, I think it will look adorable."

Lucy kept her eyes piously shut.

Snk, snk, snk.

"All right... I think that's it. You can open them now." Lucy opened her eyes and stared at her reflection.

"It looks adorable! Quick! Grab my bag and bring it in here."

"Yay!" Maxine clapped her hands together. "Maybe I'll drop out and become a full-time stylist."

Lucy turned her head this way and that, surveying her new appearance. Maxine had evened out the back with the sides and thinned out the ends making it all appear feathered and deliberately messy and rebellious. She had trimmed her fringe, so it cast a cool shadow over her eyes. "It looks really sassy."

"Yeah, well, I think a bit of sass would do you good. The Sunday school look was way over for you anyway."

"I did not look like a Sunday school girl. Hand me my bag."

"What have you got? Don't tell me you've got one of those Goth girl headbands in there with the little black bows on? That'd look too cute."

"Way better, wait."

Her hands closed over the cardboard boxes and she brought out the hair dye she'd stolen from the mall.

Maxine smile vanished. "Oh Lucy, no, no. Do you know how many chemicals there are in that stuff? It kills your hair. You'll get split ends!"

"It won't give me split ends. I want to do this."

"C'mon, Lucy. Call it a day. The school will freak, so will your mum."

Lucy's eyes narrowed at her. "Precisely. Now I've never done this before so I need your help. I don't want to botch it. Please, please."

"Oh, for the love of God. I'll grab some old towels from my room."

"Thank you, Max. I owe you for this."

"You owe me already for the haircut. Just tell no one I helped you."

Lucy unpacked the small kit inside the cardboard box and assembled it in front of her on the sink.

"Says we need to mix these two together and shake it until it turns purple. Then you have to squeeze it into my hair and rub it. Like shampooing I guess except I think the longer you leave it in, the stronger the colour will be."

Lucy turned on the hot tap and filled the sink.

"It'll probably be really uncomfortable but try to shut your eyes. The dye's got bleach in."

Lucy bowed her head down over the sink as Maxine kneaded her head with her hands. The sensation was not a pleasant one. She heard the squirt of the plastic bottle and the faint stinging sensation as the dye was being rubbed into her scalp.

"Nearly done. Stop fidgeting. You're getting dye everywhere!"

Maxine threw a towel over her head. Lucy began rubbing it frantically. She was so excited to see her transformation complete in the mirror.

"I felt like one of those witches from Salem. What is it called again, when they drowned them?"

"Ducking."

"Yeah, ducking."

"Well, you certainly look witchy now."

Lucy took the towel away. The dye had completely smothered her hair turning it from a chestnut brown to an ink black. Her skin seemed milky white and washed out in contrast. She turned her face from side to side, feeling the change move through her. Finally, she'd achieved transformation.

"Do you like it?"

"Your mum will kill us both."

Lucy smiled at the thought. There wasn't much her mother could do about it. She couldn't dye it back to brown now. The black was too strong.

A door slammed beneath their feet making them both jump. Maxine looked out of the bathroom doorway looking panicked

"Mum's home! Quick! Go back to my room. I'll tidy up here."

Maxine began frantically gathering up the dye pots and cardboard and trying to group all of Lucy's cut hair into a pile.

Lucy turned tail and tiptoed across the landing in her bare feet. She could see the top of Maxine's mother's head just below her. She was speaking to someone Lucy couldn't see.

She closed the bedroom door quietly and gathered up her things. The initial rush of skiving from school disappeared at the thought of Max's mother, who she'd never met and was, she saw, quite a large woman, catching them both. She heard running water from the bathroom, Maxine getting rid of the evidence.

Lucy could hear raised voices downstairs, a man shouting at a woman. She could see now how easily this room could become a prison with all that was going on below it. Her body tensed on the bed as she heard a crash.

Finally, Maxine slipped through the doorway, looking grim. "They're at it again, so we can't go downstairs."

"We can't stay locked in here all day."

"Well, duh. You're such an amateur." Maxine strode confidently to the one window on the far side of the room, pushed it up and slid out neat as you please onto the ledge, like a cat. "Well, are you coming?" She stepped off onto thin air, and Lucy gasped as she slid out of view down the slanted roof.

She ran to the window and looked down. Maxine was dusting herself off below. "Well? Look alive, princess."

Lucy did not like heights. She pulled herself up onto the ledge and dragged herself down slowly along the roof. It looked very far to the ground. She threw her leather satchel down first. Maxine caught it.

"Now you."

"I can't."

"It's not as high as you think. Remember, your feet will hit the ground first."

"I said I can't. Maybe I can turn around and grab onto the drainpipe and drop down."

"Oh c'mon. It's not that high. Just stand up and jump!"

Lucy got herself into a crouch. She could hear the argument from below getting louder. Someone slammed a door that seemed to shake the house. She could hear feet coming up the stairs behind her. *Oh no!*

She jumped, screaming aloud as she went through the air. The force of hitting the ground rattled her teeth and she rolled across the ground as her legs gave way.

Maxine was leaning over her with a large grin stretched across her face. "I so didn't think you'd do it."

Lucy slowly got to her feet, grabbing Maxine's hand as she pulled her up.

They walked out of the estate. Lucy turned back towards the house where there was shouting growing louder. Maxine didn't seem to hear it.

"I'm heading out into the city. I'll stay in a cafe and work or read. By the time I come home it'll hopefully be over."

"I don't know how you live with your mum being that way."

"Funny, I was going to say the same thing to you."

Lucy shut the front door quietly as she came in. She intended to creep upstairs, along the landing and into her room without talking to anyone. She would tell her parents she was not feeling well, stomach ache or something. The euphoria of her change had left her on the bus ride home from the council estate. She wondered what her mother would say when she saw her.

She saw from outside that the windows were dark. Perhaps they were out somewhere. She could grab a snack from the kitchen and then-

"Lucy, can you come in here, please?"

She froze. Her bag slipped off her shoulder and hit the floor with a rattle betraying her presence. There was her mother sitting in the kitchen. The glow from the end of a cigarette was the only light in the room

"I'm not feeling well. I need to go to bed."

Silence. Sheila continued to take deep slow drags and blew them out, filling the kitchen with a cloud of nicotine and tar. Finally she spoke: "I had a phone call today from Connie who works in the student support office. She told me you were absent. Where were you all day?"

Shit.

Sheila flipped on the kitchen light. Lucy's eyes widened when she recognised her telephone and stereo laid out on the kitchen counter, the plugs and cords tangled together like the tentacles of a mechanical octopus.

Her mother spoke again keeping her voice level. "I've spoken to your father and he's on his way home now. I thought I would give you the chance of speaking to me before he arrived. I've taken the liberty of removing your phone and stereo. Now come in here and tell me where you were tonight, or by the end of the evening your room's entire contents will be moved to the garage. Don't think I'm joking."

"Fine." Lucy walked into the room and hoisted herself onto a stool. "I was at Maxine's house."

Sheila clapped her hands together. "So! We finally come to it. You were skiving off with that little tramp from the estate. I knew it!" She stubbed out the cigarette into the ashtray with emphasis.

A small tingle came up Lucy's arms. She fought the urge to empty the ashtray over her mother's salon-blonde curls and wipe the smug look off her face.

"Do you think your father works to pay for your education just so you can go gallivanting around with some white trash?"

Lucy kept her face averted from her mother. She would not react. Let her wind herself up all she wants. Her father would be home soon. She would speak to him, not her.

"Lucy, look at me when I speak to you." Sheila reached across to put her hand on her arm and Lucy jumped back.

"Do not hit me again, Mother."

Sheila's face faltered. "I wasn't... I was not going to hit you. I'm trying to get through to you that allowing this girl to fill your head up with nonsense is destroying your education, the education your father works hard to pay for!"

"For your information, Maxine didn't take me out of school. I asked her to skive with me not the other way around, and she's not white trash."

Sheila didn't hear her. She was on her feet now in a rage. "Why on earth did you want her to go with you out of school?"

Lucy stood up too and squared up to her. She found for the first time in her life that she was actually slightly taller than her mother. "None of your damn business!"

Sheila reached up and tore the woollen cap off her head. Her black hair sprang out like a thorn bush and Sheila fell backwards grabbing the kitchen stool for support. "What on earth have you done to yourself?"

Lucy rolled her eyes. "Oh mother, you dye your hair as well. Do get grip of yourself."

Sheila raised her hand to strike her but Lucy moved faster, grabbing her wrists. "I said *don't hit me*!" She pushed her, without thinking.

Sheila hands flew out. Her heels skittered on the tiled kitchen floor and finding no purchase she tottered for a moment before going down in a heap.

Lucy moved around the kitchen, putting the table between herself and her mother who was scrambling to her feet.

"How dare you push your mother! You are grounded!"

"Oh shove it!"

Sheila came around the table with a shout. Lucy ran around to the opposite side. Sheila banged hard on the counter with her fist and ran out of the room. She heard a drawer being wrenched open. She came back into the room. The bulbs of the kitchen light reflected off the blade of the scissors, her voice was cold, betraying no emotion at all. "Come here, girl."

"No!"

Sheila came forward. Lucy backed away. Her mother's shadow reached out along the tiled floor. Sheila took long strides around the table. Lucy saw the blades of the scissors snick together. She fled for the stairs. She heard her mother screech after her.

"You come back here now!"

Some part of her, some childish part of her, actually paused on the bottom step of the stairs when she heard that tone that brooked no refusal. She shook her head against the thought that told her mother knows best, that it hurts mother more than it hurts her. She made for the second step gripping the bannister. She cried out as her mother's hands clapped down her on shoulder pulling her backwards. She landed head first on the carpeted hallway. Sheila reached down to pin her daughter to the floor. Lucy moved her head from side to side as her mother bent down with the scissors snipping.

"Hold still! You cannot go into school with that filth in your hair. I will not have you swanning around looking like a tart!"

"Fuck you!" She brought her knees up and out with a sharp kick that connected with her mother's stomach, knocking the wind from her. The scissors flew out of her hand. Lucy turned over with a sob and pushed herself forward onto the stairs, wiping snot and tears from her face with the back of her hand and ran up onto the landing. She could hear her mother pounding up the stairs behind her.

Where to go?

Her mother shouted from below her. "Stay right there!"

The bathroom.

Sheila made a grab for the space Lucy was occupying just as her body left it and stumbled forward as she overreached.

Lucy got into the bathroom and slammed the door hard just as Sheila slipped her foot into the jamb. "Ouch!"

Lucy slammed it again. Her mother cried out in pain as the wooden door collided with her foot. Sheila reached in to grab her and Lucy slapped her in the face, slamming the door a final time and turning the lock with a click.

At once the handle began to move up and down frantically as Lucy backed away from the door.

"Open this door now!" Her mother began to pound uselessly against the wood. "Open this door!" The handle of the door went up and down, the pounding continued.

She looked around the room for something she could use, something to drive her away. The porcelain tub was empty save for a decorative soap on the corner.

The curtains moved from the breeze that came through the open window.

The pounding on the door ceased. Lucy's ears pricked the same way a fox listens to the silence just before the gun fires. *What is she doing now?* She heard her mother retreat from the door and go back downstairs. *She's gone to get something to open the door.* She heard her come back up the stairs. She didn't shout out to her. Her tread was purposeful. The sound of her coming sent fear through Lucy like a cold wind. *She's got something to open the door.*

Lucy went to the window without thinking. She hated heights and was on the second storey of the house. Below her mother's Mercedes sparkled by the light of the moon. She turned her head towards the sound coming from the door. A nut came loose on the hinges and fell to the floor.

She grabbed the top of the window frame and brought her legs out into the cold air. She turned around to face the bathroom and climbed to her feet, grabbing a hold of the gutter pipe that ran along the top of the attic roof.

The bathroom door flew open with a bang. Sheila charged in like a bull, the scissors held out in front of her like a lance, the screwdriver in her other hand. The room was still, the emptiness mocking her. Her eyes moved to the window and clarity flooded through her. She would not be made a fool of. She would drag her daughter back into the house kicking and screaming if she had to.

She tasted metal as she clenched the blade of the scissors between her teeth like a pirate and grabbed hold of the window ledge, throwing herself face first into the night air, her hands outstretched into claws, her eyes narrowed with purpose.

Lucy's foot crashed into her nose, spraying her face with blood as she kicked out from where she was sitting at the roof's edge. Sheila screamed, her mouth opening wide with anger and pain. The scissors dropped onto the tiled roof. Sheila made to grab them with one hand and Lucy's ankle with another and Lucy kicked her in the face again, forcing her broken face to retreat back behind the flapping white curtains like a broken puppet. The scissors slid down the tiled roof and off, landing point end into the soft top of the Mercedes, plunging into the soft fabric of the convertible roof up to the hilt.

Lucy could hear her mother howling behind her. She looked down and tried to imagine Maxine below her with her arms open, the same smile she'd seen only hours before lighting up her features. *Do it, Lucy. Jump.*

She took a single step forwards onto nothing, letting the night air take her. She dropped and landed seat first onto the Mercedes soft roof and rolled off the car and onto the drive. She picked herself up and took off running in the direction of the bus stop, hugging herself tightly against the cold that blew in from the west.

Dayna was not going to take much more of this. "Miss, miss. Excuse me, miss."

She turned to the man who was aggressively poking her shoulder. "Yes, Sir. What is it now?"

The man in front of her was overweight wearing a blue office shirt. She saw there were sweat stains under his armpits.

"This is not Diet Coke. I ordered a Diet Coke."

Give me strength. She took the glass of Coke off him and threw it, glass and all, into the sink behind the bar, grabbed a pint glass and clicked on the hose. "Here you are, sir. One Diet Coke, as requested."

"I'd like lemon in it."

Dayna resisted the urge to throw the entire glass into his face, turned her back to him, sliced a huge segment of lemon and dropped it in. He took it from her without a thank you.

In front of her was her boss, Janina, a short stocky woman with close-cropped hair and glasses. Her beady eyes were looking up at Dayna with a look of incredulity. "Dayna, you should've gone on your break fifteen minutes ago."

"I'm sorry. I had to serve this man. He ordered a Diet Coke-"

Janina held up a hand for silence. "When I say your break is at 9pm, what do I mean?"

Dayna could see men lining up along the bar with identical expressions of anger on their faces. She could see all of them clenching notes. One man was waving at her. *Idiot.* "I'm sorry. It won't happen again."

"Just make sure you go on time from now on."

Janina turned away from her without another word and Dayna untied her apron and went out the back door into the concrete rubble-filled garden that was behind the pub. A single wobbly table and an old chair were set up for when staff wanted to take a break.

Wanda had filled out the application for her and provided a reference. She had come to the interview feeling like a tramp in her own clothes. It had been one week since the incident when she'd borrowed Wanda's clothes and she hadn't seen her since then.

Her hours were 5pm till 2am when the pub closed. She hated it. The patrons often spoke to her chest when ordering and, the first night on the job, a punter had slapped her on the behind as she was collecting glasses. She stood ramrod straight when it had happened. Janina was eyeing her behind the bar otherwise she would've turned round and bottled him.

Dayna had trouble memorising table numbers and frequently took things to the wrong place. She didn't like the way people would shout their orders at her from over the bar, or the way everything seemed to smell of yeast. After closing she would stack the chairs over the tables and bleach the floors. Janina watched her work while cashing up the till.

Looking up at the bright full moon Dayna closed her eyes and tried to see into the future. Days filled with monotonous work on minimum wage, never earning enough to get together a deposit for her own place. She imagined Wanda getting sick of her, throwing her out. Forever skimping and scraping to survive, never living, never feeling alive, and then getting older, losing what looks she had to age and despair.

She had had her twenty minutes. Break time was over. She had one foot behind the bar when a man leaned over and touched her shoulder. "Excuse me."

She turned her head slowly towards him.

"I've been trying to get served for ages. I just want a small glass of Merlot."

Dayna cast a wary eye down the long line of punters queued up, all foaming at the mouth, like savage dogs, barking at her. Janina was nowhere in sight. She took a deep breath and put on a fake smile. "Coming right up, sir." She grabbed a wine glass from under the bar and took out a bottle of wine.

"Dayna!" She nearly dropped the bottle with a jump as Janina's voice cut across the din of the room. "How many times have I told you! Don't grab the glass by the head, grab it by the stem. It leaves fingerprints on the glass."

"Yes, Janina."

Janina turned to the man who was holding out a twenty-pound note into the empty air in front of him.

"I'm very sorry, sir. She's new." The man laughed at Dayna and gave her a lecherous wink. Janina plucked the twenty from his hand.

"And a packet of pork scratchings while you're down there, love."

She banged the wine down on the bar and walked over to where they kept the crisps and nuts. She grabbed two bags of pork scratchings and threw them at the man.

"Busy tonight?" he asked.

She nodded and made to turn away.

"What time do you finish?"

"Late." She moved along the bar to the very beginning of the angry caterpillar made up of men in striped and plaid shirts that were shouting incoherently at her. Money was being waved in front of her face everywhere she looked.

"What will it be, sir?"

"Pint of Guinness, sweetheart."

"Right away." She went to the till. Janina followed, standing too close to her.

"There's far too much head on that pint. You will have to refill it. I'm sorry, sir, we will only be a moment."

Dayna could see a man in front of her banging his hand on the bar, demanding service. Something inside her snapped in two. "Nuts to this." She barged past Janina, her fingers pulling frantically at the knots in her apron.

Janina scurried after her, poking her shoulder. "Where are you going?"

Dayna dumped her apron on the bar and closed her fist over Janina's bony finger.

"Do not poke me, woman." She barged past her, ignoring the shouts from various men behind her which filled her ears.

"What about my order?"

"She's given me the wrong change!"

Fuck all of them. She got to the door, threw it open and walked out, barging through a group of lads who whistled and catcalled as she went by.

She knew she couldn't go home. It was only ten o'clock. She usually didn't come home till around three o'clock. Wanda would probably still be awake and she'd know from the moment she came in that she had walked off the job. *Well, fuck her.*

Dayna let her hair out of the bun she'd put it up in for work and let her auburn locks uncoil like a snake. She could see herself clearly in the reflection of a car window.

Rummaging in her purse, she saw she didn't have much: tips from the last two shifts at work. There was enough there for a drink, or two. She promised Wanda she wouldn't. *Promises were made to be broken.* She undid the top button of her blouse and set off in the direction of the Bad Penny.

She saw a few men turn and stare as she passed through the doors, one nudging his friend to look at her as she came in. The music was too loud tonight. She felt exposed and ugly in her polyester uniform. She plonked herself in the middle of the bar and waited patiently for the bartender to notice her. Eventually he came over, drying a glass in his hands with a rag. "What will you have?"

"Vodka tonic with ice, please."

Her brief time spent on the other side of the bar had brought her insight into why bartenders were in such bad humour. Serving drunken idiots certainly did not leave her feeling like a ball of sunshine after each shift ended.

He nodded to her. She put a note on the table and he took it and replaced it with a glass of clear liquid. *Bottoms up.* She downed the entire thing in a single gulp, relishing the way her mind began to loosen. The stress of the night was beginning to fade, but she still saw them: the faces of the men lining the bar, snarling like wolves.

"Another, please." Another drink. This time she took her time drinking it down. A man in a suit sat on the stool next to her. She kept her face turned away. He tapped her on the shoulder.

"Rough night, sweetheart? Want to talk about it?"

She slid off the stool and moved over to the one she'd occupied only a week before in the far corner of the bar. She did not scan the club for men tonight. Robbed of Wanda's pretty trinkets and queenly raiment she felt plain and alone.

Caroline turned over in the bed, moaning in the throes of a nightmare. She was wandering alone in the empty bar feeling lost. The floor was covered with filth and old sawdust. She wrinkled her nose against the stench of animal dung and wet fur hung in the air. There was movement around her in the dark. Caroline saw many eyes observing her from the recesses of the shadows.

She slowly moved through the bar stepping over snakes that were coiled up on themselves upon the floor. They bared their jaws at her as she came past making her flinch back in fright. A jackal snarled at her from where it paced back and forth along the bar, weaving in and out of the glass bottles lined along its surface glittering dully in the gloom of the room. The animal's eyes were yellow and cruel. Beneath her feet mice scurried away from her as she took steps towards the stage knowing in the way of dreams that there was where she needed to go, the only place above the stink and the predators. Something moved in the rafters above her. Feathers floated down, a sign of a struggle somewhere. *Something's up there.*

A jackal cackled maniacally somewhere in the dark. Two wolves fought over a rotting carcass, tugging at each end, sending feathers flying up into the air. Their bodies turned about on the glass table, snapping at each other's fur, tearing the feathered meat to shreds. *Please, don't let them see me.*

She hoisted herself up onto the stage and moved into the centre. The smell was appalling. All across the room crows tottered along the edges of the tables, their eyes fixed on the rodents that ran below. Caroline thought at any moment they would all swoop as one, their savagery taking over, the room coming alive in a shower of fur, blood, and feathers.

She heard the sound above her again, some doom hanging out of sight. The sound seemed to draw the eye of everything in the room. The hyena paused its pacing to gaze up; wolves ceased their squabbling, their noses pointing to the ceiling as if about to howl; the snake reared its head up and opened its jaws in desperate supplication.

Caroline gazed at each of them in turn and, unable to resist, craned her neck up to look. Dangling above the centre of the stage, bulbous and enormous, was a great dark orb suspended high by some malignant necromancy. Above all the ruined predators whose viciousness and savagery was made cowardly by its presence, the thing seemed to look upon each of them until its gaze came to Caroline.

It's found me.

She looked into the many-faceted eyes of that great spider that held court above them like a ruined king and knew that it had been searching for her, perhaps for years, and finally it had found her. Her breath stopped as she watched its eight legs spread out across the air like a hand. Caroline opened her mouth to scream.

It dropped suddenly. She fell backward with her arms up in a warding gesture. As its great body came down, she shrieked the primal sound of a cornered animal, making the wolves howl and the jackals scream.

She screamed herself awake. Sitting bolt upright in bed, she struggled against the sheets kicking frantically until she rolled out of bed and hit the ground hard.

Dayna made her way into the centre of the bar as the alcohol worked through her. She felt confident and dizzy. A group of men nodded at her with smirks on their faces as she bumped into one of them.

"You alright there, love"

She ignored them. The music was too loud. Swaying about on her feet she saw groups everywhere of suits and tarty dresses, forming a solid wall penning her in. A woman in a silvery dress pushed into her as she and her boyfriend danced out of time with the heavy beat of the bass. How anyone could dance to the racket coming out of the speakers, she didn't know.

She tried to push through the crowd to the front door but found herself in a narrow hallway that looked all too familiar to the week before where she had been molested in the toilet cubicle. *Don't go that way.*

She wanted to go home, tell Wanda what happened, tell her she would try again, a different job, maybe something in retail. Perhaps she would not blame her for walking out and let her stay with her a bit longer. She moved down the hallway to the door at the far end where she could see a sign glowing green against the dark peeling plaster of the wall up ahead. EXIT. She pushed down on the metal bar and felt the cold night air hit her face bringing the world back into focus. The air was cold and sweet. She closed the fire door against the drum and bass that leaked out dimly under the door.

Lucy's legs ached as she made her way across the flat road that led from the village cul de sac where her parents lived to the nearest town where the bus would take her out to the city, and to Maxine.

She had no way of phoning her to warn her that she was coming. She thought first of checking her usual haunts: the mall bookstore or the library and, if that failed, she would walk in the dark to the estate. She kept to the side of the road on the elevated grass knolls along the meadows that stretched out trying to think. Tonight she had hit her mother. *Good!*

But it wasn't good, not really, she knew that. She felt wicked, perhaps she was, perhaps even now her mother was at home poisoning her father against her, already packing her a suitcase, putting a call in to social services saying their daughter was out of control. *Take her away. Put her in a hostel.* Maybe she would be housed on a council estate like Maxine after a few years on a waiting list. Her stomach tightened at the thought of living in a small cramped bungalow where people go back and forth all day in front of the windows, standing on corners of the estate to deal drugs and solicit themselves. Perhaps she would be burgled. She sobbed as her imagination conjured up pictures of what her future held for her: disowned, destitute, unwanted.

She wondered what would happen to school if she were thrown out. Would she have to find a job to pay for her education? Work part time? Study part time, taking forever to complete the final year? Each thought brought fresh tears down her face. *It's all mum's fault, all because I have a friend of my own.*

Cars flitted past her, their headlights hitting her back, making her feel panicked for a moment – *Police! They've found me!* - before passing on. She could see streetlights up ahead about half a mile away. Soon she would reach the village and then on to the bus stop and out up to the city.

Headlights flashed at her back again, another car. *It's slowing down.* She felt her stomach tighten. Perhaps it was the police, or her mother.

"Excuse me, are you all right?" The car had pulled over, the engine idling. The driver's side window was down.

Lucy kept her face turned away. *Don't speak to strangers.* "I'm fine. I'm just on my way home." She walked on faster but the driver kept level with her, the car creeping along.

"Where about are you going to?"

"The village."

"Do you want me to give you a lift? It's a bit late to be walking all that way."

I could get there faster. "No, I'm fine, thank you."

"Are you sure? You're not lost?" He opened the passenger door lighting up the leather interior, so like her mother's Mercedes.

"No, I live on the edge of town, just down there."

"It's a bit cold to be walking by yourself."

Lucy stopped to look at the driver. He was good looking, probably the same age as her Dad, his face frowned at her as she peered in looking concerned.

"No, sorry."

"All right, suit yourself." He reached over and slammed the passenger door engulfing the interior in darkness. The car's engine revved up and sped off past her. She watched it go, the car headlights getting smaller in the distance.

A cold wind blew through the night making her rub her arms as she carried on wandering along the road alone.

Dayna stood in the small courtyard on the edge of the woods. Odd broken chairs and old bar stools were littered about with a few beer barrels positioned to act as tables. She noticed cigarette butts strewn about on the floor and guessed it was the place where staff took their cigarette breaks. An iron railing encircled the place. She saw a man standing at the far end with his back to her. He looked like he had come out for some fresh air. His head was tilted up to the sky and he was taking long deep breaths. *Maybe he's high. Maybe he has pills. He can give me pills, take my mind off this crap life.*

She walked to the far end and put her hands around the iron spikes. She could only see the back of his head. His attention was fixed on the sky looking up at the full moon smothered by a dark patch of cloud. He had thick dirty blonde hair in an unflattering bowl cut and denim jeans. His shoes were a distressed brown leather with spurs on. He took out a cigarette and lit it, puffing circles of smoke up into the air.

Why not go home tomorrow morning instead?

He turned around slowly and nodded to her. "Well, hello there." He tipped his cigarette to her, in a gentlemanly way.

"You wouldn't have a cigarette, would you?"

He stuck his hand in the back of his jeans and pulled one out, holding it out to her.

"Thanks."

He wore only a casual blue plaid shirt, unbuttoned at the top despite the cold, quite unlike the formal work attire that was common at the bar. He looked more like a bricklayer than an office worker.

"Wait."

She stared, her eyebrows raised.

He winked at her, stuck his cigarette in the side of his grin like a toothpick and rolled his sleeves up theatrically, exposing what Dayna thought were quite hairy arms. Strange oriental dragons snaked their way up from his wrists like vines. He moved his hands in front of her face like a magician, overlapped them in the air once and, on the second time, a thin metal lighter sprouted up in his fist from thin air.

She laughed aloud as the flame flicked out. She inhaled deeply and blew a billow of smoke through one of his rings.

"Party get too much for you, darlin?"

She felt a slight shiver of excitement move up her spine as he spoke. The Cajun accent was promising.

"Something like that. I'm not much for crowds after the day I've had."

"I understand. Don't know what in hell you call that stuff in there. It isn't music, just a load of noise."

"It's been this way since the club changed owners a few months back."

"You don't say?"

"It was different before. They had different themed nights. It was excellent. This your first time here?"

"I just moved to the area. Bought a place on the other side of the wood there. A cosy little place. Thought I'd paint the town red. You?"

She took another drag, enjoying the easy conversation.

"I just finished work and didn't want to go home."

"You're not tired after work?"

"Well, let's just say there isn't someone at home waiting for me." She dropped him a sly wink.

A large grin spread out across his face showing a few crooked yellow teeth. Dayna thought he was probably in his fifties. Still, an older man for the night could be nice. They usually had their own house, perhaps he had cash.

"I hear you. I could take you back inside and order you a drink?"

She flicked the fag end away. Already she could feel the pain of the job loss fading as the thrill of being desired filled her up.

"Lead the way!"

He opened the fire door with one arm and put his other around her as she went past him back into the bowels of the Bad Penny. He lent in as she passed and took a deep sniff of her auburn hair, whistling to himself before following her inside.

Paul had his hands locked around Shelley's wrists as she tried to force him back down to the bed. He was kicking out with his feet and shouting incoherently.

Fiona was standing in the doorway with her hands over her mouth watching the scene play out before her, feeling frozen, not knowing what to do. Shelley's voice startled her out of her paralysis. "Fiona run and get Eve now!"

The young nurse ran through the ward and fumbled her card through the reader, opening the door and running down the hall. Eve was seated serenely in the office looking at the computer.

"Shelley needs you on ward! Emergency!"

Eve swivelled her head slightly, looking the young girl up and down.

"What is it now?"

"It's Mr Graves. I think he's having a psychotic episode! He tried to climb out of the window!"

Eve's eyes widened. Her face took a focused look similar to that of a bloodhound that has just caught the scent of a wounded fox on the wind. She stood up, knocking her chair over. "You stay here". She ran across to a cabinet on the wall and took out her nurse's lanyard that was looped onto a key ring and clicked a small key into the door.

"What are you doing?" Fiona tried to peer around her wide frame to see.

Eve ignored her, taking out a small bottle and a black case that reminded Fiona of a case people kept their glasses in. She held a glass syringe up to the light.

Fiona saw it was filled with dark fluid. She flicked it with her nail.

"What's that for? Shelley said to-"

"Out of my way, you silly girl!"

Eve strode towards her, needle out. She had to jump back against the wall to avoid her as her corpulent frame passed by.

Paul was thrashing violently on the bed. "Let me go, let me go! I have to go!"

"Stop it, Mr Graves. Stop it! It's all right!"

Paul managed to pull one hand free and catch Shelley across the face sending her off balance. He made a leap from the bed to the window ledge trying to shuffle out using his elbows. He felt Shelley grab his ankle and try to pull him back in. He kicked out like a donkey, sending her flying backwards, crashing into the bed frame.

He could smell the free air; he could see the flowerbeds that bordered the ward. He was out up to the waist, then the hips. He could see the full moon above. There was still time. Someone grabbed his knees and pulled him back. He hit his chin on the ledge making his teeth rattle.

"Oh no, you don't!"

Someone strong had him. He cried out struggling to free himself but whoever it was had a grip like iron. He heard two voices arguing behind him.

"Eve, it's all right, we don't need that. He's just had a nightmare. We need to get him back in bed!"

He felt a pair of strong arms come around his waist, prising him off the ledge. Shelley slammed the window with a crash.

"They're at it again. I have to stop them!" He managed to wrench himself out of Eve's flabby arms and push her away.

Shelley came towards him with her hands out. "Mr Graves, please calm down."

Paul's eyes darted around in panic: *the double doors perhaps. No, no key. They have the key. The windows.*

Eve was getting to her feet. He had to watch her. She was dangerous like a scorpion. He wheeled around the ward, trying to keep them away. He had to keep both of them in sight. *Have to go, have to go. Not too late. Have to go.* "I have to go! I have to stop them!"

Eve waded in, the needle flashed in her hand.

Shelley cried out to her. "Eve, no!"

He felt her grab his wrist and pull him forward. He tried to pull away. Too late. He felt the scorpion sting in the side of his neck and the poison ran through him like a forest fire. As he closed his eyes to the world he saw a pale girl with auburn hair being lifted into the boot of a blue car, the pale moonlight lighting her up for just a moment before the lid came down sealing her away into darkness.

Shelley confronted Eve the moment they were back in the nurse's office.

"What was that you gave him?"

Eve busied herself by packing away the kit she'd used to drug Paul. "Just something to help him sleep. You were the one who reduced his medication. If you remember I was firmly against it." She plonked herself back down in her seat behind the computer and began typing. "And I will be writing a report of tonight's incident, noting that it took two senior nurses to prevent his escape. I'll be making strong recommendations that his normal dosage be resumed."

Shelley scowled, but saw no way around it. The report had to be made. She turned back into the hall where Fiona was standing looking lost. "Are you all right, Fi? I'm so sorry you had to be here for that. You can go home early if you like. There's two of us here."

"Why do you think he flipped out like that?"

"I've no idea. I've never seen him like that."

Fiona looked out of the window onto the corridor. "Maybe it was the moon. My nan always said when it's lit up all full and yellow like that it's a bad moon rising."

Shelley squeezed her arm before going back onto the ward to check that all the patients were sound asleep.

The blue convertible flew through the iron gates and up the hedged lane to where the house loomed up in front of him. He got out of the car slowly and limped around to the boot, letting his hands play across the lid before popping it open.

Dayna stared up at him. Her green eyes were red and puffy, streaked with tears. Her hands and ankles were bound with black tape. He leaned into the boot and ran his nose along her arms and down her torso, taking long sniffs of her auburn locks. She rocked from side to side whimpering weakly.

Charlie ran his hands up his own wrinkled face, feeling the hateful lines around his eyes and mouth. Dayna's eyes widened in fright as he peeled the blonde toupee off exposing a bald head with tufts of grey hair protruding from random places. He took out a rag from the boot and wiped his face with it, removing the makeup he'd worn to the club to conceal the worst of the liver spots and crow's feet.

He didn't have the strength to carry her up to the house. He would have to fetch the wheelchair and bring her in through the cellar. There was no chance of carrying her up the steep stairs to the front door.

He leered down at Dayna's trussed up form. "Don't you be thinking of trying to go anywhere girly girl, as ol' Charlie's been good to you so far, but you start misbehavin' and I'll have to take you up. Understand?" Dayna blinked her eyes. He reached down and ran his wrinkled hands over her face. "So sweet and sad. You will go down so nice."

She tried to twist away from his yellow fingers but the boot was too small.

"You promise not to try and run, and I'll leave the lid up so you can see the stars one more time. You misbehave and I come back and find you trying to wiggle away, I'll slam this boot and you can spend the night screaming in the dark. You hear me?"

The moon moved behind the clouds as he spoke, casting shadows across his cruel face. There was no pity in his eyes at all, only hunger.

"Blink your eyes twice if you understand me." Dayna blinked her eyes. Fresh tears broke out, running down her cheeks. He grinned and bent down, his long tongue lapped out like a wolf as he ran it down her wet cheeks. Dayna cried out through the gag trying to turn her face away.

He crooned down at her. "You be good now." He turned around and began limping around the car in the direction of the cellar.

Dayna couldn't see clearly as she came through the house. He had drugged her with something, making her dizzy and clouded. She couldn't move her arms or legs at all and she had to fight the panic that was threatening to overwhelm her. Through the fog of chloroform she could make out the dirty oven and filthy countertops of a disused kitchen

He was gone. G*ot to move. Got to get out.* Dayna had to throw her head from side to side to stay awake, to stay alive. Her hands were taped together. She could sense some feeling there and tried to rotate her hands to loosen the bonds. Her eyes darted about trying to find something she could use to free herself, a tool, or a weapon to stab him with. *He's not a him, he's an it. A horrid thing, but not a man.*

Dust came down from the ceiling as footsteps walked over where she was seated. Far above she heard doors opening and closing. She tried to turn her feet and wriggle out but the wheelchair wobbled precariously and she ceased struggling, afraid it would tip over and spill her helpless body onto the dirty floor. Dayna's eyes widened as she heard him singing as he came down the stairs, his tread heavy and deliberate.

"You were always on my mind!" *Thud. Thud.* "You were always on my-y-y mi-i-ind!" *Thud. Thud.*

Thud. He kicked the door open making Dayna shriek through her gag. She tried to move as he came but the chair only rocked her as she struggled.

He laughed at her. "I'm so sorry, I was blind." He came behind the chair and began pushing her along, the wheels leaving tracks in the dust of the kitchen floor. He bent down and sang in her ear: "I'm so sorry, I was blind. I just never found the time. You were always on my mind."

He pushed the chair into a foyer where a cobwebbed chandelier swayed precariously from side to side. Portraits hung crookedly on the walls and tables of dead flowers lined the walls. The portraits leered at her as he wheeled her by. An old grandfather clock ticked in the corner. The hands told her it was eleven thirty. *No one even knows I'm here. Wanda thinks I'm at work.* She was alone, alone at the end, in a strange house with a thing that wasn't a man. *How did I get here?*

He wheeled her across the foyer past the stairs. *Another door here, perhaps a broom cupboard.* He pushed the door inward showing what looked like a storage room. "In we go, darlin.'"

She gave a muffled scream as he gave the chair a hard push sending her into the space hitting the wall with a crash. The door slammed behind her.

Dayna screamed and lurched from side to side in the narrow room until at last the wheelchair over balanced and she was spilled onto the floor like a rag doll.

Usually he liked to draw it out. Better to leave the lambs shut in somewhere so the terror could give way to misery and increase in potency. Sometimes he would leave them in the car for hours so they wasted the brunt of their energy on pointless struggling and, when the time came to bring them in, most of their fight had been lost to despair and fatigue.

The girls rarely gave him trouble but tonight he had to hurry. It had been too long since the last one and she hadn't lasted as long as the others, not nearly as long. How quickly the signs of age had begun to show after so little time...too little! He hoped this one would be different and longed to find out.

He looked at the clock face: 11:30. *Not much time.* He came across the landing and took hold of a wheel that he had salvaged from a scrap heap years before, a remnant taken from a ship that had gone down in a storm. Putting his hands against the coarse wood he could hear the physic echo of the desperate cries of the poor souls that had gone down into the water. He loved old things. He gripped the wheel and began to turn. Before long beads of sweat began to appear on his forehead but he didn't falter. His feet dug into the floorboards as he brought her up.

He had built the elevator himself a few years before. He didn't like dragging them up the stairs. He found this panicked them and bruised them needlessly. Once a girl had struggled so much she tore away from him on the top step and, unable to move her feet because of the tape that bound her, she had overbalanced and fallen, landing head first on the staircase breaking her neck. He had had to wait an entire month for the next full moon, a total waste of life. Rose had not been pleased.

The elevator was a primitive design, a moving box through a hollowed out staircase but it did allow for a clean passage up the second floor. Beads of sweat formed on his forehead as he turned the wheel. One slip of his hands and he'd send her crashing down to the cellar, another waste. The veins in his arms stood out with the effort, but his heart lifted as he saw the top of her auburn hair come into view. She was thrashing from side to side on the floor like an injured bird, pretty as a picture, helpless as can be. He knotted the rope tight around the wheel and whistled as he strode into the lift to fetch her.

The wheels of the chair squeaked beneath her as she moved down the hallway. There were candles on the floor casting eerie shadows along the wall. A door was open at the end of the corridor, a solid wall of darkness awaited her in the open doorway, waiting to devour her.

"Here we are Rosy. Didn't I tell you she was a pretty one?"

Dayna looked about to see who he was speaking to. It seemed to be a spare room of some kind. Lit candles were on the table, the floor, all around. The heat made her feel sick. She felt like she might pass out again. Downstairs she heard the clock chime out. *Midnight.*

He lurched to the end of the room and pulled apart the drapes, letting the light from the full moon flood in, lighting up a small figure in a chair. Dayna jumped when she saw it making the wheelchair rock. She had mistaken the figure for just another piece of discarded furniture. It was a shrunken shrivelled thing reclining in an old rocking chair. The lights of the candles caught the sequinned dress that hung off its skeletal form making Dayna squint her eyes shut against the flickering light. She didn't think anything that old could be alive. The dark liver-spotted skin was pulled tight over the things bones. The eyes were sunk back into the sockets. She saw the old thing's feet wore pink fluffy slippers at odds with the dress that hung off the emaciated form.

Dayna tried to scream again as the thing lazily blinked its eyes open and became aware of Dayna for the first time, seeming to come alive before her eyes.

He began wheeling her forward. She tried to pull away and thrash as the horrid old thing grinned wide as she approached, its purple lips pulling back, exposing blackened gums in a crone's leer. It began to fetch and moan feebly in the chair, its decrepit hands opening and closing frantically and it spoke with a raspy voice in desperation. "Do it Charlie! Now!"

The clock chimed below them, counting to twelve.

Dayna screamed aloud as she saw a small blade flick out from his hand as the lighter had done only hours before. A moment of pain brought the room into clear focus before her eyes: the candles surrounding them, the old woman in the rocking chair reaching out hungrily towards her. She felt something warm trickle down her neck. The crone reached forward eagerly. He was kneeling before it in supplication, his bloody fingers anointing first its forehead then cheeks with Dayna's blood.

The clock struck eleven, twelve, thirteen chimes. *Thirteen?*

He flicked a switch on a vinyl and Carly Simon's voice filled the room like a Sabbath chant.

You walked in to the paaarty like you were walking onto her yacht.

The old crone's face filled Dayna's vision as she reached to her with her ugly hands, her fingers long like a concert pianist's fixing around Dayna's face.

Your hat strategically dipped below one eye, your scarf it was apricot.

The old woman whispered to Dayna as she struggled in the chair, screaming into her gag. "Give us a kiss, dearie."

Dayna yelped as the man tore the gag from her mouth. She opened her mouth to scream, but the sight before her caused the sound to die in her chest. Her scream never left her as she watched, in horror, the crone's jaws yawning open, her jaw unhinging as her chin dropped lower revealing a gaping hole of blackness where the mouth should have been. Her face was like a furnace door opening to the deepest circle of hell.

She tried to pull away but a hand pressed her from behind, pushing her face forward. She felt the woman's jaws clamp onto her mouth, breathing foul air down her throat from the dark caverns inside her, not hot but cold, as cold as the earth.

Dayna tried to scream as the cold wind froze the ice in her veins. Every hair on her body stood on end as her skin erupted in goose bumps. It felt as if the cold would turn her heart to glass. She had no breath to scream out as what was happening dawned on her. She saw the lines around the old woman's face tighten and disappear. The skin of the vulture talon that gripped her chin filled out into a pale feminine hand. The yellow nails receded back into the fingers and took on a manicured sheen. Blonde curls erupted from the woman's skull in a shower of gold while Dayna's own hair turned first grey then white as it broke away from the scalp, falling around the chair in clumps. The skin around her face grew loose and flabby as the vitality was drained out of her. The beating of her heart slowed as it shrivelled like a fruit withering on the vine as Rose's breasts swelled, filling out the sequinned dress she wore. Her legs were growing longer as she stepped off the chair in triumph lifting Dayna's ruined dead form up from the wheelchair as she gulped her life down greedily, finally casting the mummified remains aside like a child casting away a broken toy. The skeleton in the polyester uniform hit the floor where it shattered like old china.

Charlie was grinning as he watched Rose's transformation from the shadows of the room, her resplendent hair curling down to her waist as the stolen youth moved through her, renewing her before his eyes. She kicked the remains of Dayna cruelly aside as she moved to the covered furniture, tearing away one of the sheets revealing a tall ornate mirror propped against the wall.

He watched as she turned around and around, her head swivelling to see the fruits of her transformation.

"Rose?"

She looked away from herself, the faintest annoyance passing across her face. She had forgotten he was there.

"Rose, you promised. Please, Rosy." He fell to his knees kissing her feet, grovelling before her like a mongrel dog.

Slowly she came down to him, her crimson smile spreading as her lips met his. His mouth opened to receive the gift that only she could give. Tears of gratitude rolled down his cheeks as he inhaled the stolen youth that she blew down his throat.

Lucy was shivering in the bus shelter. She didn't know what time it was and even if the bus would come. She had visions of herself curling up on the kerb for the night and sleeping like a tramp.

The tears came again as she thought about going home and she looked wistfully back towards the way she'd come. Blackness yawned out ahead where the street lamps vanished as the farmers' fields began. She could see small lights moving in the distance, working people on their way home to their own houses. Safe houses. A line had been crossed tonight: to go back would be to give in. She would not give in; she would not surrender.

She squinted against the headlights of a car coming towards her in the dark. She turned her face away as it approached, not wanting to be seen.

"Lucy?"

Her head whipped around as she heard the familiar voice.

"Lucy, is that you?"

The car door opened lighting up the interior showing the face of her father, a picture of anger and concern. She thought of running, taking off in the opposite direction, escaping whatever punishment lay in wait for her at home. He was on her in a moment, pulling her to him.

"Where have you been? I've been driving around for hours looking or you. I am so angry with you, young lady. Do you know how worried we all are about you?"

"Dad, I didn't mean-"

"Get in the car now. I'm taking you home."

He pulled open the driver's side door and got in with a slam.

With her head bowed, Lucy opened the passenger door behind his and slid into the back seat. The car accelerated off the kerb before she even had time to close the door.

Charlie watched her from the recesses of the bed with his arms behind his head. She had dressed again after making love to him, first on the floor and then on the bed. He was hoping to have tired her out but after lying together in the darkness she had switched on the lamp and got up to play dress-up in the closet. He didn't mind; he liked watching her move and enjoy herself after taking a life.

"Charlie, this one is gorgeous!" She emerged naked holding one of the glittery dresses he'd bought at the mall. "Where on earth did you find these?"

"I bought them from a quaint little shop girl."

She plonked down in front of an old dressing table, switching on the many light bulbs that ran around the frame of the mirror and began working a comb up through her golden hair, a can of hairspray in one hand. He wrinkled his nose as the smell of the aerosol began to fill the room as she sculpted it slowly into a beehive. Her eyes were narrowed in concentration as she moved the comb through her blonde curls.

"I want to go out."

"It's three o'clock in the morning, Rosy. Everywhere will be closed now."

"Take me out for a drive. We can put the radio on and drive around."

He exhaled feigning annoyance. It was only natural. She'd been cooped indoors for weeks and wanted the fresh air. He pulled on his jeans and buttoned them. "Rose?"

"Hmm?" She was busy brushing makeup onto her cheeks, a girlish shade of bubble-gum pink.

"How long do you think this one will last?"

She stopped and looked at herself in the mirror, a figure of beauty shining like a star against the dust and disuse of the cluttered bedroom. She thought for a moment and said, "A few weeks, a month if we're lucky." She cocked her head to one side, appraising her reflection in the mirror. "She had a lot of life to live. You chose well."

He came close and kissed down her neck. "Don't I always bring the best for my girl?"

Caroline hadn't slept following the nightmare and had sat on the sofa most of the night until she felt the sunlight coming through the single window of the room, signalling her to dress and leave to go to the hospital.

Fiona looked as if she had not slept well either as they made their way together down the wide hall towards the ward entrance.

"We had an incident last night with Mr Graves."

"Paul? Is he all right?"

"We're not sure. He had what I would term a maniac episode… He attempted to climb out of a hospital window."

"Oh my goodness! Why?"

"Nurse Spencer seems to think it was a lack of medication, but I think it was due to a nightmare he had."

Caroline tried to keep her face neutral. "A nightmare?"

Fiona looked left and right making sure they were alone in the hall. "He woke up very upset. Did he mention anything that was troubling him to you when you saw him, anything at all?"

Caroline tried to picture him in their previous conversation. *"Don't stop for anyone tonight even if it's someone you think you know."*

"No, he didn't say much, just his name and I told him who I was. He was quite sleepy most of my time with him."

"He has slept most of the morning due to the sedative we gave him. We've upped the dosage on his medication so he may not be speaking much today but I think having the company will do him some good. No one ever comes to visit him." She sighed and opened the door to the visitors' room and Caroline stepped in.

Paul was sitting in the chair, facing the small window that looked out onto the lawn of the hospital. Caroline took a seat in the visitors' chair again. "Hi Paul. I've come back to see you."

Paul came to slowly as if he'd been startled awake from a nap. His fingers twitched, his eyes remained closed as he spoke.

"Are you alone?"

"Yes, no one else here."

He looked much worse than when she last saw him. His eyes looked tired and glassy and she saw large shadows under his eyes, a sign of a troubled night.

"The nurse told me you had a bad dream last night."

His glassy eyes focused on her, making Caroline feel slightly uneasy. "Do you ever have bad dreams?"

"Sometimes. Do you want to tell me what you dreamed last night?"

Paul reached a hand out to her. "I can show you."

"What do you mean?"

"You said you see things. I see things too."

She cast one eye to the door to make sure no one was standing outside listening in.

"What did you dream about last night, Caroline? Did you see *them*?"

"Who are 'they'?"

He closed his eyes, his brows furrowed together. "I don't really know. I can never see their faces. It's always too dark, but they're bad news, both of them."

"Is this what you dreamt last night?"

"It was happening out there. They took her and no one noticed."

"Took who?"

"I don't know her name. But it's always the same kind of girl. They always have a cloud of sadness coiled around them. Snoops told me about them."

"The cat?"

"He hates things like them. They dress like people, but only to hide that they're not."

The door banged open and Caroline jumped. The stocky nurse came in carrying a glass filled with a cloudy substance.

"I've come to give him his medication."

Caroline stood up and reached for the glass. "I'll give it to him. He's not really lucid at the moment, Miss-?"

"Spencer."

"Miss Spencer."

Caroline took the glass and set it down on the table. The big nurse's eyes moved from Paul in the chair to Caroline. "Make sure he takes it."

Caroline nodded and watched Eve squeak out of the room.

Paul spoke from the chair. "That one's Atropos. She's the one with the needles."

"They told me you tried to go out of a window last night. Is that true?"

"I had to try and stop them."

"Who's 'them'? The nurses?"

"They were killing the red haired girl. Her eyes sparkled in the moonlight."

"You keep saying 'they'. I don't know who 'they' are."

"They come every full moon. I've dreamed about them before, but never like last night. They felt much closer than ever before. They only take who won't be missed. People like me, although I doubt I'd be much good to them. I'm too old. They use them up until there's nothing left. They eat them alive."

"These people who won't be missed. Who are they?"

"Girls like her; girls like you."

"Girls like me?"

"You're depressed, alone, desperate. It's written all over you. No family, no one missing you. Despair's wound tight around you, and they can smell that. You may feel invisible at times but you would light up and shine like a star to these two."

Caroline felt a chill in the room. He was scaring her now. "I don't understand. Are you saying someone's been murdered? Do you want me to speak to the police?"

"Police can't help."

"Why not?"

"They only get involved if someone's reported missing. She isn't missing; she's gone."

"Who's 'she'?"

"The red-haired girl."

"Do you want me to speak to one of the nurses about this?"

"You don't believe me. It's all right." Paul turned his head to look forlornly out of the window.

"It's not that I don't believe you. It's just-"

"You said you saw things sometimes."

"I didn't mean to say that. I shouldn't have."

"I would like my medicine now."

She hesitated for a moment and then came over to him with his medicine. "If you think it will help-"

His arm shot out and gripped her wrist, making her drop the glass where it fell, shattering like a bomb on the hard floor. The room began to shift before her eyes. Flashes of images went off behind her eyes making her feel sick. *No, no, not again.*

She saw Paul as a young boy in a playground laughing and waving to a small child on a swing, transparent and foggy. She heard his mother telling him off, to stop being silly and pulling him away by the arm. She saw Paul as a teenager being shouted at by a large man who could only be his father, telling him he was a man and needed to grow out of these imaginary friends. She turned her face away as his father struck him. She saw Paul's eyes looking to his mother who stood watching without compassion from the doorway. She saw Paul as a young man lying on the grass of a cemetery on a blanket eating sandwiches alone, but not alone, talking aloud to people Caroline could not see. The scene changed and she saw Paul standing before the doors of an enormous theatre with a doll in his hands. He looked so frightened and alone.

"Paul, you have to let go now."

His eyes stared into her, his grip holding firm.

She saw Paul lying face down on the floor, pill casing empty and whisky bottle in one hand.

Enough. She wrenched her hand away and staggered back into the chair. The room rushed back into view making her want to vomit. She put her head in her hands and took long slow breaths.

"Who were the people in your room, Caroline?" She ran her hands through her hair trying to regain focus.

"What, what did you say?"

"The people marching through your room. Never seen that many before, not in one place."

"You saw that?"

He nodded gravely. "I saw it behind your eyes, a dirty room, with a big lock on the door."

"That's where I'm living."

The door opened and Fiona bustled in looking harried. "What on earth happened here? I heard a noise."

Caroline stood up quickly while Paul resumed his semi vegetative state in the chair. "I'm sorry. I accidentally dropped a glass. I was about to go and find a broom when you came in."

Fiona looked from the shattered glass on the floor to Paul in the chair. "I think that might be all for today."

"I was just in the middle of something with Paul. Do you think I can have another five minutes?"

She shook her head. "I don't want to exhaust him. He needs his rest after last night's episode."

Caroline made to move but Paul's hand shot out and gripped her cardigan. Fiona lunged in and grabbed his hand away. "That's enough. Let go now, Mr Graves. Caroline has to go." Slowly his grip lessened and withdrew.

Fiona walked her out.

"I'm so sorry about that. Why don't you come back on Monday?"

Fiona left her at the double doors of the ward. Caroline's chest was tight with all the things that she hadn't said, and questions that needed answering.

It was a week after Dayna disappeared that Wanda began to feel there was something wrong. The tell-tale signs that Dayna had passed through the flat were absent, dirty plates were not left in the kitchen and her bed had not been slept in.

Wanda went to the pub where Dayna was working and was informed by the smug manager that she had been fired the previous Friday, an entire week before.

Wanda felt as if she'd been kicked in the stomach. *She couldn't come home and tell me she'd been fired. Where did she go?*

She went to the shelter she had found her in months before, when she had first been beaten and dumped on the street by her boyfriend, but no, they had not seen her either. It was late evening on Friday when she began to get very, very worried about Dayna's whereabouts. She decided to go to the police station.

The officer on the other side of the table was leaning back with his hands behind his head looking uninterested. "And you say you had a row, yes?"

"We had an argument but she was fine when I last saw her."

"And when was that?"

"Last Friday."

"But you said you had an argument. You threatened to throw her out."

"Yes, we had an argument."

"So perhaps she's staying with a friend."

"I don't think she is. I'm her only friend."

"Are you sure about that?"

Wanda didn't like him. He had cropped ginger hair and a sallow face.

"Is there a woman officer I could speak to?"

"You can speak to me, so tell me again. You had a fight and she left?"

Wanda was getting fed up. She had been at the station for nearly forty minutes and no one was showing any concern at all.

"I've given you all the information you need. Her name is Dayna Andrews. She has auburn hair, pale skin, green eyes and she's been missing for nearly a week."

"We don't know she's missing yet. She could've gone to her parents."

"Fat chance. Her parents chucked her out when she was sixteen."

"You mentioned a boyfriend?"

"John Aldrich, yes."

"Do you have his phone number, address?"

"It's at home, but I don't think she's with him."

The officer smirked at her and closed his notebook.

"If you could drop it round to the station, I will send someone over there for you. No doubt she's there making up with him now as we speak."

"I told you, she's not with him unless she really has lost all sense of self-worth which I doubt very much."

"You said she sometimes stayed away for days if she met someone."

"She's twenty-three. She-"

"So perhaps she's off with a new boyfriend. I wouldn't worry too much. I'll speak to my sergeant and we will get someone to pop over to see Mr Aldrich. If you could phone us when you find his address." He moved around the desk and held the door open for her to leave. "Have a good day ma'am."

She opened the front door and called out hopefully to the empty flat. "Dayna, I'm home."

No answer.

She went straight to the living room where her computer was set up. She needed to keep moving, take action.

After some time she found a photo of Dayna taken just after she'd moved in. They had drunk a great deal after she had collected her things from John's house and they had snapped away with the camera happily. There was one of Dayna smiling, her pretty face alive with joy and a slight bruise on her cheek where the creep had clocked her one.

Dayna, where are you? I want you home with me.

She cropped the photo to be just her face and pasted it onto a word document. She typed in the seven letters in bold across the top of the page: MISSING. Her hands began to tremble as she began to type details of Dayna's appearance. The tears came as she hit 'print'.

Wanda trod carefully around the clothes on the spare room floor, not wanting to disturb anything. She just needed something small. She found an old cardigan with a small hole that needed darning and held it up to her nose, smelling Dayna's scent. She went back into the living room where the printer was spitting out identical black and white copies of Dayna's face smiling up to the ceiling and sat with the cardigan on her lap, leafing through her address book for John Aldrich's address, hoping against all odds that she was somehow there, and that she was safe.

Michele was seated on Caroline's sofa gripping a coffee in one hand. Caroline sat on the end of the bed looking tense. Michele's voice cut through the silence of the hostel.

"He called them 'they'?"

"Yes, he said they had taken her, this girl with red hair. He said he sees them every full moon."

"Are you sure you're not reading too much into this, Carol?"

"Meaning?"

"Meaning I found you that voluntary job to get you away from these spooks and now you've found a man who's full of them. Don't you think he could be, I don't know, delusional?"

"Do you think I'm delusional?"

"Of course not, and I wasn't talking about you. I was talking about this man. After all he doesn't live on a ward for nothing."

"He seems very lucid when we've spoken, albeit very sad and alone."

"I'm not sure you should be encouraging him with these fantasies of his, if they're making him attack staff and climb out of windows."

"He said he was trying to help the girl."

"And how did he know she was being hurt?"

"He said the cat told him."

"For heaven's sake!"

"I know, I know! And for the record I don't believe the cat has told him anything but he mentioned something to do with the nurses. What if there is something going on in that ward and he's the only one that sees it?"

"What do you mean the nurses? The one I saw seemed fine."

"He called one of them, I can't remember it was something like arachnid. She clicked her fingers trying to recall it. Atropos! He called the nasty fat one Atropos! He said she's the one with the needles. Those were his exact words."

Michele looked over to the wall, thinking. "Atropos? As in the Greek fate?"

"You've lost me."

"Atropos was the third fate, the one with the scissors. One wound the thread of life, one spun it into wool and one cut the thread bringing death. She was called Atropos, the cruel one."

"What if the nurses are hurting him and he hasn't anyone to tell? What if him trying to get out of the window was to escape? I mean, I don't know what they're giving him in that place but it can't be good for him."

"He's a paranoid schizophrenic! He's seeing things, not unlike you the week you came off your meds, seeing ghosts by the fridge."

Caroline stood up and shouted back at her. "So now we're both mental are we? Well, thank you very much for the vote of confidence! You can go now."

"Wait. Just think about this."

"There's nothing to think about. Even if it's true and they are doing something to him, I can't help him. I'm just a volunteer with an addiction problem. Who's going to listen to me? Certainly not you."

"Stop, please!"

Caroline went to shout something more at her but a noise made her turn to the window. A large cat was sitting on the sill, regarding them both with its big yellow eyes. She strode to the window and unlatched it, throwing it open. The cat dropped heavily into the room, purring. Caroline went over to it, her hand held out.

"Don't! It could be feral."

"This is Snoops."

"How on earth did it get here?"

"It must've followed me home from the hospital." She put the cat down on the chair where it immediately curled up into a ball.

Michele eyed it with suspicion. "You can't have cats here. It's in the lease. Besides it's dirty."

"I'll leave the window open. He can let himself out. He's the cat that Paul is so fond of."

"It can't be the same cat."

"Snoops is white with a black patch over one eye. Also he's a huge cat and so is this one."

"I don't believe it."

"This really is your day for not believing the obvious. Let's get out of here. We can stop by a supermarket and get some cat food for him. I'm sure Paul would appreciate me feeding him."

Rose and Charlie lay entwined together on the chaise longue in the living room. The pair had risen late in the day following their revelry in the moonlight. Rose had spent the afternoon painting her toenails pink and doing her hair for the evening ahead. The first night newly changed was special to her and attention had to be paid.

The previous night she and Charlie had driven into the woods where they rolled around on the back seat of his car like teenagers. She could smell traces of Dayna in the car: loneliness and despair, a heady bouquet that had aroused them both and kept them up till the early hours of the morning.

Charlie was on the floor with a shaving mirror, checking his hairline and moving his face from side to side, relishing the change in his appearance. "I reckon I could get away with saying I'm thirty one. What do you think? Rosy?"

But Rose was not listening. Her eyes were closed tight in concentration.

"Right now a girl over on the other side of town is telling her parents she's pregnant. They're telling her to pack a bag and get out of their house."

Charlie got up and ran his hand over her exposed naval. She was wearing one of the tasselled boob tubes he had bought her, her flat stomach was pale as snow. He ran his tongue down it like a dog. "And how would you know something like that?"

"I can hear her. She's sobbing, refusing to accept they're chucking her out. Dad's throwing her things into a suitcase. Her mother's turning away from her. It's so beautiful."

"How 'bout I run down to the car and fetch her for you. It's another full moon tonight. We could be looking nineteen years old by the time the sun rises tomorrow."

"No I don't think so. If we take too many in one month people could get suspicious."

"Who would get suspicious, the police?" He snorted.

She draped herself over him and kissed him affectionately. "Don't be greedy, Charles."

He oinked like a pig, nuzzling her neck.

"I think I will be all right till next month. Poor little girl had a lot of potential in her. You know she would've got it together in a few months. I got a flash of something when I took her, some sort of support group surrounding her, women hugging each other, that sort of thing. You did well to get her, another month or two and she would've been useless to us." She stroked his chin, admiring her handiwork. His hair was once again jet-black, thick and curly. Toned muscles stood out on his arms. His tattoos looked bright and exotic against his dark skin.

"It's different for you, getting it second-hand you don't have the side effects. I see what they would've become."

He ran his fingers through her hair. "And what would've become of our lost little girl, Rose?"

"Hard to say. I got a flash of her holding a baby, and hugging someone, an old woman, probably her mother, reconciling with her."

He smiled at her. "Too late for that now."

She smiled back at him coming in for another kiss. "Much, much too late."

"I need to go out to buy some mice. I won't be long."

"Ugh. I can't believe I let you keep that thing in the house."

He ignored her. She had never understood his pet.

"Actually, while you're out, I want you to cruise around looking for a school."

He turned back to her frowning. "A school! Why?"

"I've been thinking about what you told me. You said you smelled one in the mall."

"Two of them, wearing school blazers although I'm not sure which one it was. What are you plotting, Rosy?"

She stretched out on the chaise like a cat. He took one of her feet in his hands and began rubbing it.

"What age do we usually take them, Charlie? Twenty-three? Twenty-five? They burn out within a month, but what if we took someone younger, let's say, a depressed teen with a lot of life ahead of her? They'd have more potential, wouldn't they?"

"I suppose so, yes, but we don't take them younger. They usually get noticed."

"I've been thinking about that too, but what about if they're without a mummy or daddy?"

"They're rare and often they've been institutionalised by the social system. They've got no potential to drain, orphans and the like. They're useless, just gristle, good for a week, nothing more."

"But Miss Prep School isn't in the system. She's in a private school and you said she smelled like cherries. Our little friend from last night didn't smell that good."

He grinned down at her. "I didn't hear you complaining, but if she's in prep school with no parents then someone's looking out for her sweet little tush."

"We are going to find out who. You saw their blazers, right?"

"Dark green with a shield."

"Find the school, drive around. There can't be that many private schools around."

"Rosy, come on, think about it. Loner man hanging around the school gates, bound to attract attention."

"Or a loving father picking up his daughter from school? Besides you wouldn't need to be out of the car. Just find the school and come home."

He stood at the door. He wasn't convinced. "I don't know. It's a lot of risk."

She came over, pressing herself up against him, letting her hand move down his chest to his lower regions. He grabbed her wrist. She spoke softly into his ear. "Think what she could do for us. She could take years off me. It'd be months before she burned off."

"You've already had decades off you. You said it yourself: don't be greedy."

She slapped him hard on the face making him stagger backwards. Her temper was a terrible thing to behold and he held his hands up his face as she threw random objects at him, a vase breaking, then a lamp. "You have no vision! Don't you see! She could slow the whole process down, no more waking up with crow's feet as deep as mine shafts, or joint pain."

He whimpered in the corner as she spent her anger about the room, turning over the chaise longue, her brute strength gouging holes in the walls the size of small craters.

"Please, don't say that, Rosy. You know I don't notice things like that. You will always be the main attraction in my home theatre."

She clutched at her hair like a deranged prophet in the throes of a vision, coming towards him, her pink talons outstretched.

"It's humiliating! Every time we cycle back. Every time! And it's always worse than before!"

She lifted him high into the air by the neck. The soles of his feet kicked fruitlessly at the empty air.

"All right, all right. For you, my life, for you."

She dropped him and he scrambled to his feet throwing the door open to the hall. Rose watched from the window as his blue car pulled violently out of the driveway and through the gate.

Michele and Caroline walked back from the corner shop trying to ignore the various people lingering aimlessly on the sidewalk. Caroline jumped back as a large man barged past her, not wanting to touch him.

"When are you next going to the ward?" They stopped at the bus stop and faced each other

"The day after tomorrow."

"I wish you would be careful. I'd like to be there when you next see Paul."

"I appreciate the help, really, but I'm not sure he will talk to me with you in the room. He thinks we both have the same..." She struggled to find a word.

"Gift?" Michele said with a smile.

"Call it that for now until I think of something more fitting."

The bus was coming down the street. Michele looked at her seriously. "Promise you will call if anything happens, won't you? Even if it is nothing and you just want to talk."

"I promise."

The sun was already setting as she made her way home hurriedly wanting to be inside before dark. She turned right onto her street and stopped dead in her tracks. The shopping bag holding the cat food dropped to the floor as her grip slackened from fright. Caroline's eyes saw the telephone pole directly opposite her front door where a white A4 poster was pinned up flapping eerily in the breeze. Smiling out from it was the face of Dayna Andrews and above her photo was the word: 'MISSING'. Unable to help herself Caroline scanned the description of Dayna below the photograph. She mouthed the words: 'Auburn hair, green eyes'.

The moonlight shone through her eyes, the girl with red hair. They took her. They ate her alive. They're bad news, both of them. Go back indoors where it's safe. It's none of your business. It's nothing to do with you.

But she couldn't turn away, not now. *A girl just like you.*

And she knew as she reached out to take the poster that there was no going back.

Lucy had taken care to stay out of her mother's way since their row the previous week. She was wearing the stolen jacket and reading 'Carrie' on top of the bed. Below she heard the sounds of her parents shouting. She sat up when she heard the front door slam and a car take off from the driveway. Looking out of the window she saw her father's BMW pulling out and away from the house.

She heard someone coming up the stairs. Before she could move, her bedroom door was thrown open. Her mother stood in the doorway, her usually set hairdo was in disarray with her face devoid of make-up. Both her eyes were still purple from where Lucy had kicked her.

"What are you doing, Lucy?"

"Reading."

"What are young girls reading nowadays, I wonder?" The smell of wine leaked out of her as she strode forward and snatched the book from Lucy's hands.

"Give that back!"

Sheila appraised the cover with faint disgust and turned it over to read the blurb. Lucy watched her eyes move back and forth, her mouth twisting downwards into a snarl. "And what is this?"

Lucy made to lunge for it but Sheila turned her back to her, leafing through the book.

"Where did you get this?"

"It's mine! Not yours!"

Sheila strode out of the room. Lucy ran after her.

"Did that Minnie give you this horror book?" Lucy realised that she had put away her rage from the week before, but now it was here unfurled like an umbrella. Punishment could be delayed but never escaped.

"Maxine gave it to me."

"Aha!" Sheila turned and ran down the stairs. Lucy followed at her heels. She found her with her back to the fireplace in the living room. "Your father doesn't seem to care about the state of my face."

"You deserved it!" Lucy spat, bracing herself, waiting for her mother to move to strike her, but she only smiled.

"Is that so? Well, daddy may think that failing grades is all you've been getting up to, but when I mention to him that you've been smoking drugs with this girl Maxine he doesn't want to hear it."

"Oh for goodness sake, there are no drugs!"

"Liar!" Sheila spat. "I've tried to explain it to him and now I'm explaining it to you. That's where you've been going at night, isn't it, with this girl, to the estate where she lives to score weed or crack or whatever it is her mother's dealing in!"

Lucy laughed at the ridiculousness of it. Sheila grabbed a glass of wine off the table and took a generous swig. The logs popped on the fire behind her.

"Don't be so stupid. That stuff may go on there but Maxine is far too smart to get involved with that rubbish."

"Then where have you been going?"

"To the mall! To hang out! To get away from you!"

Sheila's eyebrows raised a fraction. She turned casually towards the fire.

"Mum, don't!"

She threw the book onto the flames.

"No!" Lucy sobbed and made to run at the fireplace, to grab the tongs, to rescue it. She saw the cover slowly curl, turning black, the flames licking greedily at the dry pages.

Sheila grabbed her wrists and shouted into her tear-streaked face. "For your own good! I'm not having that tramp fill your head up with all that rubbish!" She shook her hard, her eyebrows arching together as she felt a cold lump on the cuff of Lucy's jacket. Sheila looked down and saw the plastic security tag standing out on the sleeve.

Rose was dressed in a short pink lurex dress turning about in front of the mirror when Charlie appeared in the doorway behind her looking worried. She turned to him, raising her thin eyebrows hopefully.

"Found it, Rose. Richard Allard's School for Girls."

"Are you sure?"

"I'm sure. Old building, traditional, pricey like. Coloured flags out front, dark green, like their blazers." He sat down on the bed, a look of worry casting a shadow across his handsome face.

"Something wrong? Were they out of mice at the pet store? Pity. I guess your little friend will have to starve." She laughed to herself.

He held out a piece of folded paper to her. "I found this."

She snatched it from him. He winced when he heard her gasp. "I don't believe it." Dayna Andrew's face smiled up at them printed across the page in black and white.

He stood up with his hands in his pockets. "I didn't either. They're on every telephone pole along the way into town. Someone's missing her."

"No! No one misses them. That's the whole point of it! She had no one. I could taste it! Who on earth could be missing that stupid little tart?"

"I dunno. Not her parents for sure. A sibling, maybe?"

"No, she didn't have any siblings." Rose spoke with a conviction that he didn't dare question. "You said you picked her up from a club, was it?"

"Yeah, trendy one, business types go there to buy drugs and drink."

"Were there security cameras in there?"

"So what if there was. They'd see her talking to a fifty-something-year-old man. Nothing to see." She looked at him and nodded slowly. He began to relax. "There's nothing to find Rose and nothing to lead her back to us."

"What about the car? You insist on driving that thing to do the takes. Someone was bound to see her getting into a motor as old as that."

It was his turn to shout now. "Oh come off it! Bunch of business type wankers in polyester suits buying overpriced wine and vodka ain't gonna see nothing, you hear me? You know the type: too busy looking in the direction of the nearest piece of meat wearing a skirt, or in the toilet snorting coke. They're certainly not going to notice a girl getting into a car with a stranger. It happens every night of the week at these places. The police will put the word out. Sightings will come in from all over the globe. We sit on our hands for a month and the trail will be cold by the time we need to top up!"

He was worried he'd gone too far this time, but she seemed to accept his logic. He, after all, was the one who made the take each month. He knew what he was doing after nearly a century together.

"All right, all right. We will lay low for now. What's this bar called again?"

"The Bad Penny."

Her eyes wandered back to the mirror of the vanity table. "The Bad Penny indeed. Get your dancing boots on, Charlie, I fancy a night on the town."

She was staring down at the poster lying on the kitchen counter. *I don't know anything about her. But I could find out.*

Snoops was purring asleep on the sofa after eating a bowl of Sheba's finest. Caroline sat next to him, scratching him behind the ears. "Did Paul send you to me, kitty?" The cat purred affectionately.

Phone Michele. She had promised she would, even for something small. She even reached for the phone, picking it up off the handle and made to dial. The cat watched her with its yellow eyes. She listened to the dial tone and put it back in the cradle.

She didn't get anything from holding the paper, no flashes, not like when she had held the crowbar. Taking hold of it again and closing her eyes she concentrated hard on the photograph, looking into Dayna's bright green eyes, her happy smile. Dayna, her own sister. *Where are you, Dayna? Help me find you.*

Nothing.

Perhaps there's nothing left to find. She balled the paper up and threw it on the floor feeling frustrated. It was pointless. If Paul was right and these beings, as he called them, had taken her, then perhaps there wasn't anything left. The poster wasn't enough.

What if I had something of hers? She picked up the ball of paper and unfurled it. There along the bottom of the page were the words*:* If you have any information on Dayna Andrews' whereabouts, please contact this number.

Caroline picked up the phone and began to dial.

"Get off me mother!"

Sheila was attempting to wrestle the stolen jacket off Lucy's back. "Where did you get this?"

"I bought it!"

"Liar. Just wait till your father gets home!"

Lucy slid her arms out of the sleeve, freeing herself.

Sheila looked over the jacket, turning it inside out. She took a step towards the fire again, holding the jacket above the flames in warning.

"Give that back to me, Mother."

"Where did you get this? Did Minnie steal this for you?" One sleeve hung loose above the burning logs. The flames licked out greedily.

Lucy laughed in spite of herself. "You know, Mother, you really are dumb as a post, aren't you? I stole it!"

Sheila stared at her, momentarily struck dumb by the words that issued from her daughter's mouth. "Why?"

Lucy took some satisfaction from her mother's aghast expression. "Maybe because I liked the colour, or maybe just because I felt like it!" She screamed the last words as she lunged forward, knocking Sheila to the ground. She managed to tear the jacket out of her mother's hands and took off, running up the stairs and sliding one arm back in to the leather sleeve as she went.

Lucy had no intention of locking herself in the bathroom this time. The room she was heading towards was her mother and father's bedroom. She slammed the door and shot the bolt across as she heard her mother pounding heavily up the stairs. Pressing her ear against the door she heard the echo of footsteps moving towards the direction of Lucy's room and the bathroom.

Lucy threw open the bedroom window and clambered up onto the slanted tiles. There was no car parked beneath her this time, only the concrete slabs of her parents' back patio.

"Lucy!" a loud thump against the door. "You open this door or you will never be welcome in this house again!"

Lucy threw her legs out of the window, relishing the cold air blowing against her face, freedom beckoned. Her mother's voice shrieked from behind her.

"You leave this house and don't even think about coming back!"

She went skidding down the slanted roof tiles and rolled off the edge with a scream, landing hard on her back. She lay on the ground, looking up at the moon and the stars which twinkled brightly in the night sky. Finally she rolled onto her front and climbed to her feet, dusting herself off.

She turned, running to the edge of the property, and hopped over the wooden fence into the farmer's field and off into the wild of the night.

Caroline was sitting opposite Wanda in her living room. She couldn't help but gape around at the end tables and various decorative objects that filled the room. She felt like a trespasser, a black crow bringing ill news.

Wanda had an old cardigan in her lap that she kept pulling at absentmindedly. She spoke slowly, as if each word caused her pain. "We had a row over some things. She'd been crashing with me since her boyfriend threw her out. He knocked her about a bit."

"And you're sure she's not with him now?"

"She would've come back for her clothes. I know it. She wouldn't just disappear."

"Do you know any places she used to like to frequent?"

Wanda looked Caroline up and down, on guard. "I'm sorry but are you with the police? They weren't very interested in helping me when I went to see them."

"No I'm not. I'm just concerned. A friend of mine told me he saw a girl with auburn hair one night and then I saw your poster and grew concerned. He said she had green eyes."

Wanda eyes widened at Caroline and nodded. "The boys always liked her. Too pretty for her own good." Wanda got up and went into the hallway, opening the door to the spare room where Dayna had slept.

""The room's the way she left it. I haven't...I haven't moved anything."

Looking past Wanda she saw the single camp bed was the same as when Dayna had last slept in it, the duvet half on the bed, half on the floor. Caroline felt a pang as she saw tell-tale signs of depression around the room: cigarette butts on a plate on the window ledge, clothes strewn about the floor; so like her own room. She stepped carefully between the piles of clothes and sat down on the bed trying to cast her senses around the room.

Dayna, where are you? She tried to imagine herself in Dayna's shoes, trying to see the room through her eyes. What would she touch before going out for the last time? What would be the sort of object that she would leave an impression on? Caroline's eyes moved over the room. Her nostrils flared as she caught the scent of something exotic, something hidden beneath the stench of cigarettes, dirty laundry and stale wine. *There.*

"Wanda?" She came down the hall into the kitchen where Wanda was sitting with Dayna's cardigan in her lap, a mug of coffee in her hands.

"Did you find something?"

"Did Dayna ever borrow anything of yours? Perfume perhaps?"

Rose wrinkled her nose at the crowded dance floor. "I can't hear a thing in this racket. What's with the music? It's horrible."

He put one arm round her, leading her over to the leather stools by the bar. "Want me to take you home, peaches? Put on a bit of Nancy Sinatra and dance away in the attic?" He grinned at her.

She could see the faintest yellow tint on his teeth that had not been there the day before.

"I'm sick of being indoors, but honestly, how can they be enjoying this? Are any of them having a good time?"

He raised his nose into the air and took a deep sniff. "They're on drugs, and most are drunk. Where you going?"

Rose was pushing her way through the crowd of suits into the centre of the dance floor. "To dance, of course. Why don't you get us some cocktails?"

He watched her glittery pink dress disappearing into the crowd of dark grey and black suits and then swivelled around to face the bartender who was looking at him with a vague look of contempt. "A strawberry daiquiri and a bloody mary." He stuck his hand in his pocket and put a wad of bills on the bar.

The bartender took the bills and turned his back to Charlie to mix the drinks.

Charlie squinted, trying to make out Rose in the crowd, but he couldn't see her.

The light came on above them and Caroline gasped aloud at the various silks that hung all around her in Wanda's closet.

"She used to let herself in here and borrow things. I guess she didn't want to go out wearing her own clothes. It's one of the things we argued about, her borrowing my stuff. Excuse me, it's cramped in here."

Wanda left her alone in the closet and Caroline couldn't help but let her fingers wander over the various rich textiles that were hanging before her eyes like tantalising plums just out of reach, the sort of clothes she would never have herself.

Dayna? The envy she felt run through her fingers was not her own.

Caroline's hand brushed up against a silk satin dress that made her eyes water as she caught a flash of something.

Dayna. There it was. She reached out slowly and lifted the dress carefully down from the rail. Caroline's eyes took in the damage on it. It had holes. She saw a stain on the bust that could be wine. The dress rustled causing the beads along the hem to drop off and skitter along the floor. *Dayna, where did you go in this?*

She knew what she had to do. It came to her clearly. Caroline opened the closet a crack and called out to Wanda. "Do you mind if I use your bathroom?"

Wanda called back from the kitchen. "Yes, fine!"

Caroline crept out of the closet with the silk dress in her hands and walked into the en suite of Wanda's bedroom. She locked the door.

There was a small glass shower cubicle and a bone white porcelain sink with various soaps in a basket to the right of the door. She stripped off her T-shirt in a hurry, exposing her bare breasts to the mirror and fumbled out of her cotton skirt. She turned on the hot tap. She hoped it would come fast, whatever it was. She stepped into the black dress and pulled it up, bringing the beaded straps over her shoulders.

Dayna? She spoke aloud to the room in the drug pusher's cracked voice. "You gotta pay for these, baby…Oh, you've got more than that, a lot more."

Caroline grabbed the edges of the sink and retched as she felt the pill peddler's hands move up her skirt making her squeeze her legs together. The smell of bleach and urine seemed to fill the room like a creeping mist making her gag. The bathroom light above began blinking madly. She saw leather bar stools and glass tables. Her eyes squinted shut with her head pressed up against the shower door. She saw a blue car, shining bright with power in the light of the moon. Her hand came up and wrote the letters R A B Y N N E P D A B on the steamy glass of the shower glass door.

Caroline's eyes opened as the bile came up inside her throat. She spat out chloroform and wine into the sink and dry heaved. The dress strap came off her shoulders and the stained silk dress dropped around her feet. Slowly she came back to herself shuddering. She tried to hang onto every detail she'd seen. The dirty toilet could have been any bathroom in the country. She shivered as the tattooed drug dealer came to her mind, the way his cold hands had crept over her, and then the blue car.

The knocking on the bathroom door startled her out of her stupor. Wanda's voice brought her out of her thoughts "Are you all right in there? There's steam coming under the door!"

"Oh sorry!" she called back frantically turning off the hot tap. "One minute. I'm coming out!"

She pulled back on her T-shirt back to front and then pulled her skirt up, clinching it at the waist. One more glance in the mirror to check her hair, and then she saw the letters already dripping down from the moisture on the glass of the shower door. Turning round to their reflection in the mirror she saw spelled out clearly: BAD PENNY BAR.

Lucy stepped off the bus into the city bus station. Looking over to the shelter where she and Maxine had parted company only a week before she felt a dull pang in her chest. It felt like a lifetime ago.

She set off walking towards the mall, feeling excited and thrilled by the crowds she saw all around her enjoying their night. Couples were walking arm in arm and there was the echo of high heels on the stone street everywhere.

She'd never come to the city alone before. She loved coming with Maxine who knew her way around perfectly but she had never been after dark. *Where to go?* The mall was closed. She saw the shops along the high street were all closed with their windows dark. She thought she could go to a club and try to get in.

She looked at herself in the reflection of a shop window. Her short hair made her look older, more mature. The leather jacket and dark eyeliner she wore meant she could get away with looking eighteen. Perhaps. No harm in trying.

Caroline had stopped off briefly at the hostel to change, perceiving that wherever she was going, her T-shirt and skirt were not in the dress code. After rifling through the heaps of discarded clothes on the floor she found an old sparkly halter neck top that showed her stomach, a lost relic from her party days.

She dunked her hair in the sink and combed it out. She had crossed the city on her way to and from the hospital and knew roughly where she was going.

Walking alone she silently wished she had taken a weapon with her from the hostel: a kitchen knife or screwdriver. The crowbar would've been too conspicuous. She didn't know what manner of thing was out there tonight. Never before had she felt so alone and scared. She remembered what Paul had said: *Girls like her; girls like you.* What would happen if she disappeared tonight? Would it be her face staring out from posters on telephone poles next?

She heard a noise and jumped. A man and a woman walking arm-in-arm kissed as they ambled slowly down the street. The man swayed drunkenly on his feet. *They dress like men only to hide that they're not.*

She felt foolish. Here she was in the dark of the city, without lights or weapons, perhaps walking right into the lion's den. She kept her eyes peeled for any old cars idling on the pavement. *And what if you spot the blue car that picked up Dayna?*

She had no idea what to do, but she had to see. The Bad Penny was the place that Dayna Andrews had spent her last hours alive before being taken by two monsters. *The moonlight shone through her eyes.* They had got away with it because nobody cared whether homeless girls lived or died. Wanda had cared enough to make the posters. Caroline cared.

Her own fearful thoughts tugged at her as she moved closer into the city centre and the streets grew more crowded with people. *It's not too late to go home.* But what if they were there now? Caroline shut her eyes against the flashes of places that came to mind: mental wards, hostels, women's refuges, crash pads and halfway houses. The list was endless. So many places where they could park up on the kerb in their blue car and invite someone home for a warm meal and a hot shower. She would never sleep again knowing that those things, whatever they were, were out there, seeking out the lonely, the vulnerable, to snatch off the streets without a murmur from the authorities. Her fists curled into anger at the horror of how easily they could get away with it. The only people noticing are the mentally ill, the sensitives, the ones no one will listen to. *Except me, special me.*

She went past the church. The saints in the stain glass window frowned at her as she went through the cemetery gate alone and along the cobbled path following the musical notes that came floating through the night air making her ears tingle and her flesh creep.

The heavy music made Lucy cover her ears as she was led into the gloom of the Bad Penny. She had followed behind a trio of men, all attired in navy suits, and was now seated with them in front of the bar. She was trying to follow what they were saying over the sound of the drum and bass banging out from the speakers.

The multicoloured lights were shining down on everyone, transforming them into elfish revellers before her eyes. It was the women that held Lucy's attention dancing on the raised platforms around the stage. Each one was a picture of vitality and allure and almost all of them were clad in sequinned tops and dresses making the neon lights sparkle around them as if they were clothed in starlight. Identical looks of joy and laughter were etched across their faces as they moved around, bumping their bodies against the men who tried to surround them.

Lucy watched one of the tattooed men move close to a beautiful woman in a pink Lurex dress and try to put his hands around her waist. She twirled away from him on the stage, seemingly oblivious to everything around her, dancing in her own world. Lucy envied her.

"Here we go!" One of her company came over carrying four tumbler glasses, slamming them down on the table.

"What are those?" Lucy had not drunk alcohol before. The smell was overpowering.

"Vodka tonic, my good lady. Cheers to another week over!"

The three of them toasted together and took generous gulps. She nodded, keeping the smile on her face and slowly brought the glass up to her lips, taking slow sips at a time.

"So, Lucy, you are a student around here?"

"I'm studying at the city college. What about you?"

"We're in finance although Stan here is a data analysis expert."

"I'm a numbers droid," Stan said, winking at her.

The one sitting closest to Lucy with blonde curly hair leaned in. "Which means that Stan gets paid double what we do just to input numbers into a computer."

"Fuck off, Luke, you arsehole!" Stan shoved Luke playfully making all of them laugh hysterically.

"Language, please, gentlemen. We have a lady present."

"I'm going for a slash." Luke stood up and vanished into the crowd.

Stan leaned in close to her again. "Sorry about them. They're my colleagues so I have to go out with them after work to keep the boss happy. We can go somewhere quieter if you like." She felt his hand move onto her leg. "There's a small courtyard out back with a gorgeous view of the woods." Lucy put his hand back in his lap. "Maybe later."

He nodded, raising his drink to her before gulping it down.

She raised her own glass to her lips and took another swig beginning to feel the first tentacles of dizziness coil around her head.

Charlie had his back to the dance floor taking slow sips of scotch when he noticed the baroque framed mirror running along the back of the bar. He grinned at his reflection, his hair jet-black and thick, his eyes a bright lapis blue. Turning his face from side to side he saw creases beginning to appear around his eyes. *Shit.*

He had to take a closer look: it could have been a trick of the light, better to be sure. His eyes found Rose making a show of herself on the stage. A bloke with a tribal tattoo on his neck was grinding up against her and he felt a warm rush of anger move through him. If he was still there when he got back from the bathroom he'd knock his teeth out for him. Rose would probably like that.

He slipped off the bar stool and walked in the direction of the gent's lavatory using his muscled form like a battering ram to wade through the groups of businessmen loitering around the bar like jackals in an alley.

He came to the bathroom door which opened from within. Just as his hand brushed the surface of the wood a man in a navy suit barged past him zipping up his fly, not paying attention to Charlie at all as he went past. Charlie made to stride in when he stopped dead, his nose going into the air of its own volition, his body tensing up making the muscles on his arms bulge as he dug his feet into the floor. It was here - underneath the smell of sweat, urine, and alcohol, smelling all the sweeter against the foreground of filth - was the sweet smell of black cherries.

A wide grin spread out across his face as he made his way back into the throngs of people.

Lucy was finding it hard to keep her eyes open. She felt sick and dizzy, her eyelids began to feel heavy. Her company was becoming belligerent as they drank more and more. She stood up to leave.

"I might go to the bathroom." She got up and flinched as Luke grabbed her arm.

"Does thy lady need a noble prince to escort her?"

She could smell alcohol on his breath as he laughed hysterically into her face.

"For fuck's sake, Luke, let the girl go for a piss if she wants to. You're such a dick."

Luke's face turned from gleeful to angry. Lucy felt a tremor of fear as she watched him shove Stan back into his seat.

"Don't call me a dick."

"Don't touch me, you prick."

She saw her chance and ran onto the dance floor, pushing her way through the crowd looking for the exit. She needed fresh air. The alcohol was making her feel sick. Someone knocked into her making her trip. The crowd was too dense, the lights too bright.

"Excuse me. Sorry. Excuse me." No one paid any attention as she pushed through the din, trying to make herself as small as possible. She manoeuvred through the drunks pressing in on her from every side, finally coming out into a long corridor. *Didn't he mention something about a garden out back?*

She saw a door at the end of the hall wedged open by an old barstool. A slight wind blew in from outside. She zipped up her leather jacket and stepped out into the courtyard.

"Rose! Rose!" Charlie pushed his way up onto the stage and grabbed her by the shoulders, turning her around to face him.

The man with the tattoo on his neck pulled her back. Rose's hand flashed out catching him across the face and sent him flying off the stage, overturning a glass table.

"Should've kept his hands to himself. What is it, Charles? I was having fun there."

"She's here."

Rose played with her hair idly and planted a kiss on his bottom lip.

"Who is, sweetie? Are you feeling all right?" She reached out to his forehead.

He grabbed her wrists. "Her, the prep school girl. She's here."

"What? Are you sure?" She went rigid as she cast her eyes around the room.

"It's her. I can smell her. She's here somewhere."

"I can't smell anything. Are you sure?"

"Yeah, I'm sure. I got her in the mall. Black cherries, ripe."

Rose furrowed her brows as she took sniffs of the air. "Must be getting rusty in my old age, dear heart. I'll check the girls' bathroom."

"Want me to check the courtyard. The lonely ones tend to gravitate towards there. If she is there I'll knock her out and take her into the woods. You can bring the car around."

He made to move, but she grabbed his arm. "No, stay here, near the exit. Don't let her double back out. This is quite a find. We don't want to lose her now. What does she look like, our little princess?"

Charlie tried to think back to that day. He'd been decades older and his sight had been poor. "Sort of long brown hair, thin, medium height, maybe brown eyes, I think."

"Got anything to knock her out with?"

"No, nothing."

"It's all right. We'll just have to be creative. Don't make a move on her without me there. She will feel safer with a woman present. We offer her a lift home and, on the way, maybe we stop at our place for a nice cup of hot cocoa. It'll be tight, Charlie. The night's almost over."

He grinned at her feeling excitement in his chest. "We can do it, Rosy." He licked his lips greedily.

"Stay here and keep your eyes peeled."

Caroline couldn't see anything in the din of the club. The noise combined with the lights made her feel blind and deaf. *No way I will find any clues here. What a waste of time.* She pushed through two people dancing with glow sticks and sat on a barstool next to a man in jeans and cowboy boots whose attention was on the crowd. She spotted the barman and began waving her hand.

"Excuse me. Hello!"

The barman heard her, threw his rag over his shoulder and leaned in with a scowl on his face. "What will you have?"

"I'm looking for information about a friend of mine. I think she was here a few nights ago and I was wondering if you'd seen her." Caroline took out the fold of white paper and handed it to him. He leaned back on the bar scrutinizing the poster, then folded it up and held it out to her between two fingers.

"Nope, sorry."

"Thanks a bunch." *Asshole.* Caroline sat back and thought about the drug dealer who she'd seen when she put on Wanda's dress and decided to try the bathrooms for any trace of her presence. She felt a vague trickle of déjà vu that made her shiver when she looked up at the stage. *The spider holds court above like a ruined king.*

She couldn't place where she had seen it before. Or why it gave her such a chill.

Lucy took deep breaths of the night air gazing out into the woods. A few people loitered in the courtyard, smokers talking amongst themselves. Her head hurt from the drink. *I want to go home.* The evening was not the exhilarating night she had expected. The bar felt painted on, false fronted and seedy. Perhaps she could walk around till morning, then go to Maxine's house. Taking her last breath of clean air she headed back into the club to find the front door.

"There you are." Luke loomed up in front of her like a capering gargoyle. Another one of his shirt buttons had come undone and she saw sweat stains under his arms. "Me and the guys got you another drink here." He thrust a glass at her clumsily making the liquid slosh over the rim and spill down his front.

"Listen, I need to get going. Do you think you could show me where the door is?" Everyone around her was on their feet jumping up and down to the music that banged heavily making her head throb. He laughed at her grabbing hold of her wrists.

"You can't go yet. We haven't had a dance. You have to dance." He pulled her into the throng of people. She tried to pull away from him.

"No, it's OK. I just want to leave." She snatched her wrists out of his grip and tried to lose him in the crowd. Reaching out blindly her hands finally found the door, solid black and virtually invisible against the black paint of the walls.

Luke appeared in front of her again as she stepped out onto the street. "Come on. I wanted to get to know you better."

"It's late. I'm going."

"C'mon, Lucy." He grabbed her by the shoulders and turned her around, breathing his foul breath on her face making her feel sick. She looked around panicked but no one was paying much attention. Crowds of people were smoking and talking by the entrance. The bouncers' faces were looking dead ahead, bored.

"Get off me!" She struggled to turn away from him as he pulled her closer. His face came towards her as he leaned in to kiss. She shut her eyes against him, trying to turn her face away.

She felt a gust of air and suddenly her hands were free. Her eyes snapped open and she saw Luke lying a few feet away between two cars. A man in denim jeans towered over him menacingly.

"Leave the little lady alone. She said no."

Luke staggered to his feet, using a car door handle to pull himself upright. "OK, OK, whatever, no problem." He backed away from the newcomer with his hands up.

The man turned his blue eyes to Lucy. "Are you all right?"

"Yes, I was just leaving."

He nodded and held out a cigarette to her.

"No, thank you. I don't smoke."

He lit his own with a click of a silver lighter that appeared in his hands from nowhere and blew a smoke ring into the air. "You look a little young to be out by yourself, little lady." He looked to be her father's age. His eyes showed concern and worry.

Lucy took a step towards him. "I guess I am."

"You need a ride somewhere? I'm waiting for my wife to come out of the john. We'd be happy to give you a lift home." He took a seat on the hood of his blue car. The paint gleamed in the light of the moon.

Lucy looked about her. Perhaps she had had enough for one evening. She took another step towards the stranger.

Caroline came out of the club feeling irritated. She had found nothing of Dayna. Perhaps what Paul had stated was true. The two had picked her up and now there was nothing left, not even a ghost.

She jumped back as a man in a suit barged past her. She turned, opening her mouth to tell him to watch where he was going, and felt the words die on her lips as she saw an old blue convertible up on the sidewalk and felt a heavy stone turn over inside her belly.

Charlie grinned as he clicked the car door's silver handle. "So why don't you hop in the back and switch the radio on while you warm up. A nasty cold night to be out on your own." He heard a noise from behind and turned, just in time see a blonde woman bring a wine bottle down over his head.

Stars went off in front of his eyes as the bottle shattered, embedding glass in his scalp. He tasted blood as he rolled off the hood of the convertible and collapsed on the street.

Lucy screamed, jumping away from the car door as glass and blood sprayed over her. The man staggered sideways as fell to the ground at her feet. She bent down to help him, and her hands froze in the air as she saw him twitch on the ground and then he raised his head making her scream. His eyes were no longer blue, but yellow and reptilian like a snake.

Lucy felt something warm trickle down her leg as she backed away from the thing that was slowly rising to his feet like a broken toy wound into life. He growled like a dog, bringing one knee up, then the other, finally heaving himself up against his car. Lucy's eyes widened as she watched him reach up with both hands and pull a thick shard of glass out of his head. She watched his yellow eyes move to her and then to the blonde woman who had struck him, now trembling with the neck of the wine bottle still clenched in one hand. He bared his teeth and took a step towards his attacker.

Caroline was not a naive girl. She had survived on her wits and common sense since she'd fled home at fifteen. She had spent enough time around hostels and drug pushers to know a bad man when she saw one. There was something wrong with him. *It dresses like a man, but only to hide that it's not.*

When the thing in cowboy boots had opened the passenger door for the young girl to get in, Caroline had floated calmly towards the pair, pausing only to pick up a discarded bottle from the sidewalk. It was the first time in years she had felt so clearheaded. She raised both hands high above her head and brought the bottle down as hard as she could, marvelling at the charge that ran through her hands as it exploded over his skull.

She watched in horror as the man reached up to his forehead and pulled a chunk of glass out with a groan. His snarling mouth gave way to a mocking grin as his eyes found hers. His canine teeth flashed in the dark. A snail trail of blood ran down the side of his face as he paced towards her.

He let out a hoarse bark as he lunged forward, his hairy hands outstretched like claws. Caroline brought her elbow up and smashed it into his nose sending him back into the passenger side of the car. Before he could regain his footing, she had grabbed the handle of the car door and slammed it shut against his hand with a crunch.

"AHH!" The man-thing twisted and writhed before her eyes, screaming in agony. He was desperately trying to prise his fingers free, pulling uselessly against the metal door.

Caroline felt no sympathy as she saw plum bruises ripen on the skin of his hand. She grabbed the young girl by the shoulders, and shouted into her pale frightened face. "Run now!"

She watched the girl turn and take off running through the churchyard towards the centre of town. Caroline felt goose bumps break out over her arms as a high cold voice reached her ears.

"What happened, Charles?"

Caroline turned to look at a tall blonde woman standing passively by the vehicle door. She cracked the handle freeing him. He shrieked again, cradling his black and bloody fist in his lap, rocking back and forth on the pavement. He raised his one good hand to point at Caroline.

"Rose! It was her!"

The woman turned towards Caroline, her eyebrows raised in mild interest.

Caroline gasped as she felt a flash across her vision. It was as if a veil had been twitched aside over the spectacle before her. The man's face contorted like a jackal, his shirt stained with the blood of countless innocents. Try as she might, Caroline couldn't tear her eyes away from them. The pure horror of what she was seeing rooted her to the spot: the jackal man and his mistress, two demons in human form, blood drying on their hands.

Caroline saw the woman smile at her. *They know. Oh God, she knows I see them as they are.*

The man made to get to his feet, but the woman shoved him back down where he lay whimpering. She ignored him, her eyes never leaving Caroline's face.

When she spoke, Caroline felt the weight of the woman's power hit her like a blast of wind. "Well, well. What a special little girl. No, Charlie, let her go. Let her enjoy her little victory." An eerie half smile played around her lips. "We will be seeing you again, my dear."

Caroline fled.

Lucy was staring out of the window of the hostel. Caroline watched her, wishing she had curtains to hide the night world outside from her. Lucy had been sitting in the bus shelter when Caroline found her. She had tried to rush away until Caroline had convinced her it was safer if she came home with her.

Lucy had not spoken a word for a long time on the night bus, and after Caroline had ushered her into the bedsit she had gone straight to the window to look out for any sign of the blonde woman or the tattooed man.

"Come away from the window." Caroline gently put her arm around her and moved her away from the glass. The street outside was dark and empty apart from a man standing under the street lamp smoking. She led her back to the sofa where she sat with her knees drawn up to her stomach. Her voice came out in a whisper.

"Are you sure they didn't follow us from the club?"

"I'm positive. I need to ask you. What were you doing in that club tonight, alone?"

"Don't tell me you've never done it."

"Yes, I have, honey, but it is not a place to go to alone, and you're far too young to be going to places like that."

"Obviously, I thought it would be fun, but it wasn't really." Snoops climbed onto her lap and curled up purring. She began to pet the cat with both hands with heavy strokes.

"Would you like me to call your parents and they can pick you up?"

"No, I don't want to speak to them."

"All right, but tell me why I shouldn't. You need to be honest with me."

Her face whipped around.

"Why should I tell you anything? You're a stranger."

"Because you practically got into the car tonight with two strangers! And from what I know about them they do much worse than hurt the girls they take away. I think they're responsible for quite a few disappearances, perhaps dozens, and I'd like to know how you ended up meeting them in the first place when you should've been home tucked up in bed and away from danger."

"Why were you there then?"

Caroline sighed and took out the creased poster of Dayna and held it out to her. Lucy took it gingerly and unfolded it, her eyes moving across the page and down to the photograph.

"That bar was the last place this girl was seen alive. I was there asking about her. I believe the two beings we met tonight were responsible for her disappearance and I think they may have been targeting you for a particular reason. They seem drawn to girls who are alone or away from home. From what I can gather from talking to a friend of Dayna's, her parents haven't even noticed she's gone. They kicked her out when she was a little older than seventeen and I think it may be that way for all the victims. They're unwanted, all of them."

Lucy put the poster down and pulled the cat back onto her lap. "They would notice me not coming home. It's just that things have been bad with them recently."

"Why?"

"Because I've made a friend and my parents don't like her because she's from a poor side of town, her mum drinks and her dad is not in the picture. My parents think she is a waste of space. That's about it. My mum's a total snob and I don't want to grow up to be like her."

"How long have you been parading around in stolen clothes?" Caroline nodded to the security tag on the sleeve.

"For a few months, I guess. I can't help it honestly. I like feeling different from everyone else."

"You think stealing makes you special?"

"Things I steal make me feel special. Caroline, can I ask you something?

"Go ahead."

"Why do you think they wanted me, anyway?"

"I'm not sure but I have a friend who might know. You need to stay here tonight and stay home with your parents from now on. Do not go anywhere alone. Understand? And no going out after dark anymore."

Lucy got up and went back to the window, looking out onto the dark street. "Their eyes were the wrong colour. Did you see them? Are they vampires, do you think?"

Caroline shut her eyes. She hoped that they were vampires, that a simple crucifix would be enough to banish them, or that the light of day would destroy them, but it was doubtful. Whatever they were, she doubted the light of day held any power over them.

"I don't think so, sweetheart. I don't know what they are but I will find out, I promise. In the meantime, we have to keep you safe."

Lucy nodded, absorbing the information. Caroline saw the reality of the danger was slowly getting through to her. "Do you think she's still alive?" Lucy pointed to the poster on the table where Dayna's face was frozen in time forever on the page.

Caroline rested a hand on her shoulder. "I honestly don't think so."

Lucy began to sob quietly, picking up the cat and burying her face into his matted fur. Caroline reached out and rubbed her hand up and down her back trying to soothe her.

"He seemed so kind, and concerned."

Caroline nodded gravely behind her, picturing the man she saw: a handsome face like so many men she'd met in her life. "They always seem that way, honey."

Caroline went to the window ledge looking out into the night, knowing the man and the woman were out there, somewhere, licking their wounds like injured coyotes, and planning their next move.

Charlie was in the dirty kitchen running his inflamed hand under the tap above the sink with his teeth clenched in a grimace. Rose had had to drive them both home while he lay whimpering on the back seat of his car.

"Tell me again, Charles."

Rose hadn't even offered to dress the wound for him. His fingers were black along the tips and it looked as if he might lose some fingernails. All four fingers had a dull red welt running across where the door had struck them. The pain was constant; it felt as if his hand had been stung by hornets.

Rose was unconcerned, pacing the room with a lit cigarette clamped between her teeth. The blonde girl had bent her out of shape in a way he hadn't seen before.

"I told you, Rose. Everything was going well. I had the little nipper getting in the back seat neat as can be. I would have left her in there until you arrived, but before I could close the door: bang! I get hit in the face with a glass bottle."

Charlie carried on babbling while he wound toilet roll around his blackened fingers. "She knocked me clean over, the little bitch. Wonder what got her panties in a bunch."

"She knows what we are, Charles. She saw us."

"What do you mean?" He looked up from his hand. She was looking out of the window, her face tight with concentration.

"She saw us. She has the sight. I was standing close enough to smell the revulsion coming off her in waves."

"The sight? Are you sure? That's rare."

Rose nodded her head.

"Damn. That's bad. How much do you think she knows?"

Rose laughed, a high cold sound. "Don't get too worried. It was probably just serendipity, her turning up at the wrong time. She smelled like an addict. She doesn't understand it and has no control. Poor thing is probably living in a mental home and seeing spooks everywhere rattling their chains. I did catch the faintest whiff of antidepressants. She doesn't understand what she is. She's confused and alone, medicated to the eyeballs. I thought the Seers had died out centuries ago. She must be one of the last left in the world."

Charlie got to his feet awkwardly, using a coffee table for support as he hobbled upright. "Medication will make it easier to find her, Rosy but you're sure she saw us? As we are, I mean?"

"Without a shadow of a doubt. I saw it in her eyes." She turned back to him looking at his wounded hand with faint disgust. "She certainly got the better of you. Maybe you're getting soft in your old age."

"Hey! The little bitch caught me off guard. I'll be ready for her next time."

Rose pushed him back onto the chair. "As always, you arrive at the party long after the bill's paid, Charles. You can't go charging after her like a bull in a china shop. She will see us coming a mile off. We will have to be clever. We can't risk her going to the police."

"So what if she does? They won't believe her."

"Think, Charlie! You made a grab tonight and lost it, because of little miss second-sighted goody two shoes, and the runt you tried to collect could be in the police station as we speak. They may not believe one of them but if they back each other up the pigs would have to follow through with a report, and the club may have had CCTV. That bloody car of yours stands out like a sore thumb."

"Don't blame me, Rose. It was you who told me to stay at the front so she couldn't leave! I was comfortable waiting until next month!"

"All right, all right! Don't overreact. Besides I'm pleased she tried to stop us."

"Pleased? Look at what she did to my fucking hand!"

Rose took a deep drag of her cigarette, opening her bubble-gum pink lips wide to exhale a great cloud of smoke that obscured her from sight for a fraction of a second.

"It would've been much better for her if she hadn't intervened Charles because, in doing so, she's revealed to me something a lot better than just a warm meal."

She draped her arms around him as she spoke. "She has something I've always wanted. Think about it. We get two for one, and I get something extra in the bargain: a teenager's youth and the eyes of a Seer."

Charlie saw her eyes move from his face down to his lap where his crooked hand was lying limp like a drowned thing.

"But first things first…I am going to send her a little message"

Rose stomped up the grand staircase. Charlie limped after her using his good arm to grip the bannister while his injured one hung limp at his side. Rose had told him what she meant to do and he didn't like the sound of any of it.

"I'm not sure about this, Rosy. Why don't we leave her be for now? Let her think she's safe, let her guard down a wee bit."

Rose ignored him, moving along the hallway with unwavering focus, her heavy steps making the floorboards creak beneath her. Without a glance she passed the door to the bedroom where she had lingered in a state of living death only days before. "The little bitch needs to be taught a lesson. I want to give her a taste of who she thinks she's screwing with, make her regret sticking her nose in." She stopped outside the door to his bedroom.

He rested his one good hand on her shoulder. "Please don't, Rose. It's mine."

She shrugged him off, twisting the knob of the door and striding inside.

"I will buy you another pet, a goldfish perhaps. I need to send her a message."

"Rose! No! Please don't take her"

But she paid him no mind. She looked around the cluttered room, wrinkling her nose against the strong smell of men's deodorant and mouse faeces. A camp bed was set up in the corner for when she was too incontinent to share a bed with and then there was the glass tank on the table.

"Leave her be, Rose, please."

But Rose was already throwing off the cover flooding the room in an eerie green light. He watched from the doorway, his yellow eyes filling with tears.

Rose was moving her hand through the tank, trying to locate the thing through the many sheets of the cobweb. "Don't worry. I will give her back good as new."

Charlie wanted to intercede, but he knew he couldn't stop her. She was far older than he was and much stronger. "Poor thing," he sobbed. Charlie took such excessive care of it, feeding it two mice a day. He was so hoping to move it onto birds when it was bigger. It was a Goliath Spider, a bloated thing of shadow and darkness. The spider mewled in her grip as she brought it up from its den, its eight legs clutching at the air in desperation.

Rose barged out of the room leaving him alone with the bare tank glowing faint green and the only company the white mice caged in the corner of the room.

Rose slammed the door of her bedroom with her one free hand. The other was still closed tight around the spider struggling against the iron grip of her coral nails. She could hear Charlie fetching and sobbing through the walls. *Big cry baby.* She threw the sheets off the bed and climbed onto the mattress, tenderly placing the spider before her. It cringed back as it recovered its freedom, observing her darkly from its many-faceted eyes.

Rose let her head roll on her neck and shrugged her shoulders trying to empty herself of thought. She kept her eyes piously shut. She sensed the spider rearing up to scuttle away. She kept it pinned to the spot without effort, pressing the weight of her mind upon it. She felt its legs kick at the air, trying to push through the invisible barrier containing it. She pressed down harder feeling it struggle beneath the weight of her thoughts, slowly pushing its small mind into a corner. She needed it cowed for her plan to work.

Slowly her breathing quieted and her heartbeat slowed. Goosebumps erupted over her arms as the hairs there stood on end.

Rose had many tricks up her sleeve. If you lived long enough you picked up special things. This trick was hers alone; she'd never taught it to Charlie. He lacked the discipline for it.

The girl with the sight was out there somewhere tonight, and she would find her, make her pay for sticking her nose where it didn't belong. She sank deeper into the spider's form, feeling resistance as it tried feebly to push her out. She swatted its effort away as easily as swatting a fly. She was ancient and all-powerful and it was small and tiny before her. Like the girl.

Rose thought on the words of Nietzsche as she opened her eyes, locking gaze with the faceted stones of the spider's eyes, letting the full weight of her spirit run rampant through its alien form like a virus. *When you stare into the abyss, the abyss stares into you.*

Their eyes remained locked as Rose became aware of her new senses, the hairs on the spider's legs sending messages to her brain. She looked out through its many eyes, marvelling at the walls of the room towering up to the ceiling like skyscrapers. She twitched one finger and one leg of the spider moved. She drummed her fingers up and down on her knee and the spider kicked its back legs out sending a shower of hairs up into the room. Rose closed her eyes and concentrated.

Find the girl.

The spider turned on the spot and moved swiftly across the folds of the bedding, a passing shadow that scuttled up the wooden bedpost in a spiral, slipping out through the bedroom window and out into the night.

Charlie felt a faint unease listening to the silence in the house. Knocking on the door, he heard no answer from inside. Had Rose gone out? He felt a twinge of worry. Had she gone out to confront the Seer alone?

"Rosy?" He turned the knob and crept into the room. "Are you in here? What are you doing?" His eyes scanned the room. Her body was atop the bed. He looked around for any sign of his pet. Where was it? No doubt hidden elsewhere, poor thing. He touched Rose's chin with his hand, no response. Her eyes remained closed. He touched a few strands of her hair and frowned. Hours before it had been coiled up in a golden honey blonde beehive; now it looked like a candy-flossed ball of a spider's web. It felt old and brittle.

His hand closed around hers and he saw age spots there. Faint wrinkles etched her face. "Rosy, wake up!"

Charlie pulled up the wheelchair from the corner of the room and plonked himself down, settling himself into the creaking chair and waited patiently for her to return.

Across the city the spider moved unseen under the cloak of its own shadowy form into sewers and across the pavement. Atop the bed Rose maintained a deep concentration, inhaling deeply, trying to catch the essence of the girl on the city air. Underneath the exhaust fumes and the stench from the alleys she foraged for the rich smell of despair. She held Caroline's face behind her eyes as the spider moved ceaselessly, her thoughts bent on the woman who dared to come between her and her chosen prey.

Where are you dear? I'm looking for you.

The spider surveyed the halfway house from the shelter of the concrete drain across the street. Rose saw the front door in her mind's eye, lit in the half-dead light of the spider's vision.

Found you, dear.

Rose's nostrils flared as she breathed in the heady bouquet emanating from the house: the rich scent of ruined lives and families locked away in small rooms with nothing to cling to but each other. Underneath the stench was the rich smell of black cherries. Rose's face broke out in a grin of vulpine triumph in the gloom of the bedroom. Their latest catch was inside with the Seer. Her body tensed atop the bedspread.

Ready or not, girls, here I come.

A taxi drove across the street, its headlights blinding the spider for a moment. It flinched back inside the drain before breaking cover to scuttle across the street to the paving steps of the front garden and up the brick wall to the edge of the window.

Caroline bolted upright on the sofa as Lucy's screams woke her. She saw Lucy standing on the bed screaming and pointing accusingly. "What is it? Oh my God, what is it?"

Caroline struggled to her feet and looked down at the thing that before had been inches from her sleeping face. She jumped back with a shriek as it reared up at her and sprayed a jet of foul liquid into the air.

Caroline jumped out of the way as the foul ichor hit the wall. Lucy's shrieks were ear splitting behind her.

"Shut up Lucy!"

Lucy's scream cut off as her mouth snapped shut. Caroline moved back to the window, allowing the spider to proceed along the sofa scuttling like a thing from a dark corner of space and time, gaining ground on her. It was nearly invisible in the shadows of the room. She had to focus hard to keep it in view, jet black with its entire body shrouded in tiny hairs like a cactus, a lumbering abyss atop the arm of the sofa. Caroline saw the glisten of moisture dripping from its face as it creeped silently towards her, sending up steam from where the puddles of venom formed along the upholstery.

Get to the light switch.

"Lucy, listen. I will throw the light on. When I move, it will come for me. I need you to run to the bathroom and lock yourself in. Understand?" Lucy whimpered behind her in reply.

The spider hunched up on its rear legs, getting ready to pounce. Its eyes moved from Caroline to Lucy. She saw evil intelligence behind its dark eyes as it crept towards them. She saw it turn towards Lucy who froze on the edge of the bed.

"Hey, hey! Over here!"

It retreated at Caroline's movement. She could smell burning from the wall next to her where a small crater was forming.

"Lucy, go now!"

Lucy jumped off the bed with a scream as Caroline lurched forward, throwing on the light switch. The spider flinched back, sending a shower of hairs up in the air from its bloated belly.

She backed against the kitchen countertop, her eyes never leaving it as it glared at her, flawed black mirrors reflecting her own frightened face back at her. She could hear it whispering inside her head: *Foolish little girl. You can't save the runt. You can't even save yourself.*

She reached behind her, clutching for anything she could use to fend it off. Her hand locked around the handle of a mop Michele had brought over when she had first moved in.

Caroline shrieked as it leapt silently into the air, its eight legs spread open like a hand to smother her. She swung the mop handle around with both hands in an arc, the head of the mop connecting with its body with a meaty *plunk.* It landed on its back on the bed, its many legs pawing the air trying to gain purchase, finally correcting itself then rearing up again hissing and spitting.

She screamed as a jet of poison hit her shoulder. The smell of burning flesh filled her nostrils and her grip on the mop handle faltered for a moment as the pain broke across her shoulder like a railroad spike.

The creature scrambled up the wall and scuttled fast along the ceiling. Caroline thrust and jabbed at it with the mop head as it moved. She saw the mop head was too soft to cause it injury and she had to move around to keep it from dropping on her. She reversed the mop and prepared to shove the point of the handle into it like a spear.

Rose's torso contorted and writhed on the bedspread as three long cuts gouged into her face. Her mouth gaped open as she shrieked aloud like a banshee. Charlie flew from the chair and seized her with both hands, unmindful of the pain in his broken fingers. He tried desperately to shake her awake. Before his eyes another cut opened on her forehead. She twisted underneath him as he tried to awaken her from the agonies of the nightmare she had plunged into.

"Rose, what is it? What's happening?"

Before his eyes more cuts opened across her face, sending a fresh stream of blood onto his hands. He held on fast to her as her body hurled itself from side to side as if in the grip of a seizure. He didn't know what to do. "Rose, wake up!"

He mounted the bed forcing his knees onto her arms to stop them from thrashing around. Her entire body seemed to have an electrical current shooting through it. Her eyes remained sealed as she convulsed underneath him.

The spider came down a silk line onto the kitchen counter. Caroline jabbed at the air to keep it from coming forward. It didn't flinch, raising itself up to call her bluff. It sprayed small droplets up at her in warning.

She pounced forward with the mop handle aiming for the spider's face. It sprang onto the handle scampering up along the wooden pole to meet her face on, its black bloated form growing larger as it came forward. She dropped the mop with a shriek. Her hands came up in a warding off gesture as she felt the brush of its hairs prick her skin.

There was a hissing noise by the window and she felt something huge hit her arm. Caroline staggered and she stumbled over the mop landing hard on the floor. Her eyes widened as she saw what was happening. Like her, the spider had landed on the floor and was rearing up at Snoops from the corner of the room.

Caroline grabbed a hold of the mop handle and brought it around knocking the spider across the room with a *plop*. The cat leapt across the room with a screech, jabbing the creature with its claws and teeth. Caroline's hands scrambled over the draining board and closed over the handle of a frying pan. Clenching it tight she raised it high above her head and bore it whistling down through the air flattening the spider with a meaty crunch.

Charlie ducked as another vase shattered above him raining jagged shards onto his head. "Rose, please-"

She grabbed up an end table and hurled it across the room where it shattered against the wall. Charlie tried to shrink himself into the corner. He'd never seen her in such a rage before, pulling at her hair like a mad prophet in the midst of a vision. "That little bitch!"

She turned about with her hands, like claws grasping at empty air, wanting to rip, to tear, her face contorted in a snarl of hate. Three deep slashes were gorged into her forehead.

He gathered himself up from the corner and broke the silence that hung over the room. "Rosy, what did you do? What happened to my baby? Where is she?"

She brought her fist around colliding with the side of his cheek sending him flying backward into the wheelchair that sped back through the doorway as it took the full force of his weight.

She strode towards him. He brought his palms up in front of his face to shelter himself as she towered over him, her dull grey hair loose from its hive curling around her face like a nest of snakes, her yellow eyes peering down at him with revulsion. "Get up, you idiot. We have work to do."

"I don't understand."

"Do you have a computer here? With internet?"

He rubbed his jaw where her fist had struck. He could feel a tooth coming loose in his gum. "There's an old dial-up downstairs but why?"

"You mentioned you found the school where our little princess goes."

"Yes but-"

"I want you to hack in and bring up the photos of the students. They always have them."

"I don't know about this." He took a step back as she turned to face him like a dark idol.

"What?"

"I think we should leave her alone. Look what she did to your face."

Her hand drifted up to her cheek and felt the cut there. Her eyebrows narrowed as her fingers ran along the grooves of the wounds. Her eyes moved to his fingers still wet with her blood.

"My face?" She barged past him back into the bedroom where the wall mirror was.

"No, Rose, don't look. Please."

He fled the hallway to his bedroom as her scream rang out through the doorway. He slammed the door and sank to the floor with his hands over his ears as her shriek filled the house.

Caroline found Lucy in the foetal position in the shower cubicle. She screamed when she came in. Caroline reached forward to help her up. “It's all right, Lucy. It's dead.”

“Are you sure?”

“The cat ate it.”

“What in hell was it?”

“Just a spider.”

She followed her into the bedroom. The cat was draped across the sofa. Lucy pointed to the wall next to the bed.

“Did it do that?”

Caroline looked where Lucy was pointing and saw the craters on the wall where the poison had hit.

“I feel like it's still on me.”

“I know what you mean.” Caroline was rubbing the burn on her shoulder where the spider's ichor had hit her.

Lucy stroked Snoops affectionately. “Well done, boy.” Her fingers massaged under his neck. “That wasn't like any spider I've ever seen before.”

“Don't think about it now. It's gone.”

“The blonde woman sent it, didn't she?”

“Don't be silly. The sun will be up soon. We need to find a way of getting you home. Do you have your father’s phone number? I want him to come and take you home.”

Lucy stood up. The cat, startled, jumped to the floor. “No way! I'm staying with you. What if she comes back? What if the tattooed man comes with her?”

“You cannot stay here. You will be far safer at home. Do you understand? You'd be in danger if you stay here.” She picked up the phone and held it out to her. “You call your father or I will. Don't worry. I'm not going anywhere. I will phone you tonight after I speak to Paul."

"Who's Paul?"

"My friend, the one who told me about the missing girl."

With reluctance Lucy reached for the phone and punched in her home number. Her eyes shut as someone at the other end picked up. "Dad, it's me…"

Charlie hummed out of tune as he squatted on the dusty floorboards. His eyebrows were furrowed as his fingers worked at disentangling the wires that were coiled together like snakes. Rose sat in the rocking chair in the corner knitting. He could see out of the corner of his eye she occasionally nodded off, with her head drooping before coming awake with a start. Neither one of them spoke of how the evening's excursions had sapped her of the youth she'd only just procured. Her face was coated with a thick foundation to mask the wounds inflicted by the cat.

"OK, I think it's ready." He hoisted the computer modem up onto the table with a grunt, switching everything on. He plugged the keyboard and mouse in and waited for the dial-up tone to sound, announcing that he was connected to the World Wide Web. He grinned as the computer screen lit up like a malevolent eye opening. He felt Rose tense up from the corner. She was inherently suspicious of technology.

"I'm telling you Rose, this thing is the future. All I need to do is log into a chat room and I can get a depressed adolescent to come right to the front door, no more trolling the streets of a night with my nose in the air like a coyote."

"Just find the school, Charlie."

He typed in 'Richard Allard's School for Girls' into Ask Jeeves and clicked on the first result appearing on the screen, first pixelated and then growing into a coat of arms, shaded in green and gold. He put his hands behind his head and revolved around to face Rose, grinning. "Bingo! Now what am I looking for?"

"You're looking for our girl from last night. Check the student awards' page. They have photos of the little brats up for the parents to gloat over."

He scrolled down past identical girls all grinning into the camera wearing drab uniforms. He stopped on the photograph of a girl who, unlike the others, was not smiling, but gazing into the camera inscrutably. There was a shadow over her eyes. He leaned forward in the seat and ran his tongue down the screen.

"That's not her. Our girl was prettier. She had short black hair."

"There were two girls I smelled in the mall."

She looked from the computer screen back to him as he leaned back in the chair smugly. Understanding dawned on her and she smiled at him showing her crooked teeth. "Grab a pen and paper."

He jumped up to find a pen, feeling the warm rush of excitement, the familiarity of the hunt. "Can you read her name out?"

She hobbled over to his chair and leaned forward to squint at the screen. "Her name is M-A-X-I-N-E-C-R-O-F-T. You go to the school, Charlie. I need to get something from the garden, a little present for the Seer."

A shadow went across his face. "Are you sure you want to do this? I mean, maybe we should let it go, after what she did to your face."

He flinched back as she lifted herself from the chair. "We have to have her. She knows about us. And with her ability she's too dangerous to be left alive. The little bitch needs to be taught a lesson."

Caroline held out her hand in a still wave as Lucy was thrown into the back of her father's car. Richard Cunningham would not speak to Caroline when she had opened the front door to him. He wore a charcoal grey suit with his hair set in a well-oiled comb-over. He ignored Lucy's protests as he dragged her out of the house and down the steps where his BMW was idling on the sidewalk, out of place with the surrounding council houses.

"Dad, stop! She's my friend. She's a good person!"

"Get in the car."

"Not until you listen to me!"

Caroline watched the exchange from the window with her fists clenched. She watched him come around the car and bundle her into the back seat. Watching the car pull away she tried to turn her mind from Lucy to Paul who was waiting for her at the hospital. She said a silent prayer to herself as she got dressed.

Please let her be safe.

The events of the previous evening seemed like a nightmare, surreal. The confrontation outside the club with the two monsters, waking up in the night with the eight-legged alien in the house and then Lucy's father barging in demanding the return of his daughter and threatening to call the police on her.

Idiot.

She picked up Dayna's poster and folded it up, placing it in her back jean pocket.

"Dad, I'm sorry I will never do it again. I swear." The car took a turn too fast and Lucy grabbed hold of the car door to keep herself steady. Her father peered at her from the reflection in the overhead mirror.

"This is the second time you've run away. It's clear we've been too soft with you."

"I'm sorry, Dad, more than you know."

"I'm taking you to school. You will go straight to the library afterwards. You will stay there until I arrive to collect you. Do you understand?"

She looked out the window of the car, watching the grim city buildings and high-rise flats fly past in a blur, giving way to green fields as they headed towards the suburb where they lived. She felt herself tense as her father spoke again.

"Where did you get that jacket you're wearing?"

She took a deep breath and thought about the man with the yellow eyes. Her father's disappointment was tiny by comparison to the horrors that she'd met only the night before. She took a deep breath and unburdened herself. "I stole it, Dad. I'm sorry."

Silence filled up the inside of the car.

"What else have you taken?"

Lucy looked down in her lap. Tears began to run down her face. "Nothing else."

"Tell the truth!"

She looked up to see him still looking at her from the overhead mirror. "Hair dye from the mall and a magazine from the newsagent's. I'm sorry, Dad."

"I'm going to be speaking to the headmaster about this new friend of yours. It's clear where this newfound behaviour has come from. She's a bad influence."

"No she isn't, and neither is Caroline."

He turned around in the seat, his face a violent shade of red. "Who?"

"The woman who you met today."

He braked violently as they came into the driveway. "That woman did not look well and that place... I don't even want to think about it right now. We will discuss that woman later. She's older than you, too old and, what she's doing having young girls stay over, I have no idea."

"She helped me-"

But he only spoke over her. "Enough. You are to have a shower, change into your uniform, and then I'm taking you to school. Tonight you're to get everything together you've stolen and bring it down to my office in a bag. Then we can see about sorting your hair out. This is not over, Lucy, not by a long shot. Do you understand me?" He turned around in the seat to say these final words, his face bright crimson with a vein pulsing out from his forehead.

She nodded, wiping her eyes as she let herself out of the car.

Rose crammed the dark black toupee onto Charlie's hair and was working it with a comb. She had found him an old double-breasted suit and made him relinquish his scuffed leather boots for a pair of newly shined black loafers. "Stand up straight, Charles. Stop fidgeting."

He groaned and righted his posture. She hobbled around him surveying her handiwork. The toupee covered his balding head and layers of foundation took care of the small wrinkles that were gaining ground around his eyes and mouth. He looked like a man who might have a daughter going to a private school.

"Stop playing with your tie."

He stuffed his hands into his trouser pockets and rocked back and forth on the heels of his shoes irritably. "We never take in daylight, Rose. I don't like this."

Her gloved hand reached up to touch his wrinkled face. She had groomed him to be cautious and loved him for it but, on this occasion, the rewards were worth the risk. "You know what to do. Get her into the car, drug her, drive away."

"What if the girl with the sight turns up? I'm not getting bashed on the head again."

"You leave her to me. Just make sure you're back here with the runt before the sun goes down. All right?"

He nodded.

"Do you have everything you need?"

He whipped open his jacket. She smiled at the bottle of chloroform poking up from the inside pocket. He had a rag stuffed into his trouser pocket.

"Don't forget the glasses."

She put the spectacles on his face, admiring the intellectual look they gave him. Anyone looking at him would think he was a teacher or a parent. She pinched his nose playfully.

"Bring her back, Charlie, and by sun up tomorrow the two of us will walk around in teenage skin. Bring her back alive and unspoiled. You hear?"

"Have I ever disappointed you?"

He kissed her gloved fingers and pressed them to his mouth. He held her by her arms for a moment looking into her eyes and then went out through the back door. After a short time she heard his car rev up in the driveway and accelerate away.

Rose limped out of the back door of the kitchen carrying a wicker basket over one arm. Charlie had left a cane for her at the back door which she leaned on as she progressed down the wooden steps into the overgrown garden that stretched out behind their home and gave way to the woods beyond.

The cold wind blew through the gossamer hairs of her balding scalp. Rose felt a passing rage at the youth she'd squandered frivolously on looking for the Seer. No matter. By the time the moon rose in the coming evening she would be tied up and gagged in the attic, drugged to the eyeballs as helpless as can be. Her mouth stretched wide in a gap-toothed leer at the thought of how the girl's youth would taste.

She took deep sniffs of the scented air, using the cane to beat away the nettles and thorns that surrounded her. If only she had more time to spend in the garden. Perhaps tomorrow morning she and Charles would do gardening and afterwards, share a picnic.

She shuffled slowly across the uneven ground trying to ignore the pain in her joints as she moved deeper into the brush where the thorn bushes and brambles became thicker. Finally, she halted under the shadow of an enormous yew tree. Gnarled and twisted branches veered out in all directions. Rose took a deep sniff and looked up to see a thick rope of hemp hanging from a branch, swinging joyfully in the breeze. In the old days, this was where they dragged the guilty to be hanged. She wanted something special for the Seer and hangman's rope was just the thing.

Reaching up with one withered hand, she snatched it down with a *crack* making a murder of crows take flight from the surrounding trees. She coiled up the rope in her hands and held it up to her face, breathing in the sweet odour of murder before dropping it into a basket and then she worked her way around the tree plucking plants that grew from the desecrated ground. She took berries from the nightshade thickets and the flowers of the wolfsbane plant and finally, bending down to the base of the trunk, she snatched a few handfuls of hemlock for luck.

Caroline sat with the phone to her ear waiting for Michele to pick up on the other end.

"Michele, it's Carol. Did you find anything out about the hospital?"

"I spent the entire day in the library. It has a dotty history. People have died there, but it is a hospital. People have to drop somewhere."

"Did anything stand out to you?"

"Just that staff don't stay long. Their turnover's high. A few ghost stories published in the scandal sheets, but I doubt they're real. Most likely thought up by bitter interns getting their own back on the place that fired them. You okay?"

"I was just thinking about Paul. He's obviously not well."

"Yes, sweetheart. He's just a mentally ill man and you don't have to do this voluntary stuff if it's not helping you. You can leave anytime. Remember he's sick. You're not. Try not to get sucked in."

"Thanks, Michele. You're a good friend."

"Want me to come over tonight? I've got you a coffee machine in the back of the car."

"Not tonight. I'm not feeling well."

"Tomorrow then?"

"Probably not. I want to spend some time alone, perhaps figure some things out. Can I call you next week?"

There was a pause on Michele's end. "Sure, sweetie, that's fine. I'll leave the machine in the car. It's ready for you whenever."

Caroline closed her eyes against the feelings of guilt trying to intrude, but better to keep her away. She was safer out of it. Things had changed in such a short space of time. She wondered if she would be alive to see her again.

Stay away from the women with the beehive hairdo.

She looked over at the space next to the fridge where she had seen the dead man. "I have to go. I will be late for work."

"Call if you need anything."

"I'm really grateful for all you've done for me, and whatever happens, you tried your best for me, and you believed in me. No one else ever has. I love you like a sister."

"Right back at you."

She let the phone rest in the cradle, keeping her hand on the slim line plastic for a moment more. Then, taking a deep breath, she plunged her arm to the elbow in the upholstery of the sofa, feeling her hand close over the cold metal of the crowbar and pulled it out. She wrapped it in an old tea towel and shoved it into her shoulder bag. The business end stuck out like a nasty comment but she hoped the floral print of the cloth would disguise it. She hitched the bag up on her shoulder with a grunt and headed out of the door, slamming it hard as she went.

Richard Cunningham switched off the ignition and sat in the car staring ahead at the old school building.

"You are to stay in the library until I collect you. Do you understand me?" He kept his eyes turned away from her as she unbuckled her seat belt and opened the car door.

She watched him drive off and turned to walk in through the school gates with her back to the road, not noticing the old blue car that pulled into the spot that her father had vacated only moments before.

"He's been lucid today, Caroline, despite the increase in dosage. I told him you were coming and he seemed to understand. The episode he had seems to have faded."

"That's wonderful, Fiona."

"But Eve and I are keeping an eye on things. She's suggested that he's being over stimulated by your visits. But I don't think so. I think it's good for him to have a visitor."

Caroline was ushered into the visitors' room. Paul was once again in the wheelchair, this time facing her as she came in, away from the window. Fiona went over and checked that the latch on the window was locked before going out. Caroline unfolded the poster of Dayna and laid it on Paul's lap.

He slowly came to life like a clockwork toy being wound. His fingers took hold of the crinkled page gently and his eyes took on a focused look as he read the words on the page. His voice was slow and croaky like an old door closing. "That's her, the auburn-haired girl."

"Her name is Dayna Andrews."

"They stole her, the unlucky Rose and the Scissor Man."

"Yes, I believe they did. They tried to take someone else last night."

He looked up at her sharply. "So you saw him then, the Scissor Man?"

"Why do you call him that?"

"Have you read any Auden?"

She shook her head, watching the sky out of the window. It was already growing dark outside.

He recited aloud: "We were the whirlpool, we were the reef, we were the formal nightmare grief, and the unlucky rose... The sky is darkening like a stain, something will fall like rain, and it won't be flowers. Outside the window is the black removers' van. And now with sudden swift emergence, comes the women in dark glasses, humpbacked surgeons... and the scissor man."

Caroline shuddered, feeling a chill move through the room as he spoke. "They were trying to snatch another girl, a young girl named Lucy. I caught the man by surprise with a glass bottle. I doubt I'll be so lucky next time I see him."

"Is that why you're carrying that thing around with you?"

He extended a single bony finger to the tell-tale piece of metal poking out of her bag.

"It was horrible. He had eyes like a snake, but the woman was worse. She smiled at me."

"You saw her then, the unlucky Rose. She's afraid of you."

She let out a hollow laugh. "I doubt that very much. I scarcely got away last night, and they followed me. I'm not sure how, but they did it." She looked around to check that there was no one listening at the door.

Paul seemed to be shifting around in his seat. The wheelchair creaked as he fidgeted.

"But they sent something after me, a spider, not like one I've ever seen before. It was ancient and enormous. It hurt me." She pulled the blouse off her shoulder exposing the scabbing wound that the spider had inflicted. It was red around the edges like a burn.

He leaned forward in his chair to get a closer look.

"The cat killed it."

He smiled. "I was wondering where he had got to last night. Normally he sleeps with me."

"I don't believe the spider was ordinary, but I don't see how she could've sent it after me. She was just a woman."

Caroline jumped as the door banged open. Eve came in pushing a metal trolley ahead of her. Paul let his head roll on his shoulders as he sagged back in the chair.

"Time for his medicine. Drink this down, Mr Graves." She moved towards him and he rolled away from her in the chair. She shot a thick arm out to hold him till he moved his head from side to side. She thrust the glass to his lips. "Mr Graves, open your mouth now!"

"Eve!" Both Caroline and Eve turned to Fiona who was standing in the doorway, her youthful face flushed red with anger. "What on earth are you doing?"

Eve straightened up looking sternly back at her. "Giving Mr Graves his medication. It's four o'clock."

"You're not to force it on him. Put it down on the table. He can have it before Caroline leaves."

Eve looked from Fiona to Caroline who were both staring at her with mutual distaste. Paul was staring at the floor idly as if the present dispute held little interest for him but Caroline thought she saw a faint look of amusement behind his glassy eyes.

Eve slammed the glass down on the table and stormed out of the room.

"I'm sorry for the intrusion, Caroline. Please excuse me."

Fiona closed the door and Caroline grabbed the glass off the table, strode to the window and hurled the entire contents of the glass out into the flowerbeds.

Paul spoke softly from behind her. "Have you ever heard of spirit walking?"

She turned to face him. He looked composed in his chair, as if the intrusion by the nurses had never happened. "Think hard. Think about the ghosts you see every day."

"I don't-"

He held a hand up to stop her. "Even with the spooks you've seen, can you believe there are other things that people can do as well?"

"All right, but it's awful really. It never works how I want it to and most of the time it's only echoes, little flashes of people, and I can't ever control it."

"It takes practice."

Caroline sat back down in the chair.

"Think about the shamans of Africa, the conjure men, mystics of Asia. They send their eyes out for miles around, using crows, owls, bats."

"Spiders?' Caroline interrupted.

Paul shifted around on his seat looking worried. "I never heard of anyone putting themselves in a spider. They are different to animals."

"Different how?"

"Imagine seeing through a hundred pairs of eyes and feeling through eight pairs of legs. I don't think a person would want to do it."

"How is it that she can?"

"How do you think she can?"

"She's just a woman in her thirties by the looks of her."

"She's not a woman. Just because the thing dresses like a woman doesn't make her a woman any more than that spider Snoops killed last night was just a spider. She's got her eye fixed on you now. You got away twice and the second time I imagine you hurt her quite badly."

"What is she then and how come she can do these things? You told me it takes a lifetime to learn to do that spirit walking thing?"

"I've got a feeling she can do many things people can't do. Do you think she's really thirty years old?"

Caroline looked at her lap and pictured Rose again in her mind, the way she had smiled at her.

"She looked thirty, but what I felt when she smiled at me was like what the spider felt when it leaped at me, old, and far more to it than what I was seeing with my eyes."

"Smart girl. Whatever she is she's centuries old, and she's had hundreds of years to learn things we don't have a hope of doing."

"How do we get rid of her and the Scissor Man?"

He turned his face to look out the window. "I don't know how to get rid of them. Auden called them 'the hunchback surgeons' but I think they're just like leeches."

"You mean like parasites?"

"They're like starving dogs who never get full. They gorge on misery and loneliness. They've got noses like wolves and minds like snakes. They sniff out the lonely, the desperate, the lost girls who won't be noticed if they disappear one day."

"Why kill them, the girls? What do they get out of it?"

"How young did she look to you?"

Caroline pictured her again. The blonde woman with faint wrinkles around her eyes, grey threads running through her blonde curls. Understanding flashed through her.

Caroline exclaimed, "That's why they do it! They feed on the girls and grow a little younger!"

Paul nodded. "You said you hurt the Scissor Man?"

"I shut his fingers in the car door. The woman intervened, but I ran before they could do anything more."

"Maybe no one's hurt them before. Maybe she is curious about you. You've got away twice now and now she knows you've got gifts of your own. Like the sight you have. Maybe that's something she doesn't have and you've got youth to boot. I imagine she'd like to add your power to her bag of tricks along with the years you've got ahead of you."

Caroline began to feel very frightened.

He closed his eyes and lay back. Caroline moved her hand to his and squeezed it. She was grateful when he squeezed back. "Paul, I promise I will-"

"What are you doing?"

Caroline whipped around.

Nurse Spencer was looming in the doorway, a look of fury on her face.

"I was just saying goodbye to him."

"Get away from him. Mr Graves? Mr Graves?" Eve shook him furiously. "I told them you would tire him out! What were you doing with him?"

"We were just speaking."

"About what?"

"SHOO, CAT!" Caroline turned to see Snoops on the windowsill looking in at the three of them with interest.

Eve clapped her hands together. "OUT, CAT. SHOO!"

It turned with its bum raised in the air and disappeared out of the window which she closed with a bang.

Eve turned to face her. "I think that will be all today."

Caroline opened her mouth to say something and gasped as the smell hit her.

Eve recoiled like a scalded cat. "Oh hell, not again. Oh God. The smell! The smell! FIONA! FIONA!" Eve began shouting for assistance. Caroline caught Paul's smile as she hurried out of the room.

Eve's desperate voice bounced against the walls of the corridor. "How do you get this window back open?"

Caroline hurried out down the hall towards the double doors of the mental ward. Tears ran down her face for the love of poor Paul who was her friend, who she had to leave trapped in this place of despair and from the smell of his excrement that was now filling the hallway.

The bell signalling the end of the school day tolled mere hours after Lucy had arrived. She had spent the final hours of the day seated at the back of the class staring into space. She wanted to find Maxine and tell her about the fight with her mum, about 'Carrie' being burned in the fireplace and the horrid club she'd ended up in.

The whole classroom seemed to surge with life around her as girls packed away their pencil cases and notebooks all hurrying together to get out of the room as fast as possible. She could see the faces of loyal friends hanging around the doorway looking in at the girls who they would pair up with on their bus rides home. Maxine was not there.

Slowly she packed her things into her satchel, hitched it up on her shoulder and made her way out of the classroom towards the library.

Lucy had never needed to use the library. The textbooks found there had graffiti strewn across the covers; the O's filled in with a black marker pen. Any blank space on the pages had noughts and crosses games played by students who had long since graduated and love hearts with 'REBEKKA AND CHARLIE 4 EVER' written in biro. Lucy's parents always bought her reading list brand new. Until now she had never thought about that but as she peered down the rows of books hoping to glimpse Maxine staring into a second-hand book, she had not realized how much she had taken her life for granted.

She threw her satchel onto an empty desk, put her legs up onto the seat and took out the stolen magazine and began flipping through. The pages were creased and there were a few tears in places along the spine where she had ripped out ads to stick on the wall of her bedroom. She heard her father's voice in her head: 'You are to stay in the library until I come and collect you. Do you understand me?'

Screw this.

She slammed the magazine back into her bag and got up to leave.

Finally stepping out into the fresh air at the front of the school, Lucy's eyes scanned the small groups of girls littered around. She could see teachers edging their way towards the car park taking care to keep a distance from their fellow staff. Lucy grinned, thinking on Maxine's observation days before.

But where was Maxine? Her eyes moved over the clusters of girls at the school gates when she spotted a familiar figure just turning the corner.

"Hey, Max!' She took off running towards the gates. "Maxine, wait up!' But she was too far ahead, walking towards the bus stop, her head bowed, lost in a world of her own.

Lucy got to the gates of the school and nearly tripped as a short squat woman moved in front of her blocking her way.

"Miss Cunningham, where do you think you're going?"

Connie Francis's corpulent frame manoeuvred her backward inside the school perimeter.

"Connie, I-"

"Miss Francis," she corrected.

"Miss Francis, I'm just going to see my friend. She just-"

But Connie cut her off. "Your mother rang me today, Miss Cunningham. She told me that you are to remain in the library until your father comes to collect you, so I suggest you turn yourself around and go back inside now."

Lucy tried to step around her but Connie moved quicker, putting her lumberjack arms on Lucy's shoulders and forcing her backward. "I wanted to say hello to my friend. She's right there." She raised her hand to point to the bus stop where Maxine was standing, speaking to a tall man wearing a suit. Her eyes moved from him to the blue car parked up on the sidewalk. "Oh no!"

She lurched forward as the horror of what was happening dawned on her, sending a gust of cold blowing through her body making her stomach lurch up in her throat. "No, no! I have to-"

But the Connie took hold of her arms with her hands. "What you have to do, young lady, is go back inside the school now!"

The whole world took on a slow grey haze as she saw what was unfolding less than thirty feet away. She saw the tall man smiling at Maxine and opening his passenger car door, gesturing with his left hand. She saw Maxine turn away from him for a moment as she looked into the interior, possibly fascinated by the colour, not seeing his right hand slip into the inside of his jacket.

But Lucy saw it. She saw something in his hand, and she saw him step diagonally behind Maxine, putting himself between her and the bus stop. "NO!"

Connie pushed her hard backwards as her hands gripped her wrist.

"Let me go. I have to help her! Connie, do something!"

But Connie ignored her, refusing to turn her head and fall for whatever prank Lucy was playing. "That's enough. I'm taking you to the office. Your father can collect you there, and when he comes, young lady, I will tell him all about this.... Incident!" She spat the last word out as her vice-like grip closed around Lucy's forearm dragging her back towards the school gates.

Lucy kicked and struggled against her. She was shaking her head fervently. Many teachers were watching the scene unfold with the looks of people watching a drama on television. A few, Lucy saw, were checking their watches perhaps worried that this incident would delay them on their route home. She saw a few girls pointing at her and nodding to their friends with looks of glee plastered across their faces.

Connie was dragging her towards the front door by her elbow. Two teachers were moving towards her slowly. Panic took her, making her scream hysterically. She tore away from Connie bringing one hand around slapping her hard across the face and took off running out of the gates without looking back.

"Maxine! Maxine!" She came around the corner. The street was empty. A bus was idling up on the kerb as various students boarded, some staring at her as she ran towards them screaming. She turned about looking up and down the street for any sign of the blue car, but it had vanished, along with her friend.

"Lucy!"

She turned and saw Connie running towards her on the sidewalk looking furious, a red mark blooming on her cheek. "Come back here now!"

Lucy took a single step sideways up onto the bus and watched the double doors close just as Connie drew level with her. She raised her middle finger to the glass of the doors as the bus pulled away.

Rose looked up from her preparations in the kitchen as she heard the car pull up in the driveway. Looking out of the window she saw Charlie limping around to the back of the car and opening the boot. She watched him peel off the wig from his balding scalp and throw it into the bushes along with his glasses. He grunted and staggered as he brought the girl out of the boot and dropped her carelessly onto the ground.

Rose's eyes narrowed as she watched him bend over to catch his breath, leaning his weight against the car. He did not look well, at all. She could see deep lines and wrinkles around his face and he was moving with more than just a touch of arthritis. She'd hoped the youth would've lasted longer.

She looked down at the stove where the hemp rope was boiling in the plant infusion. The lid of the pot rattled as steam poured out filling the room with a pungent odour of decay. She wrapped her hand in an old rag and lifted off the lid. The back door banged open, and a hunchbacked Charlie limped in.

"I've got her, Rose… What is that smell?" He gagged and retched waving his hand, trying to clear the air of the stench coming up from the pot.

"Get out, you idiot!" She hit him in the face with a wooden spoon. "Take the girl upstairs. Hurry! The sun's almost down."

"What are you doing in here?" His eyes darted from the pot to her shrunken form. She hadn't looked into a mirror since returning from the garden. The look on his face told her she was obviously showing her age.

"I said bring the girl in. Now!" She raised her arm again, and he fled out of the back door down the wooden steps.

She watched him come around the front of the house with a rusted wheelbarrow, grunting and coughing as he lifted the trussed up schoolgirl into it. Rose studied the girl's bound body, noticing how her pale youthful skin seemed to shine like a pearl against the backdrop of the rusted metal. Her oily tongue slid out of her mouth and ran along her lips greedily.

Rose could see the rope lying on the bottom of the pot like a drowned thing. A thick layer of scum was forming on the surface of the potion. She would've liked to have left the rope simmering for longer but looking out of the window she saw the light from the day was already fading as the storm clouds gathered overhead. Time was short and she had to get ready. Preparations were paramount if she was to succeed.

She opened one of the kitchen drawers and rummaged inside until her hand closed over the worn handle of a butcher's knife. She ran one of her bony fingers across the crescent blade drawing blood from her forefinger. *Good, very good.* Her wrinkled hands trembled as she upturned the pot, turning her wrinkled face away from the fumes that erupted out as the poisoned contents drained away down the sink. Finally she set the pot down and waited.

She raised one crooked hand and beckoned with her fingers. Her tongue darted in and out of her mouth like a snake. She waited patiently, paying no mind to the various screams and thumps that came from the room above her.

For a moment she felt a fleck of doubt, but then slowly, very slowly, the rope emerged from the pot, descending down the metallic surface onto the counter and dropped to the kitchen floor with a dead *thud.* Then, rousing itself, moving lazily with the speed of a dazed snake, it slithered across the floor and coiled up the legs of its mistress, finally settling around her waist like a withered girdle. Rose ran the rope through her hands, relishing the feel of it prickling her skin like nettles.

There was another cry from above. Rose's gap-toothed grin spread out across her wrinkled features. It was time to go upstairs and see how Charlie was settling their new guest in.

It was raining as Caroline stepped off the bus from the hospital. She held her jacket over her head to shelter from the rain. Her thoughts were full of Paul and the brief moment of happiness they'd shared holding hands before the stupid nurse had waded in.

She wanted to get back to the hostel and phone Lucy to make sure she was home safe, and then she would turn her attention to the Scissor Man and the unlucky Rose. She hoped she could find a way to get rid of them both before she woke up with another spider in her bedroom. Her hand closed over the shape in her bag. The crowbar was still there, although it didn't bring much comfort. She thought of stories from childhood about witches being able to turn away steel but it was all she had and it would have to do.

She came up to the cracked stone pavement that led to her front door and recognized the cropped dark hair of Lucy pacing in front of the door. "What are you doing here? I told you to stay home with your parents." Caroline stumbled backward by the sheer force of Lucy's weight as she threw her arms around her sobbing.

"I saw him! I saw him! The man, the man with the blue car!"

"You what? Where?" She pin-wheeled on the spot, her eyes darting around the street.

"He was at my school. He took my friend Maxine. He took her! Right in front of me!"

"Let's get inside. You can tell me everything."

"We have to rescue her! Now!"

Caroline grabbed her by the arm and pulled her hard. "We need to get off the street!" She pushed her up the steps of the hostel. Caroline dropped her keys twice before fumbling them into the lock and got them both inside.

Rose had her pink fluffy slippers on as she shuffled into the room. She saw Charlie trying to duct-tape Maxine's wrists to the arms of the chair. She was struggling away from him. He brought his fist across her face with the back of his hand with a crack.

"Hold still, you little bitch!"

Rose cackled from the doorway. "You should have used a stronger chloroform on this one. She's a cunning little creature." Rose held the kitchen knife out to him. "Take this."

He took the handle of the knife looking puzzled. "You want me to kill her now?" Maxine's eyes opened wide as she saw the blade and began to thrash about in the chair.

Rose fetched a deep sigh. "No, you moron. She's useless to us dead before the moon rises. It looks like it will be a cloudy night which is unfortunate. I don't know how long it will take for the Seer to get here. We have to keep them all alive until the moon rises." Rose looked down at Maxine's frightened face. "Finish binding her to the chair. If she moves, cut her."

Charlie ran the blade along Maxine's cheek. "Mind your Daddy now, little princess. Don't move. Understand?"

Rose spoke from behind him. "Face her towards the window so she can watch the sun go down."

He wrapped the tape around Maxine's wrists. When she was fixed in place, he turned the chair around and wheeled it to the wide window at the end of the room. Rose shuffled into the room.

"Leave us, Charles. We need to talk, girl to girl."

Rose moved across the room, scowling as she caught sight of herself in the mirror's reflection. Her face was wrinkled like a rotten apple and her clothes hung off her emaciated form like rags on a mummy. Slowly, she turned her attention to Maxine who was sobbing quietly in the chair. She reached out to stroke her face and cackled as the young girl cringed away.

"Watch the sky, dear. The sun will set in less than an hour. Another hour and the moon will be full and high. That's how long you have to live."

When she came into the lounge, Charlie was at the kitchen table running the blade of the knife along his palms. "I'm not sure this is a good idea."

She limped to her rocking chair and sank onto the embroidered cushion making her feet no longer touch the floor.

Charlie looked up at her, his features were grim, his eyes sunken into his face. "Are you sure you're strong enough for this, Rosy?"

Rose ran her hands lovingly along the rope still coiled up in her hands. "I will be. Don't worry. Just make sure they're both locked in the upstairs room by the time the moon rises."

"What do I need the knife for?"

"Insurance. If she frees the girl, stab them both and drain as much of them as you can." She opened her eyes. He was studying her, looking worried.

"Do you want me to bring you your medicine? You don't look well."

"No. I want you to stay down here. I want you in position for when the little bitch arrives. I don't need pills or drugs. By the time the sun rises we will both be restored and I'll have the eyes of the Seer. Now be quiet. I have to concentrate."

He watched her body stiffen in the chair, her hands tightening over the arms. "What are you doing, Rose?"

She didn't answer. The chair carried on rocking back and forth. She looked like an old woman that could've nodded off while knitting.

Caroline was pacing the bedsit with her fingers pressed to her forehead trying to shut out the various shouts and bangs coming down from the ceiling. Lucy was on the floor with her knees up to her face, her eyes red from crying.

Caroline kept picking up the phone and replacing it in the receiver. She thought about phoning Michele, but she couldn't. There was too much to explain and she doubted she would believe her. She thought of phoning the hospital and demanding to speak to Paul. But Paul did not know what these beings were, or how to destroy them.

Out of the window, you see the black remover's van, the woman in the dark glasses, the hunchback surgeons, and the scissor man.

"Did you see the licence plate of the car? Think hard Lucy. It's important."

She shook her head. "I was too far away. The woman who works in my school blocked my sight, but I saw him step behind Maxine and put his hand in his pocket. He brought out something that looked like a bottle.

Caroline nodded. *Sly bastard.*

"What are we going to do?"

Caroline didn't know. She didn't know where he would take Maxine. She knew they would have to be somewhere near the city, probably somewhere on the outskirts. She tried to cast her mind back to what she'd seen when she was in Wanda's bathroom, but it was fragmented. She remembered the Bad Penny, and the churchyard in front of it.

"I need you to stay calm. Do you have anything of Maxine's? Anything she touched? Clothing perhaps?"

Lucy thought for a moment. She thought of the book Maxine had given her and felt a spark of hope alight in her chest.

"What? What is it?"

Then the cold disappointment as she saw her mother flinging it onto the logs of the fire. "No, nothing like that. I'm sorry. Do you think we should call the police?"

"Yes, we should. You're going to stay here and do that. Tell them everything you saw. They might find the car but I doubt they will find it by sundown. I'm going back to the bar where they tried to take you to see if I can think of anything."

Lucy got up. "I'm coming with you. She's my friend."

"Absolutely not. You will call the police. If I don't come back someone needs to know about Maxine. That's how they've been getting away with it. Do you understand? No one reports any of the victims missing. We will make sure that doesn't happen this time."

"What about your friend at the hospital? What did he say?"

"Paul told me they're afraid. They didn't get you the other night and are looking to make up for it. Stay here a moment." She slipped into the bathroom and closed the door. Lucy continued to speak to her through the wall.

"They're hoping you will go after her, aren't they?"

She sat down on the loo and nodded to the empty room. "I suppose they are."

Lucy's voice came quietly through the wall. "It's my fault. It's because you tried to help me the other night. They want to get you for intervening, and they took Maxine because of me."

"Don't worry about that. I will find out where they are. I need to think now, okay?"

"'Caroline?"

"Yes?"

"What hospital did you say your friend Paul was at again?"

"He's in a mental ward in Springfield Hospital. Why?"

"No reason."

She tried to slow her breathing, trying to picture them both in her mind: the unlucky Rose and the Scissor Man smiling at her from the pavement outside the Bad Penny, the black railing surrounding the stone building, the tombstones of the cemetery, the car idling in the road that led towards the city; and the other way led out into...

She opened her eyes as the thought went off in her head with a bang. She gasped aloud. *The road ran into the woods. They didn't follow us into the city in their car. It would've been easy for them to chase us down but they didn't. They went the other way down the dirt road into the trees.*

Caroline's head whipped up as she heard a slam from outside the bathroom. "Lucy?" No answer. She called out louder through the door "Lucy, are you there?" Nothing.

Caroline moved to get up, and then fell backward as the ceiling and the floor changed places. She felt the gorge rise in her throat as the tiles on the wall cracked and dissolved as she passed through the wall into a nightmare.

The long dirt road unfurled before her eyes, littered with the bones of countless girls, each taken in the dead of night and murdered far from home. A tall iron gate loomed into view. Rusted chains were coiled around it like dead snakes and, far above, towering high on the hill, rising out of the ground like a rotten tooth set in an infected gum, was the house. The moon came out from behind the clouds not white but red. Caroline felt herself move along the ground, not wanting to go into the house. The front door creaked open before her eyes. The blonde woman was hunched over a young girl, the crescent knife held aloft in the air above her heart. She heard a great grandfather clock striking twelve tolling like a church bell and the blonde woman's vulpine red lips gaped wide, her scream piercing the night as the blade came down, rising and falling again and again.

Caroline's own screams woke her. She sat up on the tiled floor, a small puddle of vomit beside her face. How long had she been passed out for? "Lucy?" She opened the bathroom door. The bedsit was empty. *No, no.* Lucy had gone.

Caroline went to close the bathroom door, and her mouth opened with horror as she saw the word painted on the mirror in lipstick making her blood curdle in her veins.

COME.

Eve was pacing the ward as the patients slept. Fiona was out on her cigarette break, slacking off. But Eve didn't mind. She liked having the ward to herself. The rain was coming hard against the glass of the windows. Eve was moving along the wall closing them one by one. She jumped when she heard a knocking behind her. Whipping around, she screamed aloud at the ghost leering in at her through the window of the ward door. Her hand went up to her heart as she realised it was not a ghost, but a girl peering in at her, knocking insistently on the door.

It was only Fiona. Eve exhaled and strode to let her in. But as she came closer to the door, her face changed from mild annoyance to a look of puzzlement. The girl on the other side of the door was not Fiona at all. This girl was a teenager. Swiping her card, Eve kept her face blank to hide the unease that was growing in her belly. “May I help you?”

The girl babbled frantically. “I'm here to see my grandfather. It's an emergency!”

“I'm afraid visiting hours are long over. Come back on Monday morning, and phone ahead next time.”

She made to close the door, but the girl slid her foot into the jamb, shoving Eve backward as she pushed her way in. “Excuse me! Excuse me!”

The girl did not acknowledge Eve, but moved down the ward pulling back curtains that enclosed the beds, exposing the bewildered faces of the patients who sat up awake one after the other.

Eve was rooted to the spot with anger, trying to think of what to do. She would have to return to the nurses’ office to phone security, but she couldn’t risk leaving the patients alone. “What do you think you're doing? EXCUSE ME! You need to leave now. I'm calling the police.”

But Lucy ignored her. “I need to speak to a man named Paul Graves. It's an emergency. I need his help. A woman named Caroline needs his help.”

“You need to leave.” She went to take the girl by the arm but the dark haired girl slapped her hand away.

“Do not touch me, woman!”

Eve was so taken aback by the young girl’s tone that she did not hear the curtain that encircled Paul

Graves' bed creep back silently. She felt movement behind her and turned to see Paul looming up from his bed like a ghost, his iron bed pan held high above his head, bringing it down on her skull making fireworks go off behind her eyes as she collapsed in an ugly heap on the hospital floor.

Lucy looked down at the nurse on the floor with her mouth hanging open. "Are you Paul?"

"Are you Caroline's friend?" Paul's eyes sharpened as he looked around the ward. "Help me get her up onto the bed."

Lucy took Eve's ankles and together they hoisted her deadweight onto the hospital bed. Paul took her nurse's ID and swipe card from the lanyard around her thick neck. Rummaging in her pockets, he pulled out crumpled up scratch cards and boxes of Marlboro cigarettes, a lighter and a set of keys. He pulled the bed sheets up to her chin and then closed the mint green shower curtain around her with a swish before turning to face Lucy. "Where is Caroline?"

"I think she's gone looking for my friend at a bar where we first saw them."

"We have to help her. She can't fight them both alone. They're too strong."

"I want to help. They stole my best friend from right in front of me, I can't stand back and do nothing"

Paul turned and drew the window up letting in a gust of cold wind. The moon was already glowing faintly from behind the clouds. "Too far to fall. We have to go out through the front door. Do you know where this bar is?"

Lucy thought for a moment. "It's past a churchyard, before the woods. I think I can retrace my steps from the bus station."

"Meet me at the entrance to the hospital. Go now and don't be seen by anyone. Do you understand?"

Lucy nodded. "Where are you going?"

Paul swiped the card through the reader and ushered her through the door. "There's something I need to get. I won't be long."

Lucy watched Paul run down the hallway with his hospital robe flapping around him like a cape as he disappeared into the nurses' office. She looked back once into the ward to where the identical beds ranged along the walls in neat rows, all veiled from sight by the monotonous green shower curtains. She shuddered to herself as she ran towards the fire exit door she'd come in by and climbed out down the fire escape.

She loitered in the bushes by the entrance. Every second that passed brought a fresh wave of fear. Were they killing Maxine now? Was she too late? She paced back and forth rubbing her hands together to stave off the cold.

She looked up to see Paul hurrying down the corridor stuffing something small into the front pocket of his scrubs. He threw his arm around Lucy's waist and kept his head down as they made their way out of the hospital. She noticed a few members of staff underneath a large oak tree smoking and both she and Paul bowed their heads as they went by, keeping her eyes fixed on the bus shelter as they progressed through the grounds.

She saw Paul's eyes being drawn up to the sky where the moon was glowing faintly from behind a whiff of dark cloud. With every step she felt thick dread move inside her like a hand closing tighter and tighter around her heart.

Fiona dropped her cigarette end and stamped it out before walking back into the nurses' office. She ground to a halt as she came inside and saw everything in disarray. *What on earth?* The cupboards to the morphine were gaping wide open; boxes containing the packets of needles and syringes were littered about the desk, crumpled and torn; and most disturbing of all she could see Eve's lanyard with the key to the medicine cabinet in the lock of the cupboard. Fiona tutted to herself as she surveyed the chaos.

There was only one thing for it. She took a seat at the computer and smiled as she typed an official complaint about her colleague who had negligently left her ID and key in the morphine cupboard and had strewn dangerous implements around the office like a mad woman. Fiona was so engrossed in what she was writing that she didn't see, out of the window, the old man and the young girl, their arms around each other running across the hospital lawn and out into the night.

It took Caroline an hour to reach the Bad Penny. The bus she was on had stopped en route making her heart sink as a recorded voice announced to the passengers that there would be a delay while the driver waited 'to regulate the service'.

After fifteen minutes of playing back the image of the blonde woman bringing the knife down over Maxine, she got off the bus and ran down the road that led into the city. She saw the line of trees looming up behind the bar and tried to picture a house on the other side of the wood, a house she had seen in her dreams standing high on the hill. She saw a narrow road that ran past the black door of the bar into the woods. *That's where they had come from the night I saw them. Monsters live in the woods.* She thought of the poem Paul had recited: *the woods have come up and are standing round in deadly crescent.*

She took the crowbar out of her shoulder bag and walked cross country towards the tree line. It seemed at once to grow colder as she stepped past the trees into the dark of the wood.

I'm going to my death. The thought came unbidden as she moved through the trees, stumbling occasionally on the uneven ground. She thought of what her life had become: a total waste of days piled up on top of each other like the neat bricks of the hostel she lived in; days on medication, waking up in the afternoon; empty looks from social workers and officials staring at her from behind their desks. She found that her impending doom came as something of a relief.

She thought of Paul trapped on the mental ward and wished she had met him sooner. She thought of Dayna, her sister whom she'd never met, but who was so like her, outcast and alone, who had been dragged through this wood to die. She thought of Maxine whom she saw in her vision bound to the wheelchair by two monsters to be slaughtered like cattle, drained of her life and discarded like a bag of rubbish. And finally poor Michele whom she would probably never see again, who right now was having dinner with her family, knowing nothing of the darkness that waited outside for those who are without love or a home, a darkness that would soon swallow her whole.

And no one will ever know where I went.

She swung the crowbar in wide arcs, knocking the brambles and nettles aside as she went deeper into the woods.

Rose was seated in front of her dressing table with a red sequined dress draped across her lap. She daubed paint across her arms, spreading it over the wrinkles and age spots. There was a blonde wig on a stand in front of her. Dusty Springfield was singing 'Son of a Preacher Man' from the record player in the corner.

From time to time Rose cast an eye out of the window, watching the progress of the moon as it crept higher in the sky, feeling her skin tingle as the night's festivities drew closer.

She popped the lid off her lipstick and applied it, pausing when Maxine's sobs broke out from the corner of the room. Rose turned to see her staring out of the window where the moon had broken through from behind the clouds.

"Oh, hush now!" Rose limped towards her with a handkerchief. "Martyrs don't cry. They offer their pain to God with joy! But you know what the worst of it is, Maxine, dear?" Rose bent down so she was level with the girl's face. "The real kick-you-in-the-teeth, spit-on-your-face of it is that you will die all alone here and no one will ever know where you went." Rose chuckled warmly, putting one hand on Maxine's tear-streaked cheek. "Your mother will probably drink herself into a puddle of self-pity, assume you ran away with a boyfriend like so many other girls your age, and you don't even know what all this is about. Life's cruel like that but don't worry, dear, a lot of things will be made clear to you before the end. I'm hoping your little raven-haired friend will try to rescue you. Yes, you know who I mean. Well, she has a new friend. I will take all of you for the fun of it, but it's the friend I really want. But I promise you this-" Rose leaned in close to Maxine who had turned away as Rose's foul breath hit her. "—I'll make sure you get to watch the other two die first." Rose inhaled deeply as the girl rocked from side to side sobbing frantically in the chair. It was two hours until midnight.

Lucy had her arm around Paul's waist as they picked their way through the churchyard. "Here it is. Do you think Caroline's here?" She could hear the sound of the music from the bar echoing across the night air. "We won't be able to get inside the club. I'm not dressed right. The bouncers will see I'm too young straightaway, and you're too old." She smiled at him and he laughed aloud. She joined him in spite of the fear that pulled at her from the surrounding trees.

Paul sat down against a crumbled tombstone, bent double. "Let me just catch my breath!"

Lucy was worried at how bad he looked. "Are you all right?"

""It was just a long walk."

"Do you think Caroline is there? We need to find her."

"She's gone into the woods. I'm sure of it."

Lucy looked beyond the club to the line of trees that stood like tall sentries, unpleasant and sinister. "She went in there? Alone?"

Paul stood up, eyeing the trees. "I believe so. You can stay here if you wish. I do not want to take you into any danger."

"I'm coming. I have to." Lucy heard a noise behind her. A cat was watching them from where it was perched on top of a tombstone, its yellow eyes shining brightly in the gloom. "Paul! Look! It's Caroline's cat. It's Snoops!"

"I wondered where he had got to." Paul crouched down as the cat dropped to the ground and ran to him meowing.

"You know him?"

"I do indeed. It was he who brought these beings to my attention in the first place."

"What do you mean?"

"In Ancient Egypt, cats were guardians of Baset, the Goddess of the moon. The cats were her messengers."

She watched the cat take off running, weaving in and out of the tombstones into the trees.

"They spill blood on the moon every month. They're against nature, a plague crawling on the skin of the earth. I think he wishes us to follow him." Paul fished for something in the pocket of his hospital johnnies.

A man outside the Bad Penny sharing a cigarette with his girlfriend jabbed her with his elbow and pointed at the old man in the white smock and the young girl running into the woods.

Caroline's sight was slow to adjust to the darkness that unfurled before her as she walked. Gradually she saw the faint outline of a house as she made her way through the brambles and thickets: a great manor, a monolith of timber and stone perched high on the hill, dwarfing the trees in its looming majesty.

She craned her neck up to count the many windows that were gouged into the framework of the house like eyes regarding her with malevolent intelligence. She passed a 'Keep Out' sign nailed to a tree and could make out the chain tied gate that she had seen in her vision. From there she would walk up to the house to meet her fate.

Charlie stood at the front door with his yellow eyes fixed on the iron gates. He knew that once the woman came through there she'd be without cover from the surrounding trees. It would be easy to take her, and then and bring her to Rose, an appeasement offering to his dark goddess.

In spite of the building excitement he felt uneasy. He had suggested to Rose that they kill the girl and skip town, leaving the other two. Why risk exposure? But Rose was insistent: all three had to go, not just because of the potential their lives offered in sustenance, but to take the woman's sight for her own.

He would not fail her. He stood guard and waited for the Seer to walk into his waiting arms. His nostrils flared as he caught something: an odour, faint but persistent. His hairy knuckles tightened on the railing as he lifted his nose up to the sky. He laughed as the smell came again; stupid of him to think that the Seer would arrive first.

The smell was there all right, coming from the woods behind the house. His teeth flashed in the dark as he growled low to himself. It would be much easier than he'd thought. He drew the chloroform and the rag out of his jeans pocket, ducked down and made his way quietly around to the back of the property, breathing in the smell of black cherries that grew stronger as he prowled through the grass.

Lucy and Paul shadowed the cat as it moved silently through the trees like a ghost. It seemed to know its own secret way and, rather than follow the dirt road up to the house, it had taken them in a straight line cutting through the woods and up into a wild overgrown garden.

Lucy could see the roof of the house was missing tiles. Only the third floor and the attic were unencumbered by the grip of vines that had taken the rest of the building. Squinting, she could see a single light on up there. The cat sat between her and Paul who was catching his breath next to her, its yellow eyes staring ahead through the trees. She felt Paul's hand on her shoulder.

"You need to stay here now."

"I'm coming with you. You can't go up there alone. Can't you feel it? It's a bad place"

He felt it. It was not a smell but something in the way the house loomed over them: its angles somehow wrong, the way the place seemed aware of presence, its evil felt on the wind making his hairs stand on end. It stood on unhallowed ground, the site of ritual murder and human sacrifice. He knew they were both standing on corpse ground.

Paul climbed to his feet.

"No!" Lucy took a single step forward before retreating behind a bramble bush. "Don't go up there!"

He turned to face her, his grey eyes looking into hers. "Be safe, Lucy." He kissed her on the cheek before turning away, bending low and hurrying through the brush and out into the clearing. Lucy watched as he made his way up to the house alone to face his nightmares.

Caroline pulled the rusted chains off the front gate. They hung limp between the bars without a padlock, an obvious invitation for her. She worried the noise of the metal grinding on metal would give her away. She doubted neither the man nor the woman would show themselves out in the open; they wanted her in the house. Her grip tightened on the crowbar. *Fine by me.*

She gazed up at the house and tried to close her eyes and rise above the fear that threatened to overwhelm her. Slowly she cast her sight out across the land, trying to feel for Maxine who was up there somewhere bound and helpless. She felt her mind come right up to the front door when something enormous slammed down like a wall of iron bringing her back to herself with a bang. She heard the echo of an old woman laughing somewhere in the corner of her mind. Rose's voice spoke from the surrounding darkness. *"No peeking, Dearie."*

Charlie's grin faded to a scowl as his poor eyesight made out the dim shape coming towards him from across the lawn, not a girl but a man. "How you doin' there, old-timer?" he growled at the intruder who was trespassing on his property. Charlie hadn't seen anything like him before. The man looked insane, half naked in hospital scrubs.

The man stopped and stared at him with faint disgust. His voice was quiet and Charlie had to strain to hear him. "Who are you calling old-timer, you old codger?"

Charlie let out the low growl of a predator as he came forward. His nostrils flared trying to find the scent of black cherries, but all he could smell was the old fool approaching him, stinking of chemicals and bed pans. He drew the crescent blade out of his jeans. "Get off my land, old-timer. I'll give you one chance. Walk away."

But Paul limped forward slowly, his grey eyes fixed on Charlie's yellow ones. He shook his head vehemently and spat on the ground between them. "I don't think so, you old dog. I've been looking forward to this for a long time. I'm not walking away from this-" Paul grinned, "and neither are you."

Charlie felt the faintest trickle of unease as the old ghost crept towards him, the odd player in the game that Rose had not foreseen. Two girls she said, no more, no less. But looking at him he saw he could barely walk. Poor sod. He was no threat at all. Still, he was trespassing and interfering in business that didn't concern him. He'd put a few holes in this old guy then go looking for the girl. It wouldn't take long. He drew out the kitchen knife and started walking down the hill to meet his challenger.

Charlie barked as he leaped through the air. He meant to wrestle the old man to the ground and snap his neck. Paul grabbed hold of him and together they rolled down the hill, looking like two old men settling a score from decades long past.

Paul gripped Charlie's wrist trying to stop him from bringing the knife down. Charlie's mouth was stretched out in a grin as Paul struggled under him, one hand closed around his wrist, the other fumbling stupidly in his breast pocket. Charlie barked into his face like a dog. He tore his hand out of Paul's grip and brought the knife down, burying the blade to the hilt in the old man's shoulder. Paul let out a scream as the blade pierced him and Charlie tried to stand up and regain his footing but was pulled back as he felt the old man's arms come around his neck.

Blood gushed over Charlie's face as they rolled together. Paul kept hold of him and Charlie stabbed down with the knife again but missed Paul's face by inches and instead planting the blade in the long grass.

Charlie rolled off him and tried to get up. As he turned away he thought he felt a bee sting him as Paul reached up and slipped the needle of the syringe into his neck. Charlie gave a shriek as his hand came up to feel where a small lump was already forming, understanding flooding through him. He tried to clamber away from the needle, but Paul held on to him fast, laughing maniacally through the haze of blood. His vision clouded as the morphine raced through him like an electric current, making him feel nauseous and sick.

Get back to Rose. She will kill the girl and restore me. Get back to the house.

The back door of the house looked to him to be miles away. He swayed on his feet pointing the blade at Paul who was clambering upright despite the blood pouring from the wound in his shoulder soaking his hospital scrubs a dull shade of crimson.

Charlie barked at him. "You stay back, you old coon!"

Paul laughed at him, the blood smeared on his face like Indian war paint. He took a step towards Charlie, one hand pressed against his shoulder, the other pulling a second syringe from his breast pocket.

Charlie knew he couldn't get to the door without turning his back on the old man. He felt panic begin to take hold of him. No, Rose would heal him. He bared his teeth at Paul like a dog. "C'mon then, you old fart!"

Paul came on, and Charlie took his weight as he bore down on top of him, meaning to tear his throat out, but something went wrong. Charlie heard a violent screech behind him and a hiss as a huge cat latched onto him, scratching at his face and hands. He felt the old man squirm out from under him as the cat gripped his face like a demon.

He dropped the knife as his hands came up to get a hold of it, to throttle it. The creature twisted in his grip hissing, its teeth darting up and down as its teeth tore at his wrinkled flesh. He finally managed to get the animal by the throat hoping to snap its neck when he heard Paul whisper softly from behind him. "Oh, don't mind him. He's just a big softie."

And then the sting of the bee as Paul slid the syringe into his neck and compressed the plunger.

Charlie felt his legs turn strange under him as they caved in. He could hear his heart thundering in his ears like a drum banging. His whole body erupted in sweat as he tried to crawl to the door but his limbs wouldn't respond. He had been poisoned by an old man in a bed sheet. No, this was not how it would end. He had seen so much. He'd lived so long. Rose told him they would live to see how the world ended.

With all his might he grabbed hold of tufts of the lawn grass and pulled himself along the ground, towards the house.

Rose was zipping up her dress when she felt a stab of pain shoot through her making her flinch. Her manicured pink fingernails flew to her neck as she felt something like a hornet sting. *Charlie.*

Something was wrong, her eyes searched the room for a sign of intrusion. She quickly shut her eyes and cast her senses out into the house like a pungent mist enveloping the property. An echo of emptiness rang around her mind. No intruder inside but still something was not right. Rose felt a cold trickle of fear creep up her back. Something had gone wrong somewhere. She could feel it. *Impossible.*

She wrenched open the door with one hand, pulling the knob off with brute force, and slammed the door, leaving Maxine alone in the darkness of the room.

Lucy felt the weight of the house pressing on her from above as she moved into the clearing. It seemed to bend towards her as she came closer, smothering her in its shadow. She found Paul face down on the ground as she reached the base of the hill, his white hospital scrubs stained red and brown with dirt. He resembled a large butterfly that had been mistreated by a gang of cruel children.

She dropped to her knees and turned him over with both hands. "Paul! Paul wake up!" He had been stabbed in two or three places that she could see. Dark red patches were blooming like roses over the pale cotton of his overalls. His face was smeared with blood. One eye was bruised and swollen shut.

She slapped his face as panic gripped her, balling up her fists and bringing them down hard on his stomach, sobbing. "Please wake up. I don't know what to do! I need you to tell me what to do!"

He let out a low groan and one eye opened slowly.

"Paul! It's me. I'm here! You've been so brave. Please don't die, not here, not in this horrid place."

His eye opened and closed. She wiped the blood away from his face with her own red-stained hands thinking that if she got it all off, he would somehow recover, and they would leave together. His hand closed over hers for a moment, and when she looked back to his face, his eyes closed again and his body was still.

She heard a cry from somewhere above and looked up to the see a large white owl take off from the trees and soar over the roof of the house, a ghost flying alone in the moonlit night.

Caroline faced the front door of the house. She tried to rid her mind of the images that tried to intrude, nasty things that scratched at the corners of her vision: images of girls she didn't recognize, girls being dragged across the lawn bound like parcels, kicking and fighting. She watched as the door seemed to creak open before her eyes releasing a foul stench of rotten meat and decay, making her stagger back in fright and cover her face. Opening her eyes she saw the door was once more closed, and solid as ever. *Just a trick.*

Reaching out for the brass knob, the door turned inward with a click and she stepped inside.

Charlie dragged himself through the back door and along the grimy tiles of the old kitchen floor. He heard the sound of dragging feet as Rose came into view, bent over her wooden cane. "Rosy, thank God. Listen we messed up. I can't move. Help me. I can't get up."

He watched her move into the room with arthritic slowness, putting one foot in front of another. His eyes climbed up her nylon clad legs where the blue veins bulged within the red lace garters strapped around her thighs and up to her face where he saw she was grinning. "Help me up Rose, please!"

She giggled to herself as she bent down to him. "Oh, Charlie, you silly thing. Where is the Seer? Did you let her get the better of you again?" She inclined her head to one side as if listening.

Somewhere he heard a door creak open. "No, I swear. She's here, the young girl, just like you said, but there was a man with her. He got me, Rose. He got me with a needle."

Her wrinkled hands snaked out towards him, one hand under his chin lifting his head up as her head came down to meet his, the other moving towards his throat.

"Heal me. Rose! Bring me the girl. I'll suck her dry and we can take the Seer together. You still need me. We can skip town, go someplace."

But she only looked down on him with a vacant look of indifference and when she spoke to him her voice was dry and raspy. "No, Charlie, I don't think I will need you at all anymore."

He realised what was happening a moment too late. Her lips met his in the familiar passionate embrace he had felt so many times before. His eyes opened wide and some part of him for a moment rejoiced, waiting for the familiar warmth of youth that she had blown into the dark well inside him so many times before. But this time it was not a warm wind of life that she blew into him, but a cold wind of cheated lives and stolen time that had come forward at last to claim its due.

He felt her grip tighten as he tried to tear himself away from her. His hands came up to push her face away, but to his horror he saw his own hands shrivel and die on the bone and the flesh peel away like burnt newspaper. The bones on his fingers with no gristle to join them clattered to the floor like discarded sticks, his skin stretched over the skull and rotted off the bone as the years caught up and in a few moments it was over.

From the reflection in the moonlight coming through the window, a woman was bent over collecting a few pieces of old laundry off the floor: a plaid shirt, some leather boots and an old belt, perhaps to donate to charity, or just to throw away.

Caroline gagged as the smell hit her: a foul stench of damp rot that emanated from the walls of the house. She clamped her hand over her face as she breathed in the scent of asbestos, mould, rotten wood and, worse than that - she knew that smell from her own bedroom - somehow worse, a hundred times worse: the smell of despair, of bad endings, she knew she was standing in a nowhere place where all train lines ended.

A cobwebbed chandelier hung from above, velvet moth-eaten curtains lined the windows hanging like dead skin, a grand staircase reared up before her eyes. She saw ropes and pulleys hanging overhead, beckoning images of traitors hanging from ceilings. Caroline could hear the thumps and sobs of past girls dragged up by that wicked contraption.

Taking a single step up on the stairs, she flinched back as a huge sound erupted from the bowels of the house, seeming to come from everywhere, filling her head, making her grip the bannister to keep her balance as the old woman's laughter filled her head, a dry hollow sound with as much humanity as a dog's bark.

The house groaned and settled around her like a giant waking from a troubled sleep. Yellowing wallpaper lined the walls. Dozens of doors stood out from the peeling plaster like sleeping sentinels where all manner of evil things could be lurking. She tried to shut out the intruding voices of young women that whispered and pleaded from the surrounding walls, the ghostly echoes of past girls dragged there to die.

She had to cover her face to hide the smell of blood and old meat that seemed to come on thicker with each step she took. Her power of second sight awoke from where it dozed inside her. Blood spatters began to appear on the walls. Caroline knew they came from a girl who had broken her restraints and fallen down the stairs. She looked back down the hallway to see a pale girl spread-eagled across the floor at the foot of the front door like a broken doll, her head around the wrong way from where her neck had broken. Caroline screamed and threw her hands over her eyes. Then she heard music drift out from the darkness. *The look... of love.... is in your eyes...*The haunting tones of Dusty Springfield were coming from the door standing slightly ajar at the end of the hall, beckoning her forward.

Lucy let Paul's head rest gently on the grass as she got to her feet. There was no sign of Caroline anywhere. She looked back up to the house that leered over her still, thinking of the day when she and Maxine had sat in the bus stop. She'd told Lucy they were sisters. '*Wherever you go, Max, promise me you will take me with you.*' That's what she'd said to her. And Maxine had told her they would always stick together, no matter what.

She looked back to the line of trees once more and down to Paul who had died to protect her. She set off marching up the hill towards the back door of the house.

Caroline screamed as the door at the end opened. She expected to see a ghost or her own self, ravaged by depression and poverty stepping out, a dark mirror to mock and cow her, but the old woman that stepped out was neither. She was shrunken and old, bent double on her walking stick with a ridiculous beehive wig balanced precariously on top of her head like an upturned ice cream cone.

Caroline couldn't help but laugh as Rose revealed herself. She'd been expecting something much worse, the devil incarnate perhaps. The sequined mini dress she wore looked like a bad joke. As she came out of the shadows of the doorway and into the moonlit hall, Caroline realized she was neither a witch nor a vampire; she was just an evil old woman with no real power at all.

Caroline held the crowbar out to Rose's face. "Where is she? Maxine?"

Rose only smiled benevolently at her, showing her rotten black gums.

"I won't ask again, old crone. What have you done with her?"

Rose looked to the door down the hall, pointing. "She's down there, dear. She will be so happy to see you."

Caroline kept the crowbar level with Rose's eyes as she strode forward. Rose chuckled and, with a flick of her wrist, flung the hemlock rope at Caroline's feet.

Caroline screamed as the rope came alive the moment it touched the floorboards, whipping around like a snake, striking her hands and face, making drops of blood fly through the air as it struck again and again.

Rose chuckled as Caroline fell through the air, wheeling her arms about, her feet rooted to the spot by the rope as it coiled around her ankles and up her legs. She tried to scramble away as Rose shuffled towards her, the moon lighting up her gaunt face.

Caroline continued to scream as the rope twined its way around her body like a vine up a tree trunk, her legs bound, her arms clamped to her sides. Finally, it came around her neck as she rocked her head from side to side. It smelled old, nasty, like burnt hair. Her screams stifled as it wound its way around her face like a gag.

"Silly little bitch."

Caroline's eyes opened wide as she saw the horrid mouth open to receive her. She saw rotted gums, yellow teeth and, worse still, a blackness that seemed alive in the depths of Rose's throat, grasping and pulling; a living void nestled there. A cold wind blew out as she leaned towards her making the blood freeze on her face. She felt the cold touch of Rose's lips press against hers and then Lucy's high voice spoke from behind them both.

"You are one ugly fucking bitch."

Rose's face whipped up in surprise, just in time to see Lucy bringing the crowbar around in a wide arc connecting with her face, sending her flying across the room and hitting the door at the far end.

"Caroline! Oh God! What is it?" Lucy dropped the crowbar to take hold of the rope that had twined around Caroline with both hands, pulling at it desperately. She could hear Caroline screaming softly through the living hemp that crawled across her mouth. "What is it? Stay still!"

Lucy's fingers came away bloody as if she'd been grabbing at a bushel of thorns. She turned around needing to know where Rose was. The end of the hall was empty. "Hold on."

She brought the business end of the crowbar up through her legs and pulled with both hands. There was a sound like a hiss as the rope snapped, the hemp ends unravelling as it withered away. Lucy pried it away from Caroline's face. Lucy saw red welts that stood out from her skin where the rope had gripped.

"How did you get here?" Caroline hugged her tight.

"Paul brought me. He's dead. I had to leave him to come and find you. I didn't want to leave him Caroline but,"

Her speech became inaudible with sobbing, Caroline held her tight until the trembling subsided. She took the crowbar from Lucy's fingers and moved past her to the door at the end of the hall. Her hand paused briefly on the knob and then she drew her foot up and kicked out sending the mouldy wood bursting off its hinges.

The pair moved into the room together, searching for any sign of Rose. They saw a tacky wall mirror with light bulbs around the frame. Sparkly clothes were strewn around like a magpie's ransom and, in the corner, bound in an old wheelchair with her head bowed as if in prayer, was Maxine.

"Lucy, no!" Caroline moved to grab her as she pushed past her towards Maxine, but Lucy ignored her, falling to her knees sobbing, her bloody hands shaking Maxine violently.

"Max! Max! Please don't be dead, not after all this!"

Caroline saw a small door was open next to the dressing table. She could see the first step of a staircase leading upwards. "She's up there."

Lucy tore the gag out of Maxine's mouth and held her as her body began to wretch and cough. "Help me, she's hurt!"

Caroline held the crowbar out to her. "Take this and get her free. Then get out, both of you. Understand?"

Lucy took the crowbar, slowly nodding, her eyes wide and red-rimmed. "But what about you?"

Caroline looked from her to Maxine who was moaning and blinking her eyes slowly as if coming out of a long sleep. Then she looked out of the window where already the first signs of a red dawn were creeping along the tree line. "I'm finishing this. Whatever you hear, make sure you both get out."

Rose had a hand clapped over her bloody mouth as she scrambled through the attic like a rat. She had to keep clutching at old furniture to navigate across the uneven floor. She wasn't done yet, not by far.

There has to be something here I can use.

Her wrinkled hands clutched and pulled at the white sheets exposing an old wooden dresser sending clouds of dust up in the air like a swarm of flies. The attic only had a single window and already she could see a faint light intruding into the room. The sun was rising in the east, but there was still time, if only she could just find something sharp.

Her eyes narrowed on something that glittered malevolently within a drawer of the dresser. She spat a glob of blood onto the floor and pulled out an old hand mirror with a large crack running through it. She carefully dislodged a jagged shard from the whole and held it up to the light. This would do. She would catch the hateful girl from behind and jam the piece of mirror into her throat. "Gloves are off now, dear," she muttered. She spat a rotten tooth out onto the floor as she examined her broken jaw in the mirror's reflection where the crowbar had struck her. *You're going to pay for that, princess.*

The light was coming stronger through the window. Rose had to squint to see where she was going. She could feel a sharp pain behind her eyes. She rubbed them as she picked her way around the furniture that was stacked all around her. She wanted to find somewhere dark to wait for the foolish girl who was even now climbing up into her lair. "Come and get me, dear. Come to Rosy."

The mirror shard glittered evilly in the dark of the corner where she squatted behind an old dress mannequin.

Caroline kept her eyes up as she ascended the staircase. She scrambled up onto the dusty floor and called out to the gloom. "It's just you and me now. No more tricks".

Looking around the attic she saw the piles of junk and disused broken furniture gained over centuries of hoarding. Boards creaked beneath her feet as she walked. Blanket-covered furniture surrounded her like ghosts. Anything could be Rose, waiting to spring out like a jack-in-a-box. "Come out and face me, woman!"

Rose's nostrils flared as she heard Caroline approach. She couldn't see well in the dark where she crouched, waiting. Going on how heavy Caroline was treading Rose could picture her in her mind's eye coming closer. Her grip tightened on the shard of mirror sending droplets of blood onto the floor.

Caroline moved forward knocking over everything within arm's reach. A vase toppled to the floor and smashed. She grabbed hold of an old sheet and flung it up in the air exposing an old mirror. Her rage built to a fever pitch as she screamed aloud. "Come out, you old witch!" She was here somewhere. Caroline could smell her.

Rose smiled to herself as she heard the girl crashing through the attic like a charging bull and drew her legs up under her, ready to pounce.

But something wasn't right. She looked about. Her free hand reached out to feel the sides of the bureau, the floor. She could hardly see a thing; a cloudiness had descended over her vision. The surrounding shapes were dark silhouettes of grey.

No, no, no.

She thought of the medicines downstairs in the cabinets of the bedroom, remedies all designed to hold off the ravages of age and sickness; all things Charlie had offered to her only hours before. She had refused because she had been so certain of herself. She screamed aloud as a grey mist enveloped her vision, blinding her.

Caroline turned as she heard a crash behind her. Rose reared up like a gorgon, her bald scalp gleaming in the morning light that came through the window, a glittering dagger clenched in her hand. She screamed as she charged forward meaning to fling Caroline to the ground and stab her to death. If she had had any sense of direction at all she would've caught Caroline unawares as her sight was on the far window that was now ablaze with the light of the oncoming day, but she reared up too far to the left and Caroline watched as Rose threw herself onto a pile of damp cardboard boxes stacked in the corner hacking away in a frenzy.

Realization rushed through Caroline as she watched Rose struggle over the mouldy boxes, stabbing up and down, the shard of mirror finally breaking apart in her bloody hands. She shrieked as her fingers tore at the cardboard spilling old clothes out onto the floor. She writhed like a snake atop the pile of laundry. "Where are you? Where are you? You little bitch!"

Caroline watched Rose clutch at the air like an animal, her eyes like boiled eggs, blinded by the cataracts that smothered them.

"Come out here! You bitch! You don't even know how lucky you are not to have to grow old!"

Caroline cocked her head to the side as she watched her progress with vague interest. Rose crawled along the floor, her mouth pouring blood from where the crowbar had hit her, the sequined dress too big for her shrivelled form and catching around her thighs as she tried to struggle to her feet.

"No, no, no!"

The light from the window moved along the room. Caroline sat passively against the old dresser as the attic flooded with the light of a new day as Rose's time ran out.

"Ahh!" Rose let out a piercing shriek as she felt her skin shrivel and die away from her bones like burning fungus. Caroline looked on in horror as Rose's small body twisted in on itself: her spine curving in a crescent, splitting her dress up the back seam, her canine mouth opening wide, tearing open along the jaw as her white eyes sank into their sockets and rotted away.

Centuries of stolen time spread over the corpse like spiders web as the skull's face caved in on itself and Caroline finally tore her eyes away from the horrid smell that filled the attic as Rose's twisted skeleton withered away like burning twigs leaving a pile of bones wrapped in sequined rags.

Caroline turned to leave. She felt her way slowly around the odd furniture not wanting to touch anything. She felt something shift in the room behind her. She turned slowly and saw a great shadow rising up from Rose's remains, emerging out from the pile of old bones that lay on the floor. Like a death's-head moth emerging from a cocoon the black fog spread out, rising up like a great cloud of mould. Caroline's mouth opened to scream as she felt its cold tendrils reach out to her before a strong wind blew in from the window, catching the tendrils on the air like a candle flame being snuffed out.

Before her eyes the fog came apart like wet tissue, it's power broken and impudent turning to motes of dust hanging in the air.

Caroline found Lucy and Maxine huddled together at the top of the staircase with their arms around each other like two children from a fairy-tale woodcut. Lucy was covered in drying blood while Maxine was pale and still dizzy from the chloroform that the two had used to snatch her.

Caroline could not believe it had taken her mere minutes to get down from the attic and along the hallway. The house had seemed much larger before, a place outside of the laws of reality. Now with the morning light spilling through the dusty windows it seemed that whatever power had held court over it was broken, and the house was just an abandoned building where tramps broke in to sleep during winter months and that in time would crumble into ruin.

Caroline had Maxine's arms around her neck as she carried her down the staircase, and by the time they reached the front door she was able to walk. Lucy kept one arm around her shoulders at all times and Caroline was proud to see that neither girl looked back as they stumbled down the hill into the daylight. Caroline pushed open the iron gates with a great heave, letting the two girls out onto the road.

As she closed them she risked a single look back to the house and was not surprised to see Paul sitting casually in the doorway, his transparent form wavering in and out of view in the stillness of the morning. He raised a single hand to Caroline in a wave and she raised her own hand in return. She heard his warm voice speak aloud in her head, "Be good to yourself." She nodded to him and smiled, and felt something pulling at her arm.

Lucy was looking up at her enquiringly. "What is it? Is something wrong?"

Caroline saw the look of panic on her face subside as she smiled down at her. She glanced back to the empty doorway where Paul had stood only moments before and said, "No, everything is going to be all right now. I promise."

The three young women followed the winding road out through the woods and into the city arm in arm, bonded together by something deeper than friendship, each feeling safe in the knowledge that a great evil had been banished from the world and that the long darkness was over.

The End

Did you enjoy this book? Please leave a review on Amazon and Goodreads if you did it helps so much

If you would like a signed bookmark of the cover art or to receive news of future books go to

Facebook.com/witchywriteralex

Printed in Great Britain
by Amazon